Dancing with Darkness...

🌙 Tired of the tight leash that she and her
sisters are kept on by their parents,
Rachel Durham is seeking for a way out: and one
night, she unexpectedly finds one in their
Chesapeake Bay home.

As the pull of the night world grows inexorably
stronger upon Rachel, her anxious father enlists
the aid of Paul Fester (soldier, medic, juggler,
and ninja) to find out what his daughters are up
to.

With the father's tentative consent, Paul
embarks on a daring but difficult balancing act
to win the girls' trust—before it's too late.

The Midnight Dancers: a Fairy Tale Retold
by Regina Doman

The Midnight Dancers

a fairy tale
retold
by regina doman

CHESTERTON PRESS
FRONT ROYAL, VIRGINIA

2008 cover design and interior by Regina Doman
Typefaces "Little People" and "Decadence" are freeware fonts
created by Emerald City Fontwerks.

Chesterton Press
P.O. Box 949
Front Royal, Virginia
www.fairytalenovels.com
www.reginadoman.com

Summary: When teenaged Rachel Durham finds a way
that she and her eleven stepsisters can sneak out of their
Chesapeake Bayside home after midnight, their worried
fundamentalist father enlists the help of Paul Fester, an ex-
soldier and traveling juggler, to find out what the girls are
up to. A modern retelling of the classic Brothers Grimm
fairytale "The Twelve Dancing Princesses."

ISBN: 978-0-981-93186-9

Printed in the United States of America

To my very own siblings,
Alicia, Martin, David, Jessy,
John, Paul, Maria, Joseph, and Anna
So glad to have all of you.
                    This one's for you.

☾

Once upon a time, there was a king who had twelve beautiful daughters, each one more lovely than the next.

— Grimm

The king was beset by a curious problem...

—— Grimm

Paul felt a prickle in his spine as he set down his duffle bag at the airstrip. That usually made him think that something significant was going to happen. Most of the time, it was only his imagination, but occasionally, the prickle was right, so he paid attention. For a while, he kept glancing up at the other soldiers, officers, and Middle Eastern allied military that sporadically passed him by, wondering what it could mean.

Maybe he was about to meet someone. His heart skipped a bit eagerly at the thought, though by now—he was twenty-three years old—he had experienced enough heartache to not be completely optimistic. And there didn't seem to be any winsome girls strolling around the Army base terminal in this Middle Eastern desert. He tried to put the thought aside, but given his personality, he knew it would be difficult to do.

Who knows? Maybe she's inside the terminal, frustrated that her flight's gotten delayed, and she's on her way outside to catch some rays... That elusive she. He shook his head to dispel the thought. *Better focus on getting ready for med school in the fall. Only a few more weeks till your tour of duty's up...only a few more "fews" left to go!*

Still, he sighed as he pulled out his flute case. He was settling himself for a long wait. Another military delay meant that their flight wouldn't be happening for an hour.

He watched the heat shimmering in hypnotic waves over the desert sand as he assembled his slim silver instrument. There were few other people outside just now. Just the other guys in his squad leaning against their bags and dozing off in the hot sunshine, hats over their eyes, earplugs in, listening to music or Armed Forces Radio broadcasts.

One officer was standing a short distance from him, leaning on a railing and staring out at the desert, apparently lost in thought. When Paul began blowing softly into his flute, the officer turned with surprise and smiled. An older man, ruddy-faced, wearing his ACUs, with a black eagle on his uniform,

1

marking him as a full-bird colonel. He listened for a moment, then turned back to the desert and his own solitude, and pulled out his wallet. Paul could tell he was still listening, and encouraged, felt his way through the melody, making it up as he went along.

Then he heard the sound.

He opened his eyes and lowered his flute at the whistling sound starting in the distance. But too quickly he recognized the high-pitched scream.

"Incoming!" he and two other squad members shouted simultaneously. As Paul threw himself face forward on the ground, he barely registered the colonel turning away from the railing as something exploded against the concrete wall of the terminal.

There was a bright light, confusion and pandemonium, but the members of Paul's squad went into action immediately. Paul, who had been knocked over by the explosion, scrambled to his feet and half-hobbled, half-sprinted to the colonel. The officer was moaning, lying in a twisted position against the wall of the air terminal sprinkled with concrete dust and debris. Paul and another infantryman pulled him back away from the smoking mass the mortar round had left.

"Medic!" the infantryman yelled as the other members of Paul's squad hurried around him.

"On it!" Paul was already checking the man's vital signs. The officer was still in obvious pain, clutching his arm breathing fast. Paul pulled out his medic's kit and focused on the wounded man. His color was good, he was breathing okay. "What's your name, sir?"

"Durham. Colonel Robert Durham, Internal Affairs."

"You in pain?"

"Lots."

"Your arm?"

"Think I landed on it when I fell," the man grunted.

Paul did a check of the man's limbs and quickly discovered that his left arm was indeed broken. "Anything else hurting?" He put on his stethoscope and took a quick listen to the man's lungs, then tried to ascertain if there were any other injuries.

"Just my arm."

Paul glanced around. Apparently the colonel was the only victim of the mortar round: everyone else had cleared the vicinity.

"I'm going to try to splint your arm, sir, okay?"

But as soon as he started to lift the arm, the colonel gasped in pain. "Hold on, just a moment, sir," Paul said, pulling a pen from his pocket.

Probing for the right spot, he pressed it gently and firmly in the indentation of the man's upper ear, an acupressure point for pain. The colonel's panic seemed to subside. Paul carefully set the broken arm in a splint and wrapped it with an ace bandage.

"My wallet..." the colonel said. "I had it out when I fell..."

Paul glanced around and saw the wallet lying on the ground, its contents scattered around him. Getting to his feet, he retrieved it. "Is this it sir?"

"Yes, it is," Colonel Durham said, and feebly tried to take it with his good arm.

"Don't move," Paul said. "Let me put it back together for you." He replaced the ID cards, money, and photographs. There was a prayer card with a wooden cross glued to it, and Paul brushed the debris off it and gave it a quick kiss of reverence before replacing it.

"You a Christian, corporal?" the colonel asked.

"Yup. Catholic, actually," Paul said.

"Hmph," the colonel said. He tried to look up. "They doing a QRF?"

Paul glanced around. One member of the squad was busy calling in a 9-line MEDIVAC report for the colonel's injury, and his squad leader was organizing the other members. "Yes sir, looks like they're going to go check out the fence line to see if they can get a shot at the OPFOR who shot off that round."

"Hope we get them before they hit us again," the colonel said, twisting around.

"Hope so too, sir. Just relax. We'll get you transport out of here." Paul decided to keep the colonel conscious and relaxed as long as possible. "Sir, if you don't mind my asking, are these all your kids?"

The officer glanced up at the photo Paul was holding. "They are now," he said. "Plus two more, both boys. That's our wedding photo. Sallie and I each brought six kids into the marriage."

"Six kids—each?" Paul looked closely at the photo and counted. In the photo, Colonel Durham stood next to a woman in a simple white dress, and two rows of six girls flanked them. "Twelve?"

The colonel cocked his head. "It's a bit unusual," he said. "My first wife died in a car accident. About a year later, our church was raising money for a woman whose husband died in a construction accident. She had six daughters too. That struck me, so I asked our pastor if he could put me in touch with her. Five years ago, we were married."

"Wow," Paul said. "What a great story! My own parents have eight kids. Trying to fit eight kids into a split-level growing up was uh—an experience! But fourteen: that must be crazy! But fun," he added.

"Well, it's definitely crazy," the colonel admitted with a sigh.

At last Paul spotted a medic humvee coming towards them and breathed a sigh of relief. Paul's squad sergeant was hurrying over to him.

"You okay?"

The colonel didn't answer, but Paul answered for him, "A broken arm, but I think he's okay otherwise."

"I meant you, corporal."

Paul blinked and looked down. There was blood spreading over his pants leg, and he was suddenly aware of a throbbing pain in his thigh. His adrenaline rush must have masked it. "Uh, yeah, I guess I'll need some treatment."

"Where's your flute, corporal?"

Paul, who had been dozing in his hospital bed, woke up with a start to find the colonel staring down at him, grinning, his arm in a sling. He returned the smile a bit faintly.

"I'm not sure, actually. I think my squad leader got my stuff," Paul said, trying to sit up.

"At ease, soldier. I just wanted to come by and see the medic who helped get me through that close call. God bless you," he shook his head. "They said you took some shrapnel to the leg."

"Yeah, but they think I'll be all right." Paul said. "Lucky it missed the joint. If I can rest through the spring, I'll be fine by the summer."

"They sending you back stateside?"

"Yes sir. My tour of duty was almost up. And you?"

"I'm thinking it's time for me to take the early retirement option." The colonel laughed and sat down in the chair by Paul's bed. "So where'd you learn to play the flute?"

"Oh, in college. A few friends and I had a juggling group. We used to go to festivals to juggle, and I learned so that I had something to play along in the background."

"Sounds like a fun job."

"It was, actually. If I recoup all right, I'm going to do some more of that this summer."

"Now," the colonel said in a fatherly tone, "I hope the army's preparing you to do more than just juggle."

"Well, I do acrobatics and aikido as well." Paul couldn't help saying. He grinned. "Sorry, that was a joke. No, juggling's just a hobby. Actually, the Army's paying for me to go to medical school. I'll start in the fall."

"Oh, really? Good for you. But if you're pre-med, I'm surprised they didn't place you in a medical core."

"Well, I sort of liked being in a squad, you know? A bit more action. Plus my specialty is emergency medicine."

"I can say you did a good job there. By the way, what was that you were doing in my ear that stopped the pain?"

"Acupressure points. I've been interested in acupuncture and Eastern medicine since high school. I'd like to get training in Eastern and Western medicine and use both in my practice."

"Some would say there are profound differences between the two systems that make them incompatible," the man said cautiously.

Paul shrugged. "I just don't buy the whole Eastern versus Western divide. Human beings live in both places, and they all need healing."

"Hmph," the colonel said, "Well, that's an interesting take on things. I wish you well in your recovery. Hope your folks weren't too worried about you when they heard about your injury."

"They're glad I'm all right. And your family, sir?"

"Sallie thinks it's God intervening on her behalf to get me back home to Maryland. I've been saying for the last couple years that I needed to stay stateside for a while. Our girls are mostly teenagers by now, and it's probably better if I'm there to help out with the parenting." He looked a bit gloomy.

"Sounds like a big job, handling a dozen teenagers," Paul said, since the man had fallen silent.

"It is. You know, teenaged girls. Typical." He changed the subject. "So, are you going to juggle at any festivals this summer?"

"Yes, actually," Paul said. "My friends are all trying to hold down real jobs now, so I'm the only one left who can still do it. And the organizers at the Bayside Colonial Festival in Maryland wanted me to come back. So that's where I'll be going."

"Bayside, Maryland?" The colonel looked surprised. "That's our town!"

"Really?" Paul said. "Great little town. Right on the Chesapeake Bay, too."

The colonel beamed as he stood up. "It is a great town," he said, pulling a card out of his wallet. "Look us up when you get there and come visit."

"Thanks! I'll look forward to it," Paul took the card.

The Durham Family

Robert Durham≈≈≈≈≈Sallie Fendelman

Rachel, 18	Cheryl, 18
Miriam, 17	Tammy, 17
Priscilla, 15	Taren, 17
Rebecca, 14	Brittany, 15
Lydia, 13	Melanie, 13
Deborah, 11	Linette, 11

Robbie, 3

Jabez, 1

one

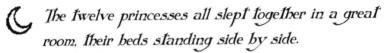 *The twelve princesses all slept together in a great room, their beds standing side by side.*

— *Grimm*

Rachel!"

Rachel Durham heard the voice distantly, but it was still far enough away to ignore. She had time. Chances were that Sallie would find another sister to help before thinking to call her oldest stepdaughter again.

So Rachel continued to lean out of the kitchen door and look down the lawn over the trees sloping to the bay. Soon the night would come. The wind was making flurries of ripples on the water, and the summer sunset was simmering off in the west, leaving a streak of pink like a road that seemed to be beckoning her to follow.

If only I could run away right now, she thought. The breeze was alluring, refreshing, and inside the house was stale and stifling, even in the air conditioning. She wanted to run through the woods and go down to the water, just to sit on a rock out in the bay. Just a taste of freedom…

"RACHEL!"

She whirled around. "What?"

The kitchen door slapped shut behind her, trapping her back in the light and noise and routine of the household. "Look at Jabez!" The sound of Sallie's voice cut through her senses as Rachel's eyes adjusted to the brightness of the kitchen. Her stepmother, thin blond hair falling out of a ponytail, was pointing into the pantry with one hand like a condemning Old Testament prophet. Her other hand was clutching a basket full of laundry.

Rolling her eyes, Rachel looked into the pantry, and then grimaced. Eighteen-month old Jabez was sitting on the floor, with one chubby hand poked shoulder deep into a container of bread flour. Hearing his name, he raised his eyes, puckered over with brown stubs of eyebrow. His baby mouth was a round O. "Am I not supposed to be doing this?" his gaze clearly said.

"Please get him cleaned up!" Sallie said brusquely. "And finish the kitchen."

"The kitchen *is* finished!" Rachel said incredulously, looking around at the enormous room with its historical stone fireplace and newly-installed cabinets and appliances. The dishes were drip-drying on the countertop, while her sisters busied themselves with a few final chores.

"Why weren't you girls watching Jabez?" Sallie retorted, instead of apologizing.

"Maybe because we were too busy doing the kitchen," Rachel muttered, throwing down her towel and leaning down to get her baby brother. Sallie exited the kitchen, calling for the twins to come and get the laundry.

"Bad baby," Rachel pronounced, prying Jabez's hands gently off the flour container and tucking him under her arm like a sack. The pantry was a mess, but, she decided, that wasn't her problem. She was the oldest sister in the house: she could delegate.

Since seventeen-year-old Miriam, the second-in-command, was drying dishes, and Liddy and Becca were sweeping the floors, Rachel made up her mind that cleaning up the pantry was Prisca's job. But the fifteen-year old sister was nowhere to be seen. *Prisca's goofing off, as usual.*

Gritting her teeth, Rachel tried to diffuse her irritation by talking to Jabez. "Bad boy, bad boy," she chanted as she dusted him off, and he chuckled at her. She pressed a small kiss on his head, and he gleefully shoved both fists into her face, exuberantly careless in his affection. She sighed, appreciating his small-scale male energy in a house with so many girls.

"Got to put you to bed," Rachel said, putting him under her arm again. "And find the slacker."

She caught sight of herself in the mirror over the sideboard and half-smiled. She had skin with a touch of olive, mahogany hair and bright blue-green eyes she was quite proud of. Rachel Durham was attractive, and she knew it.

Whooshing a laughing Jabez along in her arms, she turned a corner to look into the side parlor. Her youngest sister Debbie was vacuuming, but no sign of Prisca. She turned another corner to go check the library. Sometimes Rachel was happy to be living in a rambling historical house, but at times like this, she wished there were less nooks and crannies where siblings skipping chores could hide.

Jabez was getting heavy, and he was about to start whining. Looking around for someone to take him, Rachel spotted Cheryl in the downstairs bathroom, leaning against the side of the shower wall, almost hidden by the curtain.

Her oldest stepsister was supposed to be cleaning, but Rachel guessed, from the bend of her head and the light glinting off her glasses, that she was reading a book. Cheryl was six months younger, and very different from Rachel: a nervous, insecure, dreamy type who was chronically disorganized.

Rachel's policy was to use a soft touch when it came to Sallie's daughters. In their blended family, there were enough problems without looking for more. Keeping her mouth shut, Rachel walked past the bathroom, getting more and more irritated with Prisca every moment.

Moving Jabez onto her shoulders, Rachel hurried up the steps to the girls' bedroom on the top floor. "Pris—CA!" she bellowed.

Her fifteen-year-old sister was crouched over on the lower bunk of her bed, reading a magazine, which she immediately rolled over to hide. "What?" Prisca said defensively.

"The kitchen floor's not mopped," Rachel said.

"I did it!"

Rachel shrugged. "Could have fooled me. Anyway, you'll have to do the pantry over. Jabez got into the flour."

Prisca swore, stuffed the magazine under her pillow and stormed downstairs, still spitting out profanity.

Rachel followed her out and down the steps. "You better not let Dad hear you talking like that."

"Oh, shut up!" Prisca said, her voice rising piercingly as she hurried downstairs. Prisca had always been a tad temperamental, but lately she had been even more so. Not wanting to exasperate the situation further, Rachel decided to give Prisca some space for the moment.

She met Brittany, one of the more easy-going Fendelman girls, coming out of the boys' bedroom with the vacuum cleaner. "Want to get him ready for bed?" Rachel said, indicating Jabez. "He had a flour adventure. I'll take the vacuum downstairs." Over Brittany's pompom ponytail, Rachel saw that the room was cleaned and straightened. "Hey, good job."

Instead of answering, Brittany shrugged, and then puffed out her cheeks in a goofy face for Jabez, who burst into riotous giggles. Brittany whisked him out of Rachel's arms and around the bedroom in some basketball moves.

Having gotten rid of her toddler burden, Rachel walked downstairs with the vacuum, rubbing her shoulder. She needed to make sure that Prisca had actually gotten to the kitchen.

She stowed the vacuum, and found Prisca in the pantry, sweeping up flour with quick angry strokes. The dish rack was empty and the girls were scattered. There was scum in the sink, and she picked a sponge and wiped it off, then looked around.

Done for the night. It had been a long day. Trucking her siblings to swimming lessons in the morning, grocery shopping in the afternoon, weeding the garden, picking raspberries from their bushes, making supper, and cleaning up—*man, summer is supposed to be a vacation,* she thought. *And I've barely done anything except work.*

I need a shower, she thought. *And some time to relax.* Thinking of the fashion magazine under Prisca's pillow, she turned her path towards the upstairs again. But as she opened the door to the back staircase, Dad's voice rang out, "Girls! Time for family devotions!"

She groaned out loud, and regretted it at once. Her dad's head snapped around the corner from the living room, his eyes hard. "What was that, young lady?"

"Nothing," Rachel said, massaging her shoulder and wincing as though she had just banged it. "Just hit myself with the door."

Her dad looked at her suspiciously, but Rachel, feigning innocence, slouched past him into the living room.

Ever since Dad had gotten back from his tour of duty, he had decreed that the time after dinner was "family hour." He wanted everyone hanging out in the living room for an hour or more so that they could have "quality time." But by the end of the day, Rachel was sick and tired of her family, and being around Dad wasn't helping much. He just didn't have the energy to deal with them all now, and Rachel knew it. She wished Dad would admit it to himself that his idea of a nice, happy time with his daughters just wasn't working out.

Only a few family members were in the living room. Rachel noticed that Linette had suddenly reappeared: the youngest Fendelman had vanished after dinner, leaving someone else to clear the table, and Cheryl hadn't done anything about it. Now Linette, adorable with blond curling hair and large brown eyes, was snuggling up against Sallie and listening to her read a library book. As usual she was pretending to be younger than her eleven years and skipping chores with no consequences. The Fendelmans were lousy at the chain of command.

With satisfaction, Rachel noticed that the youngest Durham sister, eleven-year-old Debbie, was industriously vacuuming crumbs under the dining room table. Noticing Rachel, Debbie made a face and rolled her eyes at Linette. Rachel grinned back knowingly. With dark hair and blue eyes, Debbie was arguably prettier than Linette. But Debbie was no slouch, even if she was a scamp.

"Devotions!" her dad called again, but no one was coming. Rachel sat down, and realized how long it had been since she had. A sigh escaped her, and she leaned back in the armchair and picked up one of Sallie's women's magazines. Recipes were not her thing, but she was bored. She turned the pages to an article on bedroom makeovers.

"Why can't we go on vacation there?" Debbie asked over her shoulder, pointing to an advertisement of a girl sunbathing on a Caribbean isle.

"Ask Dad," Rachel said absently.

"Dad!" Debbie started, but Rachel, realizing she had misspoken, pinched her.

"I didn't mean you should *really* ask him," Rachel said hastily. "Look at those dresses: aren't they gorgeous?"

Sallie looked up. "I don't think you should be looking at that magazine during devotions," she said, putting out a hand.

But we aren't even having devotions yet, Rachel silently fumed as she handed over the magazine. She stared at her denim skirt, which seemed to her to be unforgivably plain. The other girls were drifting into the living room now. Three-year-old Robbie bolted through the door and leapt onto the couch. Jabez, now in pajamas, toddled through the door after him, tripped, and fell face-down on the carpet.

Amidst the wails, Rachel heard the phone on the end table ringing and picked it up. "Hello?"

"Uh, is Rachel there?"

Warmth spread through her. "This is Rachel," she said quietly.

"Hey, what's up? It's Alan."

"Hi!" She glanced circumspectly around. Only a few of the girls noticed she was on the phone: Sallie was busy with Jabez.

"Hey, remember that CD we bought at the mall? I was wondering when I could get it back from you."

"Um, let me see," Rachel ran through her head. "Maybe on Monday when I go to the library..."

"Who are you talking to?"

Out of nowhere, her dad had appeared in front of her and was fixing her with a steely glance. Great. Perfect timing. Not only had Alan called, but he had managed to time his call to the moment when all fourteen children were finally in the living room.

"Uh—hey, I got to go," Rachel hedged. "Family devotions." She quickly hung up the phone and looked at her dad. "What?"

"Who were you talking to?"

"A friend from church. I need to return a CD, that's all."

"Which friend?" He put out his hand for the phone. Rachel knew she was sunk: Alan's name was on the caller ID.

"Alan." There was no helping it now.

"That Vonnegun boy, right?"

"Dad, he goes to our *church*."

Her dad looked at her, arms folded. "Did you get the CD from him at church?"

"I ran into him at the mall," Rachel said defensively.

"Did you run into him, or did you meet him there?"

Rachel threw up her hands. "Dad, I don't see what the big deal is! What difference does it make?"

"Because you girls know that you are not allowed to be with boys unsupervised. That's the rule in our house. You were disobeying. And setting a bad example for your younger sisters." Her father's blue eyes bored into her. "I want to talk with you about this after devotions."

"Fine," she said, and stared at the ground. The other girls waited in silence while Dad walked to his chair, picked up his Bible, sat down, and opened it. Devotions began.

Afterwards, Dad closed the Bible and said, "Rachel, I want to speak with you upstairs."

She inclined her head and got up stiffly. Dad walked her upstairs, talking to her all the time. "You know perfectly well that you should not be sneaking off to hang out with boys. That is our family rule. You are eighteen years old, the oldest girl in this house, and you set the tone for the rest by how you behave. Do you understand me?"

"I understand you, Dad," she said.

"Then why don't you exhibit it in your actions?" he raised his eyebrows. "I don't understand it. And I don't understand why you can't respond to a simple request without flouncing around. I don't appreciate it. Your mother – " he barely paused, "doesn't appreciate it. How can I keep the rest of your sisters in order if you don't listen to me?"

Rachel pursed her lips but didn't reply. As they walked up the stairs to the attic, her father went on, "It's my responsibility before God to raise you up in the way you should go. I take that responsibility seriously. Have I made it clear to you, Rachel, the way you are supposed to behave? Haven't I shown you what goodness is, what the right way is? Have I made that clear to you?"

"Yes," she said, when his question became more than rhetorical.

"Then if you know the way, why you don't follow it?"

Because it's boring, stifling and rigid—like some kind of military exercise. But even Rachel didn't dare to say something like that to her father, not when he was like this. She looked away from him, knowing how she was supposed to respond, but unable to do so, any more than she could bend her knees backwards.

"I want you to go to your bedroom and think about what I've just said to you," her father said, and opened the door to the top floor. "You know I love you, Rachel. Good night."

He shut the door, and she stood in the room, hot tears on her face, a rage growing in her that even she could see was out of proportion to the situation. She flicked the fan switch "on," flung herself on her bed, grabbed her pillow fiercely, and thrust her face into it. Her tears stopped almost immediately, but the turbulence inside didn't die down. *Why is it always like this? He treats me like a child and sends me to my room.* Ever since Dad had gotten back from the Middle East ... *no, ever since Mom died ... he just doesn't know me. He just doesn't understand.*

Her eye caught the black and white photograph encased in a frame sitting on her dresser. It was a picture of her mother, laughing and looking extremely gorgeous in a black dress and pearls. To Rachel, that picture seemed to represent an era of her life that was unreachable. She was beyond wishing that Mom was still alive: she just felt bleak, grim acceptance.

After a moment, she heard the door close softly, footsteps came up the steps, and then thirteen-year-old Melanie Fendelman sat down on the bed. "Hey Ray," she said in her soft drawl, rubbing her fingers over her older stepsister's back.

That was Melanie for you, loyal and wanting to help out any way she could. Rachel had known that her younger stepsister would seek her out, and she was grateful.

"Thanks," Rachel turned over with a sigh at last, wiping her eyes. She stared at the sloped ceiling of their rooftop room and listened to the whirring of the fan. "You didn't need to come up."

"I know. How are you?"

"Stinky." Despite her anger, Rachel couldn't resist a smile as she looked at her young stepsister. She considered Melanie the prettiest of the Fendelman girls. Though not conventionally beautiful, Melanie had a round, still childlike face with amber eyes that squinted easily up into laugh lines, honey-colored wavy hair, and an open demeanor that made you love her as soon as you looked at her. It always gave Rachel a twinge of remorse, wishing that she could be more like Melanie, peaceful and friendly and accepting. She would trade all the Fendelmans plus a few of the Durhams, Rachel thought, so long as she could still have Melanie as her sister.

"What do you think, Melanie? I just don't get Dad. And he is just clueless about me. What do you think?"

Melanie chewed the side of her mouth. "Maybe you're just too much alike."

"Yes, that's possible," Rachel said, rolling over. She stared at the ceiling. "Dear God, I just want out of here. I just want out. I'm just sick and tired of it."

The door to the attic opened again, and Miriam came up, followed by Tammy, one of the Fendelman twins.

"Hi there!" Miriam said brightly. "All full of sunshine and candy?" A bit on the heavy side, she could always be counted on for a sarcastic comment.

Rachel snorted. "Yeah. Sour balls."

Miriam chuckled and pushed open one of the large windows a bit further, then sat on her bunk bed, bumping her head. Exclaiming, she rubbed her dark brown hair. "You know, as soon as I get out of this house and get a job, do you know what I am going to do with my first credit card?"

"What?" Tammy asked, swinging onto her bed and throwing back her straight blond hair.

"I'm going to buy a huge California king-sized bed," Miriam said impressively. "I will never ever sleep in a bunk bed again. Forgetaboutit!"

"You can switch with me sometime," Tammy offered. She and Taren, her twin, slept in their own single beds.

"Oh, come on!" Rachel cried out. "I think bunk beds are so romantic! When I get married, I'll tell my husband, 'if you don't want to sleep in a bunk bed, this is off!'"

The others giggled. "He won't like that," Tammy opined.

"Oh, I'll let him choose whether he wants the top bunk or the bottom," Rachel said generously. She rolled to her feet and sat up, staring around the room. "Come on. Let's rearrange the room."

The girls stared at their room, which Dad had been promising to break up into smaller sections ever since they had bought the house, but which he had never seemed to find time or money to have done. The vast whitewashed room had three bunk beds (staggered in the middle of the room, to take advantage of the highest point in the sloped ceiling), two single beds, and two double beds, along with a big long-mirrored dresser and two little dressers and a vanity. "No matter what we do with it, it's still going to look like a camp cabin," Miriam said dryly.

Rachel shrugged. "I need a new perspective. Something. Come on, let's give a try. Tammy, help me with the big bed. It's been in front of the chimney forever. Oh, here's Cheryl. Give us a hand."

"With what?" The oldest Fendelman girl had just walked upstairs.

"We're rearranging furniture again," Tammy said.

"Again? Why? At this hour?" Cheryl had her book in her hands, and she did look tired.

"Oh, come on. The room's clean. If all five of us do it, it won't take long." Rachel said.

Reluctantly, the blond girl put down her book and found a place at the footboard. "Where are we moving this?"

As each of the beds had drawers beneath for storage, moving them was a chore. "Good thing you came in. It'll take all five of us to move it, for sure." Tammy figured.

"I just want to move it over by the window. And we can move the two dressers here, and put them together to make one big dresser. Well, sort of. It's something I've thought about for a while," Rachel said.

"That might look cool," Melanie agreed. Cheryl sized up the situation, and began to get interested.

"We might be able to hang a canopy over the bed, from the ceiling beams," she said.

"Hm! Yes, that's a great idea!" Rachel said appreciatively. Good, she had a team.

So all four of them shoved the double bed out from the wall with Miriam complaining about the uneven floorboards.

"This room is too ancient," she grumbled.

"I like old rooms," Rachel retorted, struggling to get her hands under the headboard for another push. "It was once a sewing room—excuse me, a weaving room—when this house was built, before the Civil War. That's why there's so many windows—to let in light to work by." She grunted and shoved and the bed slowly creaked forward three feet.

"You know, this will look very different," Melanie said, as they paused to rest. "We've rearranged before, but we've never moved this bed."

"Wonder why?" Miriam puffed sarcastically, putting an elbow on the footboard to rest.

"We always had it shoved up against the kitchen chimney," Cheryl pointed out. Rachel had chosen that spot for the biggest bed because the wide brick chimney against the wall was a natural focal point.

"Isn't there something funny about that chimney?" Tammy said abruptly. "It looks too wide."

"Too wide?" Rachel queried, running her hands over the worn red bricks, smoothed by time.

"Well, wider than the kitchen hearth is. I don't know. Brittany would be able to tell you. It's a spatial thing."

Rachel stretched out her arms. "That's how wide the kitchen chimney is," she said. "I almost can't get my hands around it."

"I think the chimney up here is wider. Measure and see," Tammy said.

Rachel did, and was surprised. "You're right, it's about a foot and a half wider."

"I always wondered why they needed such a wide chimney," Melanie said. "It's just to let smoke out with, right?"

"Right," Rachel agreed, ironically. "There's actually a hearth in the master bedroom—well, what used to be the master bedroom, which is now your mom's sewing room. I used to wish there was a hearth up here. It sure would be nice to have a fire in winter."

Tammy, intrigued, had gotten up and was trying to see if she could get her hands around the wide expanse of brick. "That's weird. You'd think they could measure. It's almost as though—hey!"

She put her hand on the wall board to the right side of the chimney, and it moved slightly. "This board is loose."

Rachel scrambled to her feet. "Let me see," she said, with proprietor's interest. She felt the board of the paneling. "What do you mean? It's not warped—the nails are in solidly."

"No, no. Push it in," Tammy said. "It's like, soft."

"Soft?"

"Well, it gives under your hand."

Rachel pushed on the board, and to her amazement, it—and several boards next to it—moved inward on an invisible hinge, a door about eighteen inches wide and five feet high.

"That's too strange," she said. "What is it? A broom closet?"

"Yeah, for one broom," Miriam said.

Rachel pushed the door in as far as it could go, and the scent of air hit her nostrils—a clean, cool breath. The breath of adventure.

two

Their room was locked with a great bolt and there was no way that the princesses should have been able to leave, but yet...

— *Grimm*

achel's voice dropped to a low tone. "This is not a broom closet."

"What is it?" Cheryl asked, in a hushed voice.

They looked at the narrow opening.

"Miriam, get me a flashlight. Quickly, and quietly, and *don't* draw attention to yourself," Rachel said.

Miriam, stirred by her sister's voice, obeyed instantly.

Rachel felt inside the door. She had expected the chimney wall to form the left side of the closet, but instead there was no wall. Exploring with her hands, she found that what appeared to be, outside the closet, the side of the chimney was actually an extra two columns of bricks, placed to make the chimney appear wider than it was.

"I think," she said at last, "that this was designed for a person."

"But how?" Cheryl asked, pushing back her glasses with a finger.

"Look, the door bends all the way back. The hinges must be hidden in the paneling somehow. You slide through this narrow crack into this area here—" Rachel, unafraid, stepped into the darkness. "And then shut the door. Yes, there's a handle on this side. It's a hiding place—no!"

"What!" all three girls chorused at once.

Her foot had slipped into air. "No, it's not a closet. It's a hole—No! It's a step, a step down!"

"Is it a stair?" Melanie asked.

"I'm not sure," Rachel said, a rush of adrenaline pumping through her veins. "Where is Miriam?" She was giddy with that first step into the dark, but didn't want to go further without some guiding light.

Miriam came inside the bedroom and shut the door softly behind her, holding the flashlight. She flashed a wicked grin. "Should I lock the door downstairs?"

"Yes—no. Wait." Rachel took the flashlight and clicked it on. It shone into the narrow darkness. All the girls peered around the slit. There was a narrow staircase, leading down and around.

"Oh, this is too weird," Miriam breathed.

"Let's go in." Rachel said suddenly. "All of us."

"In there?" Cheryl asked, suddenly looking scared.

"Come on," Rachel insisted. She was nervous too, but figured if they were all in it together, she would be less scared.

"What if the staircase collapses?" Tammy demanded.

"Then the ones behind could pull us out. Come on!"

"I don't like dark narrow places," Cheryl objected.

"It's got to open out soon. Come on, let's give it a try," Rachel coaxed.

"I'll go with you," Melanie said, and Tammy nodded. Cheryl reluctantly bobbed her head, and they crowded into the slit, Rachel leading the way.

At first it was terrifyingly cramped. Rachel counted down as she edged along the wall, sideways. One step down. Two steps down. Three steps down. Four steps down. Five steps down. "Are we all inside?"

"Barely," said Miriam, "but I think I can make it."

"Then shut the door."

The room light was cut off abruptly, and the girls were alone in the confined space with only the flashlight cutting a narrow beam through the deep brown darkness.

"Right," Rachel whispered. "Slowly now!"

The stairs were steep and uneven, and the spiral made them tricky to navigate. Rachel felt them make a full circle turn as they descended down, still stepping sideways. After about twenty steps, Rachel found it hard to judge just how far down they had gone. "Are we at the level of the first floor?" she hissed.

"I can't tell," Cheryl said, second to last in line. "Listen."

They all halted. Faintly, they could hear the sound of the dishwasher running.

"We must be near the kitchen. Are there more steps?"

"Yes," Rachel said. "Gosh, we must be going down into the basement."

They continued treading downwards, the air growing fresher and cooler, until Rachel unexpectedly turned into a wooden wall. "Stop!" she breathed, and the girls came to a stop.

"Is it another door?" Cheryl asked anxiously.

"I think so—wait—no, on this side—" Rachel found a worn iron handle and pulled in. She stepped forward unexpectedly down, into open space, on gravel, and stumbled forwards. "I'm out! Watch your step! That last one is steep!"

They were still in blackness, but they could hear outdoor sounds—trees rustling in the wind, the noise of water, bird calls. "Where are we now?" Melanie asked, puzzled.

Rachel shone her flashlight around. A jumble of metal parts and spokes flickered in the light. "Bicycles!" Suddenly it all fit together. "We're in the bike cave!"

Their house was set on a slight outcropping, and they had long ago discovered that if you went down to the bayside in a certain way, you would find a shallow cave in the side of the cliff, a place just big enough to keep things like bicycles out of the elements. Of course it had been exciting at the time to discover the bike cave, which Dad had said must have been a root cellar at one time, but that discovery seemed terribly tame compared to this one.

"The steps are behind the shelves," Rachel said, shining her flashlight. "See? There's the shelves of the old root cellar. We never thought to look behind them…"

There was silence for a moment, and then Rachel picked her way out around the bikes to the outside of the cave. The others followed her. They were now in a woody path leading down to the beach.

"What *was* that?" Melanie asked after a minute.

There was silence, but then Cheryl spoke up. "Maybe it was for the Underground Railroad. Remember? When we first bought this house, the people who lived in it told Mom that they thought it had once been a station on the Underground Railroad. You know, where they hid escaped slaves."

"I see. They would hide the escaped slaves in the weaving room, and if they needed to get away fast, they could hide in the hidden staircase, and maybe escape out through the woods. Then out to the bay. That must have been convenient," Rachel said.

Cheryl began to get excited. "Then we've made an important historical discovery! We could tell the museum folks and get pictures taken. I bet there's some important archeological evidence around here…"

Rachel interrupted her. "No." She shone the flashlight around the huddled group, looking at each of them in turn. "We don't tell anyone."

"Why not?" Tammy spoke up first.

"Because," Rachel said calmly. "we can use this staircase now. For ourselves. To get out of the house at night, whenever we want to."

"What for?" Cheryl asked.

Rachel looked up at the trees, and felt a wave of excitement come over her, carried on the night breeze. "After everyone goes to sleep," she said. "we can come down here and go swimming."

There was a current of excitement in the air, because Miriam squealed, and the other sisters shushed her quickly.

"Look around," Rachel dropped the flashlight, and without its white radiance, the world around them changed from black to dark blue and silver. The moonlight glimmered on the beech trees overhead. "It's a different world, waiting to be explored. So we must keep this a dead secret. Understand?"

She looked around at the darkened faces of her sisters, and saw them bob yes, one by one. "Okay," she said. "Let's go back up."

Rachel insisted on going up the secret staircase first, and listened long and hard at the door to ascertain if any of the other sisters were in the room, even lying on the bed and reading. When she finally opened the door a crack and found it empty and the bedroom door shut, she breathed a sigh of relief and slipped in. The others followed her.

"What should we do now?" Tammy asked, but Rachel shook her head.

In a low voice she said, "We never talk about *that* out here."

There was a respectful pause, and then Tammy said, "I mean, about the bed. Are we going to move it, or not?"

Rachel thought. If they moved the bed now, it would open up the chimney area, and someone else might discover the board. But they needed to keep the board door open somehow, in order to use it.

"Move it slightly to this side," she said, after a moment. "Here. If we move down the next two dressers an inch or two, we can do it."

"All right," Cheryl said cheerfully, and they moved the furniture.

They were moving the last bunk bed when Prisca came up the steps and started. "Where were you guys?" she exclaimed.

Rachel, with presence of mind, shut the door, and then made Prisca sit down.

"I am serious," Prisca said. "I was about to freak. I heard you all in here talking, then I went to the bathroom. Then I came back, and found you all gone. Where did you go?"

Rachel said only, "Did you tell anyone we were gone?"

Prisca, confused, said, "No. I thought I was imagining things, until I found you back in here. What gives?"

Rachel eyed each of her sisters, and poised the question at Cheryl and Miriam. Cheryl nodded, and Rachel, deciding to incline to her wishes, asked, "Can you keep a secret, Pris?"

"You know I can," Prisca said. "What?"

"First, lower your voice. We'll show you—but after the others are asleep," Rachel dropped her voice as Taren and Linette came in. Prisca nodded her head dumbly.

The sisters who knew the secret got ready for bed in unusual silence. Tammy edged over to Rachel during an opportune moment and said in a low voice. "I can't keep a secret from my twin," and Rachel understood.

"Okay then," she said.

When they were all in bed, Rachel kept the light on, reading. She heard her father and Sallie come up the steps and go into their bedroom. Fairly soon the sounds from their room faded into silence. It was late at night, nearly midnight. Outside the window, the silver moonlight and black shadows beckoned.

She carefully kept an eye on the other sisters, and when she was sure all those not in on the secret had dropped off to sleep, she got out of bed, walked quietly to the bedroom door, and locked it. Miriam and Cheryl were alerted, and got noiselessly out of bed. Melanie had been dropping off, but she climbed down from her bunk as well. Rachel touched Prisca, who rolled over and looked at her, then got out of bed. Rachel pressed a finger to her lips, warning quiet. Prisca nodded, and looked around at the others.

Then Tammy touched Taren, who had actually fallen asleep. Taren gave a huge yawn and raised her head. "What's going on?" she asked.

"Shhh!" came from all corners. Linette and Debbie instantly sat up in their beds. Miriam gave an audible groan.

"Are you guys having a secret meeting?" Debbie asked hopefully.

"No. Go back to sleep," hissed Miriam, but Rachel shook her head wearily.

"Let them come," she said. "We might as well bring everyone along. Wake up Liddy and Becca and Brittany too. But keep everyone quiet!"

What the heck, she figured. They might as well start out with having everyone involved. It would be easier in the long run.

When she saw that everyone was awake and hushed, she got out the flashlight from her pillow, and strode to the center of the room a finger on her lips. She looked around, confident that she had everyone's attention, and then approached the hidden door. It now looked so solid that her senses told her she was mistaken. But when she put a hand on the wood and pushed gently, the paneling yielded beneath her fingers. There were muffled gasps from some of the girls. The black crack widened, and Rachel clicked on the flashlight. Inside she went, into that second reality, and the darkness wrapped around her like a cloak.

She followed the beam of the light cautiously down the steps around and around, hearing her sisters behind her, breathing and making hushed exclamations. When she reached the bottom and had fiddled with the little clasp on the door, she pulled the shelving door open and stepped down, her bare foot touching cool gravel, a shimmer of excitement went through her. She bounded through the cave to the woods beyond, laughing to herself for the sheer delight of secret freedom.

Once outside, she clicked off the light and let herself be bathed in the glow of the full moon, the ground around her blotched with the shadows of the trees. It was an entirely different sensation from being bathed in sunlight.

She tossed her hair—she had coal and cobalt hair in the moonlight—back over her shoulders and looked at her sisters. A few of them were looking around uncertainly. Cheryl was explaining the possible origins of the secret stair to the younger ones.

"What are we going to do?" Liddy asked, her voice uncertain.

Rachel raised one eyebrow. "Whatever we like."

"But what if Dad and Sallie find out?" Liddy pressed, her blue eyes shadowed with concern.

"They won't find out," Rachel said, putting the flashlight into a hollow by the door where she could easily find it on the way home. Over her shoulder, she cast a look around the circle. "So long as no one tells them."

She meant that Dad would never find out, that none of the sisters would dream of breathing a word to him or Sallie. But she couldn't impress that on them now. She had to show them how to explore the possibilities first.

"Come on," she invited. "Let's go swimming!"

She plunged along the path through the woods to the bay, and with muffled squeals and protests, her sisters followed. After about a quarter mile they came out of the woods to a short slope leading to the beach.

"But we don't have our swimsuits!" Debbie pointed out, scrambling down beside Rachel breathlessly.

Rachel shrugged at her youngest sister. "Next time, we'll wear our swimsuits to bed. So long as we can get them quietly without Dad and Sallie finding out." She sat down on the pebble beach overhung with a willow tree, and said, "Tomorrow I'll put our swimsuits in the dryer during dinner and bring them upstairs with the laundry. Now, remember, try not to make too much noise."

She stripped down to her underwear and splashed into the water. A few yards out she dove into the plum black water and swam. The colors of the water were so different now, beneath the moon—she plunged upward and out of the water, into the night. Looking over her shoulder, she saw the rest leaping into the bay, and heard their laughter echoing across the waves.

The water was warm, still heated by the long summer day, and she swam slowly, meditatively, feeling herself wrapped in its black beauty. Her hair hung down her back like a heavy seal-fur curtain, sleek as otter skin. She was beautiful in the night, and she knew it.

After a while, she swam to the rock near the shore and climbed lightly atop it to watch the rest. While they frolicked, she planned. Dad must never know about the door. They needed a strategy, a system, and most of all, a combined group secret. It was fortunate that Cheryl had been present for the discovery of the door, and that Tammy had discovered it. That made this a Fendelman effort as surely as a Durham effort. Both sets of girls had equal stake in the discovery. If she could present it to them in the right way, she could bring all of them to an understanding that this secret was too valuable to lose. And they would be unified.

And from there ... Rachel stretched. The horizons were limitless. They could do almost anything they pleased, here in the night. She looked up and down the Bay Shore, from one side to the other, and her eyes fell on the island.

It stood in the middle of their corner of the bay, dark spiky firs and green velvet lawns. In the embrace of the firs stood a fine house, nestled in its evergreens like a movie star wrapped in a mink coat. It was the summerhouse of a rich family, rarely used. Caretakers came and went occasionally by boat during the day, but it seemed to be deserted most of the time.

Deserted or no, there was enough wood and valley on the island's ample shore to hide a dozen girls. If only they had a boat. But their father didn't see a need for a boat, aside from an old canoe the girls used occasionally. And there was no way all twelve of them could fit into the canoe.

The rumble of a motor made her turn her head, and she saw, across the bay, a speedboat slicking through the wavelets like a silver knife cutting through butter, scattering glittering wakes as it passed, generously heaping up the waves. Rachel smiled. That was how it would have to be done. Other people—men—had boats. She would have to be brave, and cunning, and careful, but it could be done.

"I *will* get to that island before the summer is over," she promised herself. She slid off the rock and threw herself back into the purple waves and stroked back to the shore.

"Ready?" she said, all business once more. "Time to go back. Get your things together—be careful not to leave anything. If we're going to keep this secret, we have to be careful. Prisca, get your other sock. Taren, is that yours? Right. All together? Then back up to the cave."

Once they were at the door of the cave, Rachel surveyed the near-dozen wet and breathless faces.

"Okay," Rachel said. "This is our secret. We tell nobody. Not our best friends, not Mom, not Dad, nobody. This is just for us sisters. But we never talk about it during the day. We never use it during the day, not for nipping out of chores, or anything. It doesn't exist during the day. The only time we use it is when we all go down together, at night. After everyone else is asleep. We keep it a dead secret. We don't volunteer that it exists, and if anyone asks us, we don't admit to knowing anything. All agreed?"

Rachel looked at each of the Fendelman girls in turn. "Cheryl? Tammy? Taren? Brittany? Melanie? Linette?" They were with her. Then she looked at her biological sisters. "Miriam? Prisca? Becca? Liddy? Debbie? Anyone object? Anyone too scared?"

"I won't be scared," Liddy said, "not if we stick together."

Rachel nodded. "That's the whole point," she said. "We sisters have got to stick together on this. It's what we can do together, without anyone else supervising us or giving us rules. Right?"

All the girls—Fendelman and Durham—nodded.

"Good," Rachel breathed. She had succeeded. They were all in on this as one. "Now back upstairs. I'll keep this flashlight under my bed. Remember, keep quiet. When we get upstairs, no whispering, no talking. Just straight to sleep. Miriam, go last and latch the bottom door behind us."

She led the way back up the stairs, and opened the top door quietly. She tiptoed inside and held the door open for each sister. Miriam came up last, nodding that everything was okay. Rachel shut the door quietly, pushed the flashlight under the bed, and lay down.

They had pulled it off.

three

A poor soldier, recently returned from the wars, heard of the king's mysterious problem...

—— *Grimm*

Paul reached the campgrounds after a long but carefree walk from the bus station. He paid the fee, and started to get settled in on his vacation. He wasn't thinking about anything in particular, just relishing the sweet taste of freedom. His doctor had declared him fully recovered from his war injury. Medical school didn't begin till the fall. So his tour was done, school was yet to start, and within this brief window, he could do as he pleased.

Trimming expenses to the absolute minimum meant that he had decided to go without a car for the summer. He had packed everything he needed into his backpack and the large colorful bag that held his juggling gear.

He took a bit of time to pick a campsite, and finally chose one within reach of the Bay, but sheltered from the constant breezes that swept over the waters. Clearing the ground and pitching his tent were done in the same leisurely fashion. When everything was arranged, he settled down on a fallen log and just sat for a while, feeling no inclination to move or do anything but be still.

This was his holiday, his treat before starting medical school, and he rejoiced within its limits. He planned to spend the next several weeks camping, hiking, and doing some stints as a street musician and juggler at the Maryland Colonial Festival. Entertaining would pay for the campsite and some food for the next few weeks. If not, he could always ask his parents or one of his seven siblings for money to see him through, but he hoped he wouldn't need to fall back on that.

He started to whistle and picked up a stick, tossing it gently from hand to hand, planning a new tune for his flute. While he had to make time to practice his juggling routine for the festival, which started next week, for now, he could relax. He decided to start with a walk on the beach, maybe go for a swim.

So after tidying up his campsite, he walked down to the beach that bordered the campgrounds. The bay curved around him, and he looked with satisfaction at the green shore stretching out into the distance on either side of him. A few miles down the beach to the left were houses, but to his right the trees came right down to the water, and the land jutted out into a promontory on the bay. There was a house up there: he could see its chimneys through the trees. They must have a beautiful view of the surrounding bay.

He started down the beach to the left, enjoying the brisk breezes. After a while he broke into a jog.

The beach ahead was mostly deserted, but as he jogged on, he saw an older man walking in his direction wearing khakis and a windbreaker. As Paul drew near, the man paused and looked out at the bay. There was something familiar about him. When Paul was close enough, he thought he recognized him.

"Excuse me—Colonel Durham?"

The colonel turned, and his troubled expression was replaced with surprise. "That's right." He brightened up. "Corporal—what was your name? Jester?"

"Fester," Paul said with a grin.

"That's right," the man said, shaking Paul's hand warmly. "How's your leg doing?"

"Doing really well," Paul said. "How about your arm?"

The colonel lifted his arm. "It's OK. My back's a little stiff, but that would happen just by getting old," he said. "It almost doesn't count. But I'm working a desk job now. No more work overseas. My wife is grateful. So what are you doing now?"

"For the next few weeks, I'll be at the Colonial Festival."

The colonel snapped his fingers. "That's right. Fester, jester. You juggle. I remember now. So what are you doing after that? You thinking of staying in the army?"

"Well, at least to get through medical school," Paul said. "I start in the fall. It's the only way I could afford to go."

"Take my advice: don't stay in if you get married."

"Why do you say that, sir?"

The colonel looked out at the bay. "Too hard on the family. I've been in the army since I was nineteen. I've been on tour a lot. It's always tough for the family, but you know, we worked through it. Even after I got married again, everything seemed okay. But coming back this time, it's been different.

It's like I don't know my kids and they don't know me. I'm wondering if I paid too high a price."

After a moment, Paul said, "My dad was military too. He was a captain, in the Marines. We moved around a lot, until he retired a few years ago in Chicago. I don't know what he did differently, but you know, it was okay with us kids. I'm really proud of him."

He noticed the colonel was studying him. "Did you get along with your parents when you were a teenager?"

"Me? I did, I guess. I mean, we had a pretty open relationship."

"You'd tell them what was going on in your life?"

"Sure. Well, sometimes I wanted my own space, but yeah, I'd talk to them a lot."

"It's a mystery to me how that happens," Colonel Durham said. "I can't get my girls to talk to me at all. And they've been very—secretive lately."

"Maybe they're just getting to know you again," Paul ventured. "It takes time."

The colonel shook his head. "There's something going on with them," he said positively. "I can tell they're hiding something. The odd thing is that it's all of them: from the oldest right down to the youngest ones."

"Have you asked them about it?"

"Sure. Flat denial, all down the line. Sallie's asked them about it. Nothing. We finally just let it go, but I can't get the idea out of my head that they're up to something. I've been trying other tactics, but I'm up against a wall." He sighed heavily. "I have no idea what else I can do."

"Maybe it'll come out, in time," Paul said. "Maybe they'll tell you."

Again, Colonel Durham shook his head. "You don't know my daughters," he said positively. He seemed to change the subject. "Would you like to come to dinner, now that you're in town?"

"That would be great."

"How about tonight?"

Paul was taken aback. "Sure. If it's no trouble."

"No, no, it's fine." Colonel Durham said. "Besides, I'd like you to meet my girls. I'm sure you'll have a lot in common." He pointed up the beach in the direction from which Paul had come. "Our house is right up there. But you can reach it by the road as well. Will 5:30 work for you?"

"I'm free," Paul said, grinning. It was good to be on vacation.

"Rachel, look. That must be him, coming up the drive," Prisca said, pushing aside the linen curtains with one finger.

"The new guy that Dad invited?" Rachel rolled her eyes, casting a glance at the other three older sisters sitting in the sewing room, where they were sorting laundry. "I bet he's another spy."

"Dad said he's staying at the campsite near our house," Miriam said.

They all studied the newcomer surreptitiously as he came up the drive.

"What a goofball," Rachel said. "Will you look at those clothes? Who wears striped shirts these days?"

Tammy craned her neck. "So what, Rachel? He's got a nice set of muscles."

Her twin, Taren, agreed after a judicious look. "Plus a rather nice face, from what I can see. Kind of cute."

"He looks too clean cut. Like a grown-up baby. No thanks! How much you want to bet he's an upright young Christian man?" Rachel pronounced mockingly. "Dad would never invite over someone from the military unless he was a *nice* young man. A *very* nice young man." The others stifled giggles.

Prisca said beneath her breath, "Who cares? At least he's a man." Which generated more mirth from everyone except Rachel.

"Whatever." She sat down again, grabbed a fistful of socks, and began turning them over and laying them down one by one, looking for matches as though she were playing solitaire. "Well, he's here, and we're going to have to put up with him now."

After the others left to deliver laundry or spy on the visitor, Rachel deliberately took her time in front of the mirror, putting up her hair. She was tired. Part of the secret pact, as she thought of it, was that when the sisters went out on one of their midnight adventures, no one was allowed to complain about being tired the next day, so as not to arouse suspicion. The sisters had taken to going to bed earlier, and snatching naps for themselves during the day (getting up later was not an option in the Durham family). Today had been a no-nap day for Rachel. At the moment she wasn't feeling up to another outing tonight.

Still, swimming at night was so relaxing. And she had laid other plans, if only they would work out. Maybe tonight they would... Rachel chewed the end of her fingertip and cursed inwardly when she heard the doorbell.

Paul liked to approach people of any sort with a bold and friendly demeanor. However, when he had rounded the curve of the hidden driveway and saw the Durham house, he felt as though he had gone out of his league.

The large, obviously historical house sat on a promontory of land that jutted out into the bay. Three brick chimneys protruded from its weathered tile roof. This was the house Colonel Durham had pointed out to Paul earlier that morning on the beach. Paul guessed that the Durhams must own all the woodlands extending down to the campsite, and probably the beach running around the promontory as well. A low whistle escaped him, and he felt a sudden humility. This was a far cry from his parent's house in the Chicago suburbs. *Oh great*, he said under his breath, feeling apprehensive.

When he knocked on the door, it had been opened by, as he expected, a girl. This girl was about twelve years old, strikingly pretty, with bright blue eyes and long dark brown hair, wearing a skirt printed with small blue flowers and a white shirt. "Hi," said the girl, with a bright and careless attitude. "What do you want?"

Maybe she thought he was a landscaping assistant or a deliveryman. Paul asked, following the script, "Uh, is your father home?"

"Sure. Let me get him." She bounced off, swinging her arms. Paul could see a flagstone interior, and a simply furnished period style entranceway. He swallowed, and looked down again at his canvas shorts and striped shirt. He hadn't expected to be invited to anyone's house for dinner while on vacation, let alone to a house as upscale as this one.

Another brown haired girl came into the entranceway, wearing a denim jumper and pulling her hair up into a ponytail. She had a wide-eyed, faintly surprised expression. "Are you the guy who's coming to dinner?" she asked.

"Um, yes."

"Daddy said you were coming. I'll go get him," and she turned away and clattered up the stairs in sandaled feet.

"That's okay…" Paul tried to say, and gave up. He thrust his hands into his pockets and took them out again, unsure of how to look.

Then suddenly Colonel Durham was striding into the entranceway, beaming and smiling, trailed by the pretty younger girl. Seeing Paul on the doorstep, he took the girl's shoulders and said, "Debbie, we don't let our guests stand outside, we invite them in. Now, go fix your hair." And extending his hand to Paul, he said heartily, "Welcome! Come in!"

Paul returned the handshake and stepped into the house. "Thanks, again, very much," he said, relieved to see the man again. "This is a lovely house. When was it built?"

"I believe 1822—but that's a question you can ask my wife—come on in, and I'll introduce you," Colonel Durham led him through a dining room to a living room, where the willowy blond woman he recognized from the picture sat on the sofa, wearing a cotton print dress with a high neck and nursing a boy toddler. With large brown eyes and straight pale hair in a bun, she looked more subdued than her husband. A girl, a smaller copy of her, sat on the couch reading a book.

"Sallie, this is Paul Fester, the medic that put me back together after that mortar round almost took me out."

"Paul. So glad to meet you," Sallie said, lifting her eyes to his briefly with a smile. She dropped them right away, as though she were shy, or uncomfortable.

"Let me introduce you to some of my children," Colonel Durham said. "This is our son Jabez, and this here on the couch—stand up, please, Linette—is Linette."

"Hello," said Linette, not meeting his eyes.

Colonel Durham was looking around. "I just saw someone—oh, there you are. Brittany and Melanie, I'd like you to meet Paul Fester."

Two young teen girls, blond curly hair in ponytails, both wearing cotton print skirts that came below the knee. Paul was starting to see the pattern. The Durhams must belong to a church that believed that women and girls should always wear skirts, he guessed.

By the time they started to sit down at a table on the porch for dinner, he had met about seven girls, mostly younger ones. Some were blond and shy: others were brown-haired and energetic. It was easy to figure out which parent had begotten which children.

Some oldest girls came down last, as a group: three brunettes—tall and full-figured, and two blonds—twins with long straight hair pulled back from their slim tan faces. Despite the fact that they were wearing the same kind of clothing as their younger sisters, they carried themselves differently. There was an air of dismal sophistication about them, as though they were cuisine reviewers at a very poor restaurant. He was introduced to Rachel, Miriam, Priscilla, Tammy and Taren, and felt as though he was beneath their notice.

Colonel Durham had been mistaken, Paul saw clearly. *We don't have anything in common.*

"Let's sit down," Colonel Durham said, leading the way to a long table on the screened-in patio on one side of the house. They all took their places, and as they bowed their heads for grace, Paul automatically made the sign of the cross, and sensed eyes upon him. He felt a little self-conscious as he crosssed himself again when the prayer ended. *But after all, I'm Catholic. I can't hide it.*

When he looked up, he found himself under the bold, inquisitive stare of the girl he had heard introduced as Rachel. She was sitting right across from him. Up until now, he hadn't been sure she had noticed his existence, but she had clearly noted the Catholic gesture. She said nothing, but lowered her thick lashes as though she were hiding a smile in her blue-green eyes. He noticed again that her face and figure were quite attractive, but in a way that was almost too smooth and conventionally obvious to capture his lasting attention. He had known girls like that in high school—the class beauties, the prom queens—and he had never felt the slightest interest in them, nor they in him. Briefly, he wondered if Rachel Durham's world was allowed to include prom queens or beauty pageants.

So Paul focused his attention on the younger girls, who seemed to regard him more congenially. One of them, with wavy hair and tranquil eyes, sat next to Rachel.

"You're Melanie, right?" he asked.

She nodded, and a wide smile came over her face that he couldn't help returning.

"How old are you, Melanie?"

"Thirteen." Her soft voice had a slight drawl.

"What grade are you in school?"

"I'll be in eighth grade this year at Bayside Christian."

To Paul's surprise, Rachel, said, again with lowered lashes, "That's our school. It's a private Christian academy run by our church."

"Oh. Bayside Christian Fellowship, right?" Paul remembered.

Colonel Durham spoke up, "That's right. We joined the church around five years ago. It's been a real blessing." Paul noted a smile barely touched Rachel's lips at that remark. "We're all quite involved in the church. I'm on the board of directors, I lead the men's group, and Sallie hosts a woman's group. The girls are all part of the Young Christians group at our church, too." Colonel Durham passed down a dish to Paul. "Peas from our garden. The girls shelled them."

"That's great," Paul said. "My parents did gardening, too."

"How many kids were in your family again?"

"Eight."

"Really?" Sallie seemed surprised. "Where do you fall in?"

"I'm number seven," Paul answered after swallowing his food.

Rachel's eyebrows rose.

"Is that so?" Sallie said, "Robbie's number seven in our family."

Her husband caught her eye and chuckled, "He's number seven for both of us, that is."

Conversation continued rather agreeably for the remainder of dinner, and afterwards, Paul volunteered to help with the dishes. This seemed to soften the older girls' attitude towards him considerably, and they quickly set him up with soap and a scrubbing brush.

"Ah, back to boot camp, eh?" Colonel Durham looked into the kitchen. "If you'll excuse me, Paul, I've got to answer some email." Paul nodded, realizing that the colonel had deliberately left him alone with his daughters.

Paul doubted that the daughters were enthused. Rachel looked at him with narrowed eyes for a moment, and when one of the girls said something about "...when we're down on the beach," Rachel shushed her abruptly.

"So why are you here for the summer?" queried the stocky dark-haired girl with striking eyebrows over blue eyes, who he remembered was called Miriam. "Do you have a job here or are you on vacation?"

"Actually, a combination of both. I'll be entertaining at Colonial Festival this summer," Paul said, scrubbing the bottom of a pot.

"Really? Are you dressing up as a Revolutionary War soldier then?" Cheryl asked. She was the tallest of the blonds, with glasses, freckles, and short bobbed hair.

"No, I'm actually dressed as a harlequin. I have a routine I do—some juggling, some acrobatics, a few magic tricks, and playing the flute—that sort of thing."

"What's a harlequin?" Miriam asked.

"'Harlequin'—as in 'Harlequin Romance,'" Rachel put in, scraping leftover peas into a plastic container. "The little clown in diamond-patterned tights with a funny black hat. He's on their logo."

Paul colored slightly at her dismissive tone. "The harlequin's one of the traditional figures in the Italian commedia dell'arte. There was a dell'arte group at my college, and since I'm the tall acrobatic type, I got to play harlequin. My costume is mostly black, with a diamond-patched vest."

"What does that have to do with the Revolutionary War?" Cheryl asked, a little incredulous.

"Not much. The Harlequin tradition is pretty old, and I suppose they had them around during the Revolutionary War," Paul said. He could tell by their faintly smirking expressions that the older girls did not think that this was an appropriate activity for a guy. He tried hard not to let it bother him. *They're sheltered*, he realized. All the same, he was anxious to change the topic.

"You're right on the shore," he said, squinting out the kitchen window. "Do you get any chance to go boating on the bay?"

"I wish," Miriam said dismally, drying a serving bowl. "We have a canoe, but Dad won't buy us a motorboat."

"Mom's afraid of us drowning," one of the twins said airily, setting down a stack of plates.

"No, he's afraid we'll escape," a black-haired girl said.

"No, it's because we don't have a dock," another girl contradicted. "The old one was rotting when we bought the house, so Daddy had it knocked down. And he didn't want to spend the money to get a new one built and buy a boat."

"It's not fair. Our neighbors up and down on either side have docks and most of them have three or four boats. But here we are, the nicest house of the lot, and we don't have anything." Miriam complained, clattering the pots and pans as she put the dry ones away. "We're totally backward in this family. I mean, what's the point of having a house on the bay if you don't have a boat?"

"'Never been boating? Well, what have you been doing then?'" Paul quoted. The female faces around him looked blank. "From *The Wind in the Willows*," he explained. There was a silence. "Haven't any of you read it?"

"I've heard of it, but the literature teacher at Bayside Christian said she thought it had pagan parts to it, so I didn't read it," the blond twin said.

"Oh," Paul scanned his memory. "What, because of the scene with Pan? I guess so. Well, that's a shame you didn't read it. It's really a good book. I read it in college." He set the large pan he was washing in the dish drain. "It sounds like your school is pretty strict."

"Yes," Miriam said emphatically. "My gosh, you'd think we were in the Middle Ages."

"Well, actually, the High Middle Ages were a time of great intellectual inquiry," Paul said. "Maybe you mean, 'the Dark Ages?'"

She stared at him again quizzically. "Yeah, whatever."

Only Cheryl seemed to appreciate his remark. She tittered. "Seriously, they are *so* close-minded at our school. We're not allowed to read hardly anything except what they call 'Great Christian Classics,' like *The Pilgrim's Progress*. I keep in touch with my friends from North Carolina who are in public school and we aren't reading the same books at all."

"You might not be missing much. In Catholic school, we read some pretty trashy modern books in literature class," Paul said. "It's a shame that most high schools don't teach the real classics."

"Are you Catholic?" several voices asked.

"Yes," Paul said.

"But are you a Christian?" Melanie asked. She had been leaning on the counter, listening, but hadn't spoken until now.

"Of course he is. Catholics are Christians," Rachel said, a bit edgily. Paul was surprised to hear her speak up.

"Not necessarily," Cheryl said. "Just because you were born Catholic doesn't make you a Christian, you know."

"Oh, stop being stupid, Cheryl. There are Catholics at Bayside Christian Academy, and you know it. We're not supposed to interrogate guests about their religious convictions. It's not polite," Rachel said, her voice sharpening.

Cheryl flushed, and Paul said, "Really, it's all right. I'm not offended. I had several Protestant friends growing up and they were always asking me questions like that about my faith. I'm used to it."

He looked at Melanie. "So what do you do around here for fun?" he asked. "Go swimming?"

She shrugged. "We don't get much chance during the day,"

Two of the younger girls suddenly started smiling.

"We keep ourselves busy," One of the blond twins, said airily, giving what was intended to be a sly wink to the others, some of whom tittered.

"Mostly after hours," one of the younger ones said with a laugh, and was shushed by an older one.

"We sew," Miriam said dryly, casting a hard look at the younger ones.

Melanie said, "We do things with our church group. But lately we've just been at home."

Bored and up to something "after hours"—at night? Paul thought to himself. But he doubted that any of them were going to confide in a stranger like him.

"Do you really know how to juggle?" the youngest dark-haired girl, asked. For answer, Paul grabbed a handful of cooking utensils from the sink and began tossing them in the air. A spatula, ladle, serving spoon and wooden spoon were worked into a fountain. He juggled them for a few passes and then stopped, letting them splash back down one by one into the soapy water. He stared at the water.

"Yeah, I think so," he said.

There were muffled giggles, and a little blond girl breathed, "That was so cool."

Juggling is a great icebreaker, he thought.

four

For the king had caused it to be proclaimed that whoever could discover the princesses' secret would have a rich reward...

—— Grimm

achel, seeing that Paul was washing pots and keeping the younger entertained enough to actually finish their jobs, decided she was going to slough off her own chores. She shrugged off her denim apron which she had put over her summer dress. Conveniently, the phone rang just then, and she said, "I've got it," scooped up the handset, and stepped outside. "Hello?"

"Hi Rachel! Uh, *is* this Rachel?" It was Keith Kramer, from her class at school. Her antennae pricked up. Keith was a friend, but he never called the Durhams. It was odd.

"You know it is, Keith," she said. "What's up?" She was sure she had heard someone pick up the phone on the other end.

"I, uh, wanted to give Colonel Durham a message about the Bible outreach."

"Okay, I'll go get him." But Rachel stood still. If her dad had picked up, he could just intervene, right now.

"That's okay. Just tell him my dad and I won't be able to make the meeting on Wednesday. Uh—how have things been, Rachel?"

"Okay," she said, wondering if her dad was listening on the line or not. Was he testing her or something? Trying to see if she was going to obey him or not?

"Having a good summer?"

"Yeah, it's been quiet around here since graduation," Rachel said. If her dad was listening, it had to be clear to him that it was Keith Kramer, not her, who was initiating the conversation.

"So—what have you been up to?"

37

Aha, maybe that was it. Dad didn't need to listen in on the conversation. Dad was hoping that Keith would be a spy for him. Just like Dad was hoping that Paul would be a spy.

Flushed with anger, Rachel suddenly felt reckless. "Wouldn't you like to know?" she said softly.

"What was that?"

"Oh, come on Keith," Rachel said in a soft voice, staring at the golden row of windows on the house. "Wouldn't you like to know what I've been up to?"

There was a silence that seemed too long and Rachel wondered again, her heart racing, if her dad was listening on the phone after all. If he was, she had just given herself away. On a sudden impulse, she walked swiftly around the house.

"Uh," Keith said with an effort. "Yeah, that's why I'm asking."

Rachel didn't answer because she was hurrying, as fast as she could without breathing hard, around the house to the place where her dad's study was. Slowing to a halt, she peered in the window.

Her dad was typing on the computer. The phone was in its receiver—but maybe he had it on speakerphone?

I'm being way too paranoid, she chided herself. She had an idea. "Well, then," she said with a laugh. "Maybe you should talk to Taylor."

"Taylor from our class?"

"Yeah, maybe you should talk to him," she said. She had talked to Taylor at church last week. She had figured out that even though Taylor was in her dad's study group too, he wasn't going to be a spy.

"Okay, I'll do that," Keith said. "Uh, make sure you give your dad that message."

"Sure I will," she said, and hung up the phone.

She wandered up the path that ran between the vegetable gardens, feeling the breeze tugging her hair out of the bun, and planning. Glancing up, she saw Paul through the kitchen window and wondered idly if he were watching her. He probably thought she looked like some kind of old-fashioned heroine in her too-long skirt and blouse. *He would be mistaken,* she thought. *I'm trapped in this quaint Christian life by day, but now I have an escape.*

And that thought alone was invigorating.

After Paul had finished the dishes and helped the girls with the kitchen, the evening had darkened. Colonel Durham returned and offered to drive Paul back to his campsite.

Paul had a feeling that the man wanted to talk with him alone, so he said yes. After saying goodnight to the girls and Mrs. Durham, Paul got into the passenger side of the colonel's large town car. It was a comfortable car, but not ostentatious. The Durhams, he was starting to see, were well-off, but didn't live extravagantly. It was interesting to see Christian parents who took the challenge to live simply seriously. He admired that principle, although he could see the teenagers were chafing under it.

"Thanks very much for having me over," Paul said.

"We enjoyed having you as well," Mr. Durham said.

As they drove, Colonel Durham was quiet for a moment then said abruptly, "So, now you've met my daughters. You see the problem?"

Paul searched for words. "They're all very beautiful young ladies," he said slowly.

The Colonel gave a wry smile. "Yes, they are. I wonder if that's half the trouble. I wish God had given me godly daughters, but instead He gave me beautiful daughters. And that makes my job twice as hard. I don't know what it is about females and beauty, but if a girl's beautiful, she seems to think that she has a right to focus on that. But I guess that's human nature."

"Does there have to be a conflict between being beautiful and being good?" Paul couldn't help saying.

The colonel frowned. "I don't know if there *has* to, but in my experience, there often *is*," he said.

Fingering the medal around his neck and silently asking for guidance, Paul tried to think of where to start. "I was wondering…just thinking about how my own dad related to my sisters…Have you had much time to spend with them? How much do you see them during the week?"

"I'm working from home three days a week and Sallie's almost always home. They're practically never out of our sight. That's what's so puzzling to me. I don't see what they could be hiding. They couldn't be doing anything at nighttime: they'd have to walk right past our bedroom to get downstairs, and we always keep our door open. Yet I'm sure there's something going on. I just can't figure out what it is or when it's happening."

"Have you looked into getting any help?" Paul asked.

The man harrumphed. "I've tried to sound out some of their friends from church about it. A couple of their male classmates are in my Bible study group. I've asked them to try to find out. You know how sometimes teens will only talk to other teens, and I know my girls are always trying to talk to these boys anyhow. But the boys have no idea. Either that, or they know what's going on and they're not telling me either."

"I meant, have you tried seeing a family counselor or something," Paul amended.

The colonel shook his head. "Been there, done that," he said. "We did the whole counseling thing when my first wife died. I don't know that it did much good." He turned off the car—they had reached the campsite. "Besides, I don't think this is psychological. It's all about trust. The girls don't trust me. I don't trust them. And frankly, I don't see what can be done about it."

He coughed and looked uncomfortable. "Like I said, I asked a couple of their friends already if they could find out what was going on. And I'm not sure if I can trust what they're telling me. I don't know if you'd consider trying your own hand, to see if you can find out what they're up to?"

Paul stared at him. "So you're asking me to spy on your daughters?"

"Well, I wouldn't say that. If you were to talk to them…get to know them…and happen to figure out what it is they're up to…you could let me know." He looked a bit aggravated. "I know it's an awkward request. I just don't see what else I can do, short of bugging the house or having chips implanted in their arms. The situation has deteriorated to this point."

Paul could see how frustrated the colonel was. The man was in a tough spot: he was spying on his daughters but he didn't want to have to spy.

Thoughtful, Paul leaned forward and looked down at his feet. "Let me ask you this," he said at last. "Which would you prefer—to have someone tell you what it is your daughters are doing? Or to have your daughters tell you themselves?"

"I'd rather my daughters told me themselves, of course," Colonel Durham said, looking searchingly at Paul. "Why? Do you think you could get them to do that? How?"

Paul drummed his fingers on his knees, thinking of the snatches of the girls' conversation he had inadvertently overheard. "Well, I don't know if I could. Part of it would depend on how much you're willing to trust me," he said at last.

The Colonel sat there, frowning and looking hard at Paul, suddenly looking formidable, the way that Army commanders can look when the need arises. Paul knew he was being scrutinized.

At last, the Colonel spoke. "Trust you—how?"

Paul took a deep breath, "I'll need to know if I can have your permission for two things."

"All right," Colonel Durham said. "So what are they?"

"I would like your permission to be on your beach at night, without your knowledge. I mean, I would come and scout around the beach late at night, randomly, just to observe. I would come and go without attracting attention to myself, sir." Paul realized he had fallen back automatically into the military manner of speaking.

Colonel Durham looked at Paul quizzically. "You think the girls are up to something on the beach at night?"

Paul continued deliberately. "And the second thing—and this is bigger—if I do find out, I need to be free to not tell you anything until I can persuade your daughters to tell you themselves. Like you said you would prefer."

Colonel Durham was silent for a long moment, staring over the steering wheel into the darkness. Then he put his clasped hands to his chin and closed his eyes. When he opened his eyes a few seconds later, he looked at Paul.

"All right, corporal," he said. "I'll trust you."

"Okay," Paul said. "I'll see what I can do." He felt a pit opening out in his stomach as though he had just agreed to walk across a high-wire buffeted by crosswinds. In the dark.

Rachel waited until she was sure her parents were asleep for the night, then she rose out of bed. The other girls, alerted, followed, some stifling yawns. Most of them didn't get changed into their night clothes any more, but simply put on comfortable clothes to go to bed, in anticipation of an outing.

But to Rachel's surprise, Prisca got out of bed wearing an emerald green dress. "What are you doing?" Rachel hissed. The dress was an old semi-formal dress of their mother's that had been hanging in the storage closet for as long as anyone could remember.

Prisca just shrugged, "I just wanted to wear Mom's dress. Is that a problem?"

"Suit yourself." Rachel let it go.

They filed quickly down the stairs to the cave, through the woods, and out into the cool moonlight on the beach. Rachel stretched and arched her back.

"So why are you dressed up?" Linette piped.

"I just wanted to," Prisca said, raising her eyebrows. She put her hands on her hips and spun around. The dress flared out, showing off her legs. "Rachel said we could do whatever we wanted."

"Sure. Whatever floats your boat," Rachel said. "Just make sure you don't ruin the dress."

"I felt like getting dressed up tonight." Prisca produced the zippered pencil case that served as her secret makeup bag. She usually hid it in her backpack during the school year, to make up her face as discreetly as possible after she reached school. Makeup was banned at Bayside Christian, but that didn't stop the girl students from trying to get away with as much as possible.

"Do my face too, Prisca, please!" Liddy begged.

"Let me do my own face first." Prisca spread out her makeup on a smooth rock, and began to pick out eye shadow. "That is, if I can," she said, "I don't have a light. This will be interesting." It was a full moon, but still different from daylight.

"I'll do your makeup for you," Becca said. "I can see to do you, and then you can do me."

"And me," Liddy insisted.

"Antsy pantsy. All right."

Rachel wandered away from the makeover to the water. The other girls followed her.

"Well! That was an ordeal at dinner tonight," she said. "What a name— Fester. Paul Fester. I wanted to laugh when we were introduced. Can you imagine having to go through life with a name like that?"

"Oh, come on," said Miriam. "He was okay."

"He's a geek," Rachel said. "What normal guy dresses up in a clown suit and goes out juggling?"

"Paul said he would teach me and Debbie to juggle," Linette said, skipping through the sand. "I showed him how I could do a frontward walkover, and he said he would teach me to do it backwards. He said that if we were really good we might be able to be in his act with him. He said he could jump through a flaming hoop if he had someone brave enough to hold it up for him. I said I wouldn't do it but Debbie said she would, if he showed her how."

Rachel rolled her eyes at Miriam. "Well, he certainly gets on well with the youngsters."

"That's probably why he wants to be a clown," Cheryl added.

"I like him. He's cool," Brittany spoke up unexpectedly.

"You're too young to know what cool is," said Taren disdainfully.

Brittany said nothing, but crossed her eyes, stuck out her tongue and touched her nose with it.

As they talked, they were making their way down the beach. Further down the shore, the beach turned into woods. Halting a few yards from the first trees, Rachel threw herself down on a sandy spot and sighed. "I'm so bored," she said.

"Maybe we should get Paul to come down here and juggle for us," Miriam suggested, and Rachel coughed, laughing.

"That's good," she said appreciatively. She kicked at a pebble with her toe, picked it up and threw it in the water. Inside she wondered if Taylor would come through tonight. She searched the deserted bay again for the hundredth time, disappointed.

Then she caught sight of a white plume rolling across the waters to her. A wake? A boat?

She stood up, hearing a motor, and scanned the darkness. Then she saw it. A motorboat. *Two* motorboats. Coming in their direction.

Now, not wanting to look too eager, she sat back down again on the sand. And that was okay, because the other girls were standing up, peering at the boats.

"I think they're coming this way," Miriam said in disbelief.

"Are they?" Cheryl said anxiously. "I'm going back up."

Rachel cast a glance at Cheryl, who was decently clothed. Fortunately no one had yet gone swimming tonight. "Just stay here. Wait."

Cheryl paused and the girls all watched as the two boats came close and cut their engines. Then they began to drift towards the shore.

"Hi there," came a voice from one of them.

Rachel stood up, attempting languidity. "Taylor?" she called.

"The same," the familiar voice said, and the twins exchanged delighted glances.

"You took your sweet time," Rachel said.

"Sorry."

"Well, come on in."

"Where's the best place to pull up?" a voice from the other boat asked. Rachel recognized Keith Kramer and smiled to herself.

"There's a deep spot there, under the willows. Maybe if you can get the nose of the boat in there…"

"All right," Taylor said.

The other girls had been listening to this exchange in silence. Rachel glanced at them. "Relax. It's just Keith and Taylor from school," she said. "Who else is with you?" she called.

"Rich and Pete."

"Pete! Omigosh, hi Pete!" Prisca's voice came shrilly from further up the beach. She scrambled down, her green dress shimmering in the moonlight. She was wearing far more makeup than she could have gotten away with either at Bayside Christian or in front of her father, and looking much more mature than her fifteen years. It was actually a bit scary.

"Hi Prisca," Pete said. "Uh, wow, you're dressed up."

"Oh, yeah, sort of. I was just trying it on. What are you doing here?"

"Rachel told us to come by, so we did."

All the girls looked at Rachel, who, raising an eyebrow, smiled. Taylor was edging his boat towards the willows. After a bit of maneuvering, he managed to get close enough for him to stagger onto the shore, followed by Pete and Rich, who were seniors like Rachel and Cheryl. The second boat followed, and Keith Kramer and Alan Vonnegun got out.

"Hey Alan," Rachel said. "Glad you could make it."

"So am I," he said. "Hey, when you are going to get me that CD?"

She laughed. Alan was a good friend: she was glad he had come along. "I'll get it to you."

"So what are you girls up to?" Taylor asked as he reached the girls.

Rachel grinned. "Escaping parental supervision."

"Seriously? Are all of you down here?"

"Yes. Like I told you, we've been doing this for the past couple weeks or so. It's been fun, but you know, it's always great to have company." She smiled artfully at Keith, who flushed.

Taylor was checking out the beach. "This is really private. Your parents can't see you from the house, can they?"

"No. Their bedroom faces the other way. I'm glad you cut your motors when you did. Just in case they could hear anything."

Rachel was dying to get off the beach, but she saw some preliminary socializing would be in order. So she sat down on the sand while the girls clustered around Taylor, Alan, Pete and Rich, chatting eagerly.

"So how did you make it out here?" Rachel asked, as Keith Kramer sat down beside her.

"Oh, my parents went to bed. Then I just took off," Keith said, with some exaggerated casualness. Rachel could see that he was reveling in the freedom of this nighttime adventure.

"And your parents let you take the boat out at night?" Rachel said innocently.

"Well, not exactly," he said, "but if I fill up the tank with gas, my dad will never notice I was out."

"So your parents don't know what you're up to," she said with a smile.

"Uh...no." He swallowed.

"Well," Rachel teased, knowing she had him. "*I* won't tell on you if *you* don't tell on me."

She sounded joking, but she had a feeling that Keith picked up on the threat, and realized he had made a big mistake.

"Nah, I'd never tell on you," he said, a bit indignantly. He looked around. "Like Taylor said, this is a really neat... beach you have here."

Keith scrambled to his feet and hurried over to Prisca, who was standing with the other boys, shrugging her shoulders, fluttering her eyelashes, and giggling to her heart's content.

Rachel wanted to laugh. *So much for Dad's spy.* But instead she walked down to the water where the youngest girls, who had quickly tired of the conversations, were splashing around. She started a splashing game with them, and then Taylor joined in. It was fun, but Rachel wasn't anxious to get too wet, so after a few minutes, she sat down on a rock and Taylor sat next to her. As they talked, Melanie slipped over to sit with them, putting her head on Rachel's shoulder.

After about a quarter hour, Rachel looked at Taylor and said coaxingly, "Taylor, take us for a boat ride."

Taylor said, hesitantly, "Sure, but are you all going to come?"

"Just me and Melanie and Cheryl," Rachel said. "The rest can stay here or go with Keith."

"Man, Alan should have brought his family's boat. I told him he should have. It's huge."

"He should have," exclaimed Rachel, disappointed.

"Well... maybe I can ask him to bring it tomorrow."

"Good." She stood up. "Come on, Cheryl! Melanie and I are going for a boat ride."

Rachel had picked Cheryl deliberately because she sensed the older girl was irritated by the twins' flirting with boys who were Cheryl's classmates. Also, Rachel calculated that Cheryl would hesitate to go on a boat ride at first, but would probably enjoy it once she got out there. A small outing like this was the perfect time to persuade her conservative stepsister that they had nothing to fear.

Cheryl grudgingly joined them, after Taylor asked her to, and Melanie seemed happy so long as she was accompanying Rachel. They clambered into the swaying boat and settled themselves. Cheryl asked for, and got, a life jacket for herself and Melanie, but Rachel sat up front in the boat next to Taylor, letting the wind stream around her neck and through her hair as the powerful engine gunned to life and pulled her away.

For the next half hour she lived in the rush of the wind and water, and by the time they headed back towards the shore, she was yearning for more. Only the need to keep their secret safe impelled her back home.

"Never been boating? Well, what have you been doing then?" The quotation came back to her—where had she heard that? She realized, disconcerted, that she had heard it that evening, from Paul Fester.

"Taylor," she said, as he let the boat drift back towards shore. "You have to tell the other guys that they can't let on to anyone that they saw us here. Right?"

"Oh, yeah, sure. I'll make sure I'll tell them," Taylor said, seriously.

"Keith won't chicken out, will he?"

"He better not, or he'll get us all in trouble," Taylor said. "Are you worried that your dad will try to crack him?"

"Yeah, sort of," Rachel said. "I mean, you know my dad. General Patton."

"He's been sounding out the guys in Bible group about what you girls have been up to. I was the only one who knew what he was getting at, and you know I won't tell." He grinned. "And now that the rest of them have been out here, I doubt they're going to tell him either. I mean, we'd have to admit to Colonel 'Patton' that we were out with his daughters at night—alone!"

"Yeah, right!" Rachel laughed. This was exactly as she had hoped. Now she didn't need to worry. "Thanks so much for coming by. Can you come again?"

"Absolutely."

"Good." Rachel felt another thrill go through her. This was working. She looked out at the island standing aloof in the bay, and appraised it like a diamond.

five

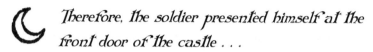 *Therefore, the soldier presented himself at the
front door of the castle . . .*

— *Grimm*

aul stood on the Durham's doorstep around ten o'clock the next
morning, steeled with determination, and knocked. He wasn't
entirely sure of what to do next, but it had occurred to him that this
might be a decent idea.

When one of the girls answered the door, he asked to see their mother.
In a few minutes, Sallie came to the door. She was dressed in a blue cotton
jumper, and was holding baby Jabez, who looked recently cleaned.

"Good morning, Paul," she said, and her eyes were still a bit nervous,
although she smiled. "What can I do for you?"

"I wanted to say thanks again for the great dinner last night. I really
appreciated it."

"Well, you're very welcome, I'm sure."

"Last night, I had told your younger daughters, Debbie and Linette, that I
could teach them juggling. They seemed to be interested so I wanted to find
out if that was all right with you, and when would be a good time."

Sallie looked hesitant. "I would have to ask my husband. That's very kind
of you to offer. Would you want to be paid for it?"

Paul shook his head. "Not at all. Actually, I'm scheduled to do this show
next week at the Colonial festival. I could really use some assistants. If you
and Colonel Durham were willing, and the girls as well, they could be my
assistants in the show."

"Oh my! Well, that would keep them busy! Are you sure you could teach
them in time?"

"Even if they learn a few things, they can help me out. It's really not that
difficult."

She paused. "I'd have to check with my husband first. If he says it's okay, then maybe you could come by at noon to teach them? If the girls are finished with their chores. Would that work for you?"

"Sounds great!"

"All right," Sallie said, still seeming a little guarded. "I'll see you then, Mr. Fester."

"Call me Paul, please. Goodbye."

Paul walked away as the door closed, breathing deeply. He was fairly certain Colonel Durham would allow the lessons. The only difficulty was that he was sure he would be tired by noon.

I'd better go back to the tent and make up my sleep now, he thought. *And I hope Debbie and Linette manage to make up their sleep too.*

Rachel yawned over the laundry. *I must, I must get some sleep today.* She thought of the hammock outside in the sun. After she was done here, she would steal down there and doze off, if none of her sisters got there first.

Stepping up her pace, she finished the laundry a bit more quickly than usual, dabbed on some sunscreen, and slipped outside, stifling another yawn. The hammock hung in a corner of the yard, unoccupied. She lay down, closed her eyes against the sun, and was asleep almost instantly, swaying in the breeze.

A bit later on, she drifted to the surface of sleep and became aware of shrieks of laughter and shouts. She opened one eye, and saw some figures cavorting on the lawn. After watching them in a bored perplexity for some time, she remembered that Paul was supposed to come over to teach Debbie and Linette juggling, or tumbling, or something like that. She closed her eyes again.

Then she heard giggles coming closer. She opened an eye a bit irritated, and saw her two younger biological sisters Liddy and Becca, dressed in fancy dresses, come dancing up to the hammock, carrying a big plastic hamper between them.

"What are you doing?" she asked, a bit sharply.

Liddy, resplendent in royal blue, with ample costume jewelry said, "Becca and I are going to play dress up. In the cave."

"Won't Sallie think you're a bit old for dress-up?" Rachel asked mildly.

"Oh no. She saw us, and she said we looked very cute," said fourteen-year-old Becca. "Of course, we were doing it with the young ones, before Paul came and stole them away from us. So we're just bringing the rest of the dresses down to the cave to wait for them."

"I see," Rachel said, "and you might just forget and leave them down there."

"We might," Liddy giggled.

"I see," Rachel said, and closed her eyes again. She wondered to herself if there was a dress somewhere in the house that she could wear. There was something about seeing guys on summer nights that made her want to dress up. But she didn't exactly want to go in an old dress-up gown or discarded bridesmaid dress. Her own bridesmaid dress from her father's second marriage had been made for her before she really hit her growth spurt—no question of her fitting into it now. Besides, it was pale blue cotton with ivory roses on it. At the time, she had picked out the fabric herself. But now it seemed like fabric for a naïve little girl, not for someone—well, like herself.

Remembering picking out the bridesmaid dresses turned over painful memories. Her mother's death was something she had pushed to the furthest reaches of her mind. For a long time her father had seemed so anxious that she not be psychologically disturbed by the tragedy, and had arranged a plethora of counseling services for her, and would probably do so again, instantly, if he had any idea that she was still struggling with it. But she was weary of talking about the pain, and just wanted it to die away quietly in the back of her mind, alone and unnoticed.

The one good outcome of Mom's dying was that for a while, it seemed, she and her father had been very close. He depended on her, the oldest, to keep the other girls together, to soak up their grief and more than that, to look after them, cook for them, feed them, keep them clothed, to run the household, especially when his military duties called.

Then he had met Sallie, and things had begun to change. Rachel remembered bitterly the night Dad had taken her, Rachel, out to dinner, and told her about his plans to marry again. "You've been taking on the responsibilities of an adult, and you shouldn't have to do that yet at your age. I want you to be free to be a child again, and enjoy being a young person."

Perhaps he meant it to be comforting, but for Rachel, he was stripping her of her newfound maturity. He was taking away part of her identity, even though he hadn't realized it. So here she was, capable of running a house, but unable to do it as she wanted, because it was no longer her house. Yet she still had to live under her father's roof, and be a child, and she was sick of being a child.

And her father, who at one point had begun to treat her as an equal, repented to her (at their new pastor's prodding) for placing too many burdens on her shoulders, and had proceeded, through his deeper involvement in their church, to become more and more clueless. He didn't understand her silent outrage at having to listen to Sallie, whose haphazard housekeeping drove Rachel nuts, or her resentment towards the church and its various ministries.

Her father had turned to the church for support in his time of bereavement, and now seemed to be caught in its stranglehold. Everything in the family schedule revolved around church groups, share groups, youth groups, men's groups, and women's groups. Church annual retreats had become more important than Christmas and Easter, it seemed. But Rachel could see how much comfort and happiness her father and his wife derived from the church and their church family. She didn't dare suggest they leave or pull back. Who was she, she thought dismally, to wreck the happiness of so many people?

So she was finding her own version of happiness, in different places. *Yes, what I need*, she thought, *is a dress*. A sleek black dress, not too formal, not too casual. And black sandals, with thin straps. There was nothing in her wardrobe—or her sisters'—or Sallie's—that remotely resembled the dress she was envisioning. Such dresses were common enough in the outside world, but not in the cotton-print fabric of their church and family life.

The other girls would need dresses, too. Dresses to dance in. Because they would go dancing, somehow. She felt the island would be a perfect place for a midnight dance.

She counted up dollars on her fingers. Last week she had gotten paid for several hours of filing at the church office. Perhaps next time she went into town, she could go to the Mission store—or better yet, the bargain-price clothing store that sold slightly defective brand name clothes. Next time she and Prisca went grocery shopping, they could arrange to split up and have one of them go to the store while the other went clothes shopping. Yes, that might work.

Turning over, she sighed, and gazed lazily over at the juggling class. She could see Linette tossing a club in the air and dropping it, while Paul stood in front of her, coaching her. Debbie was working with two clubs, and seemed to be doing just fine.

She wished she could get two sweet dresses for the younger girls as well, something still girlish and not too alluring. Part of her regretted that Debbie and Linette had found out about the secret. They were really too young, even though Debbie was a tremendous flirt in her Sunday school class, attracting and casting off boys like an unusually pugnacious flower. No doubt she was more interested in Paul and his juggling than in any boy near her age.

"Rachel," Cheryl's voice called. Rachel groaned and rolled over in the hammock, wishing she had stayed asleep. The insistent note meant she was needed for something. She closed her eyes until her stepsister was standing right by the hammock, shaking her by the shoulder.

"What?" Rachel moaned pathetically.

"Mom wants you. You're supposed to make bread today. For the Sabbath."

"A pox on the Sabbath day," Rachel murmured.

Cheryl, shocked, said reprovingly, "You really shouldn't say that."

Rachel opened one eye and saw Cheryl's hand hanging down by her side, holding a book, her finger keeping her place. It was an older cloth-covered volume with scrolled black writing and an ominous title: *Babylon Mystery Religion.* Beneath the words was a lithograph of a rather crude statue of a woman holding a baby.

"What are you reading?" she asked.

"One of mom's books. It's all about the Roman Church."

"You mean the Catholic Church?"

"It's not really a church, Rachel. It's a satanic system. See the statue on the front? Doesn't it look like the statue of the Virgin Mary with Jesus you see in Catholic churches? But it's actually a statue of the Babylonian goddesses Ishthar with her son, Nimrod the sun god. She was the moon goddess. Catholics are really just pagans under another name, worshipping the sun and moon."

Rachel regarded the suggestive title with some amusement. "So Paul is an agent of Satan, trying to get us to...worship idols or something?"

"I hope not," Cheryl said, her eyes worried. "This book is old, Rachel, and Mom said it's still in print. It's possible that not everything that it says is true, but there's so much the author says that you just can't argue with. It's actually frightening."

"Cheryl, you read too much," Rachel blew her hair out of her eyes. "Just because a book is in print doesn't mean anything. I mean, isn't the Satanic Bible old? And that's probably still in print." She was irritated and got to her feet.

But as she stalked towards the house, she couldn't help casting a furtive glance in Paul's direction, picturing him as Cheryl's agent of the devil, horns sprouting out of his short-cropped curly hair. The picture didn't fit.

Everything about Paul screamed "Wholesome." *What a simply tremendous disguise,* she marveled sarcastically. *You would never guess.*

Paul turned a full somersault and landed near her on the grass, breathless. He was sweating in the hot summer sun. A silver medal bounced on a chain around his neck, along with a couple of strings. Wiping his forehead, he picked up the medal, untangled it from the strings, and tucked it back under his shirt. Then he turned he seemed to become aware of her presence and started.

"Sorry, didn't see you there," he murmured.

Rachel raised an eyebrow. "What's that around your neck?" she asked.

"Oh, that. Just a medal, and a cross, and a scapular. They tend to get all tangled when I'm tumbling."

"What kind of medal? For bravery?" she pursued. Debbie giggled behind Paul's back.

"Heck no. Not that kind of medal, just a Catholic thing." He held out the medal. "It's got a picture of Mary on it."

She looked, but could barely make out a figure of a woman on it. To step closer would mean stepping closer to a tall, sweating man, and she was too aware of Paul's masculine presence to do that. "Hm! Pretty."

"What's the string thing?" Debbie wanted to know.

"A scapular. Here—wait, I'll take it off. Sorry, it's pretty soaked. It's made of wool."

Paul held out a strange contraption, two brown felt squares dangling at the ends of two rather dirty brown strings. Another medal was strung on the string.

"What's it for?" Debbie demanded, taking it. Rachel cast a glance at it, and saw that embroidered on the felt was a woman holding a baby, remarkably similar to the Babylonian goddess on Cheryl's book. She felt an odd twinge in her stomach.

"It's a sign of my devotion to the Mother of Christ," Paul said, and held out his hand. Debbie gave it back, and he put it quickly to his lips then pulled the loop of string over his shoulders so one square hung down in the back and the other on the front. He tucked both back under his shirt. The girls all watched him with interest, not knowing what to make of this.

"Imagine, a pagan in our midst," Rachel said to Cheryl as they strolled to the house.

"I can't believe it—did you see that? Just like in the book!" Cheryl said in wonder. "He was kissing it like it was an idol."

"Cheryl," Rachel switched topics, "do you want to go to town with me?"

"What for?"

"Let's see if your mom wants us to go to the grocery store. I feel a sudden urge for a new dress."

That night, none of the girls wanted to be caught unawares again. If there were going to be boys on the beach, the girls were going to make the most of the opportunity. Rachel woke them up a bit sooner, and they pattered about upstairs for a bit, getting together a few essentials, which took so long that Rachel became impatient and shooed them all down the steps, despite protests.

In the cave, Prisca and Liddy pulled out the chest of dresses from against the wall. They had spent the afternoon clearing out the cave and stacking bikes against the wall so that there was considerably more room. "We tried to get one dress for everybody," Prisca said. "There's at least fourteen here, but I'm not sure who will fit into what."

Taren exclaimed in dismay, "But some of these are so old! And out of style! You expect us to see boys in these?"

"Take your pick—the dresses or your PJs," Prisca said briskly. "Or perhaps you'd rather get back into one of your ultra-cool denim jumpers?"

"Then at least give me the dark blue one. It will look black," Taren begged.

"But that's the one I picked out for Rachel!" Prisca objected.

"Whatever," Rachel shrugged. "I'll wear the green one. I don't care. I'm saving up my money to buy a new dress anyhow." She and Cheryl had made a quick trip to a fashion-clothing store to investigate styles and prices, and the lowest priced outfit was at least $60.

The statement seemed to inspire the girls. "Yeah, I'm going to save up my money too!" Liddy exclaimed, buttoning up a periwinkle blue dress that had once been Sallie's.

"We can get whatever kind of dress we want, can't we?" Becca said. "There is this adorable purple dress I've been longing to get, but I'm sure Sallie and Dad would say it's too short."

"I didn't see anything I cared for at the store," Cheryl announced, putting on a pink flounced sundress that had been in the costume box for years, still relatively intact. "I'm probably just going to buy some fabric and make a dress."

"Make a dress? How are you going to get away with that?" Tammy demanded.

"I'll sew when Mom's downstairs, or out at a meeting. If we take turns watching, we can get a lot of dresses made that way," Cheryl said. "I want something long and flowing and lacy and maybe white."

Rachel rolled her eyes as she got into the green dress Prisca had worn last night. It was a bit snug, but she could still fit in it.

"Hello?" said Miriam. "This dress is not my size, not even if I were half of what I am."

In the end, dresses were switched, modified, and taken on and off at least six times before all of them pronounced themselves at least temporarily satisfied.

"Gosh, we don't have any time," Prisca said. "I'm going to do my makeup now, quick!"

Rachel had already done hers upstairs in the bedroom, and now strolled outside the cave in her mom's old green dress. In the moonlight, you couldn't tell what color it was. She sidled down to the beach in her bare feet—she didn't have any shoes appropriate to the dress—and folded her legs under her, awaiting the boats.

The moon was an oval tonight, voluptuous and silver, and its reflection danced on the waves. Rachel had mulled over the problem of what to wear for a long time. Their church held that only modest dresses were appropriate for women and girls, as pants were man's attire and unfitting for females. Rachel privately thought this was insanity. The more moderate parents in the church allowed their teenage daughters to wear nice jeans and tops on some occasions. Perhaps she should spend her money on getting a nice pants outfit—but no. She had a good figure, and she *was* a girl, after all, and she wanted to make the most of it. A dress—not a homely plain dress, but a really cool dress—that was what she wanted.

Dresses to dance in, she thought. With short skirts skimming the thighs or swinging about the knees, and flirtatiously short sleeves or no sleeves at all. Somehow or other, she wanted to find a way to go dancing, in the darkness and warmth of summer nights.

There was a faint roar, and she saw the boats coming, and felt that breathless anticipation. Just for the fun of it, she put a hand in the bay water and ran it through her hair, so that it would glisten in the moonlight.

Three boats tonight—Taylor's, Alan's, Keith's. Rich and Pete were sitting in Taylor's boat. Thankfully, Taylor remembered to cut the engines before cutting in closer, and called to Alan to turn off his. Alan pulled out a paddle and started maneuvering his overlarge open fishing boat towards the willows. Seeing Rachel, he started pretending to sing an Italian boating song, which the other guys picked up. The other sisters, hearing the motors, ran down to the beach, skidding down the sandy bank in their dresses, laughing and shushing each other.

As before, the boys edged their boats beneath the overhanging willows and tied them to the trunk.

"Man, are you girls going to a party or something?" Taylor asked, seeing the girls all decked out.

Rachel shrugged. "Are you bringing us to one?"

"We brought the party with us!" Alan cracked, pulling out a pack of cigarettes.

"Of course you did," Prisca said. "Rachel, Alan is our own personal party."

Taylor shot a glance over his shoulder and lowered his voice, "I did bring some drinks."

"Really?" Rachel said, "You mean, alcohol?"

"I mean beer. Is that all right?"

Rachel considered swiftly. "It's fine with me if you guys drink," she said as she thought, rapidly sifting through her sisters' potential reactions. "Don't let the little girls have any. And you know we're all dead if our dad finds empty cans on the beach."

"Sure. Want one?"

"Maybe later. Thanks." Rachel had to gauge the risk. She had never had a beer herself, though she suspected she would enjoy one. However, didn't alcohol stay on the breath? The last thing she wanted was Sallie getting a whiff of something on one of the girls—that would be a dead giveaway. It was clear that Rachel would have to have a meeting with the girls and decide on rules for these types of situations ahead of time. Making decisions on the fly like this increased the risk dangerously.

She decided the best tactic would be to prevent the guys from breaking out the beers right away. "But first," she said, "can you bring us all out for a ride? I'm dying to get out on the water."

The other girls chorused agreement and Taylor said, "Sure. Who's with me?"

Rachel, Cheryl, Debbie, and Linette chose to go with Taylor. The other sisters quickly clustered around their choices—Tammy and Taren were angling in on Keith and Rich, and went in Keith's boat with Becca and Liddy.

Prisca had attached herself to Alan tonight, and Miriam went along with her and Pete ("Partly to keep Pete from getting ticked off at Prisca," Miriam said beneath her breath to Rachel. "Man, she's a flirt!"), and Brittany and Melanie, the odd two out, went along for the ride.

Getting into the boats in the dark of the willows was tricky, and it was a difficult fit. "Sorry it's a little crowded," Taylor said regretfully, gunning the motor and they cruised out into the bay.

"That's all right," Rachel said over the noise of the engine. She looked behind her. Cheryl sat in the back, an arm around each of the little sisters. Rachel noticed that Cheryl's face, which had been guardedly concerned since beer was mentioned, looked far more relaxed. Rachel smiled at her, took a deep breath and turned her face ahead into the night wind.

They rode for a while over the waves, and then Taylor said, "Where do you want to go now?"

Rachel looked over to the midnight jewel in the center of the bay. "Take us to the island," she cried over the noise of the motor.

Taylor cast a glance at the island and said, "What? You want to go on there? You're crazy. It's private."

"Yeah, but who's ever there?" she challenged.

"Why do you want to go there?"

"Just because it's there," she said mischievously. "Come on, take us there."

Taylor didn't look too happy at the thought. "We could get in real trouble."

Rachel pulled back. "Why not just ride around it and see if anyone's home?" she suggested. "If someone's there, there'll be a boat in the dock."

"Or a helicopter in the heliport," Taylor said, dubiously.

"A helicopter?"

"Yeah. You can't see it from your side of the bay, but there's a heliport on the other side of the island. That's how the rich people get on and off."

"Oh. Shoot." Rachel hadn't considered this.

"Well, I'll drive around it," Taylor said. "It's pretty big."

He made a wide circle around the island. Rachel eagerly scanned the coastline, taking in new images of the island. The further side revealed more of the house, a lovely mansion lifting a stone-and-timber face to the ocean. The sight took Rachel's breath away. She put her chin on her hand and drank it in. It would be beyond her dreams to actually enter a house like that. She didn't dare to think much about that, not yet.

Taylor pointed out the heliport, a swath of flat green grass where the trees had been carefully shaved back.

"It's empty," Rachel said hopefully.

"Yes," Taylor said. But Rachel could see that it wouldn't be prudent to push him farther tonight. She had made the suggestion, and she would let it sink in.

They counted four boats in the dock, but they were all covered with canvas, a sign that they were not being used. "If they weren't coming back, they'd be stored on dry land, though," Taylor commented. Rachel had to agree.

"Look!" she said, and pointed to a flat stone dock on the far side of the island. Trees lined it, and there were no lights nearby. But in the moonlight, she could see a flat stone portico, obviously a receiving area. Stone steps led up to the house.

"It's another dock," Taylor said, oblivious to the implications. Rachel decided to remain silent about those. She would ease him into her plan. She had seen in a moment—it was a perfect outdoor dance floor.

"We have to go there," she said beneath her breath. It was going to happen. She could taste it.

six

That night, the soldier slipped on his cloak of invisibility . . .

— *Grimm*

achel."

Rachel winced at her father's voice and looked up sharply. "Yes?"

"I talked to Mrs. Pearson at church yesterday, and she said she could use some help over at the parsonage on Monday afternoon. I told her that you and some of your sisters would go over there today to help serve her."

Rachel cringed. Mrs. Pearson was the pastor's wife, and she almost always needed someone to help serve her. "But we were going to take the little girls and boys to go to the Andrews' pool this afternoon!" she objected. "Sallie said it was okay."

"I'm sorry you've made other plans, but I think the needs of the church come before our personal desires, don't you?"

Rachel murmured something incomprehensible.

"I'm sorry, I didn't hear what you said."

"I didn't say anything," Rachel said defiantly. "Nothing worth repeating."

Her father looked over at her. "It shouldn't take too long. You know how difficult it is to be a pastor's wife. She needs our support."

Rachel nodded, and turned back into the other room. "Yes, but does she need my personal support?" she asked bitingly in her mind.

"The problem is, our family has no life outside of this church," she said aloud as she came into the basement, hauling a load of laundry.

"Tell me about it!" Prisca agreed. "My gosh, it's like we're enslaved to this group of people."

"The pastor's personal slaves," Miriam minced words. "If there's a job to be done—'oh, call those Durhams. He's got plenty of kids—he can spare a few!'"

"'Your daughters are so capable,'" Rachel quoted, pressing her hands to her breast. "'They have been such a blessing to our church.'"

She was referencing the last church anniversary, where the pastor's wife had stood up before the congregation and praised the Durham family. The girls had been singled out as models of hard work and zeal for God, which had thoroughly embarrassed them, mostly because Rachel thought it wasn't true.

"They don't know anything about us," she said. "For all of the 'sharing' and 'testifying' that goes on, they don't really know what any of us likes, or wants, or cares about."

Prisca tittered. "If they found out what we really wanted, they wouldn't like us very much, would they?"

Rachel gave a bitter smile. "No, I doubt they would." She had been around the parents enough to overhear their gossip about teenagers in the congregation that were perceived as 'rebellious.' "They'd hold us at arm's length," she said. Another thought occurred to her, and she went on grimly. "They'd start to think less of Dad and Sallie, too. They'd start out saying, 'Poor Colonel Durham. Such a heart for God, but his daughters are out of control,' and then they'd start carefully disconnecting themselves from him and Sallie. They'd pity them," she spoke the last words distastefully.

"Damn them!" Prisca spoke out suddenly. "I hate the church! I hate it!" She slammed down her laundry basket.

"Don't say that," Rachel hissed, throwing a glance upstairs.

"Don't curse," Liddy said, eyes wide.

"But I do! I hate them! They don't love us. Not really. And I hate having to bow to them!"

"Prisca," Rachel said, thoughts running through her brain, "it's wrong to hate."

"So what?" Prisca looked up at her wildly. "I still hate them. I hate them all. I hate what they're doing."

"You can't hate the church of God," Liddy said, attempting to be reasonable. "That's like hating Christ."

"Oh shut up! Shut up!" Prisca sat down, folding her arms, and started sobbing.

There was silence. Rachel sat down next to her younger sister, and put a tentative arm around her. It frightened her when Prisca was like this, so violently emotional. But she steeled herself. *Distract her*, she thought.

"Prisca," she said, invitingly, "we haven't gone to Goodwill yet."

Prisca wiped her eyes with the heels of her hands. "Can we go there after we get done slaving for Mrs. Pearson?"

"Absolutely," Rachel squeezed her hand.

The cellar door banged, and Tammy bellowed downstairs, "Linette! Debbie!"

"They're not down here," Rachel called up warningly.

"Paul's here for their lesson," Tammy yelled, and walked away.

Rachel raised an eyebrow. "They won't have to go to the Pearsons. Lucky Paul is in Dad's good graces."

"For now," Prisca said. "Wait until he finds out that Paul's actually a Babylonian Mystery Worshipper." The joke had been making its rounds among the sisters, and hadn't gotten old yet.

Rachel took out a load of bedspreads to hang up on the old clothesline. The dryer was full, and they would dry faster in the hot sun. Besides, she liked the smell of sun-dried sheets and spreads. As she hung up the spreads, she watched Paul coaching the young girls through some cartwheels and walkovers.

After she finished, he turned to her and said, "Gorgeous day, isn't it?"

"Yes," she said. *For swimming,* she thought bitterly. "Any plans for the day after your lesson with my sisters?"

"Nope. That's the fun of being on vacation."

She smiled at him sardonically. "All of us should be so blessed."

He looked at her quizzically, and then cast his eyes around the property. "You girls must feel pretty lucky, growing up here."

"I suppose we should."

"I mean, you have so much land. And the bay. I guess since I grew up on a postage stamp in the suburbs, I'm jealous." He grinned his baby boy's grin at her. *So naïve,* she thought.

"I guess the kids have it good," she said flippantly. "My little brothers get to run around and play as much as they like. And the young girls. They're lucky."

"Aren't you lucky?" he asked.

"I suppose some people would think so," she said slowly. "I'm supposed to be grateful, aren't I? After all, I have father and stepmother who are married to each other, a nice house, and a good Christian upbringing. Yes, I should feel very grateful, shouldn't I?"

Her eyes bored into his.

"But you're not," he said quietly. "Why?"

The thought of Prisca's fierce tears curled her lips with disdain. But that was not something she could tell him. Would tell him.

"If you can't understand that, I'm not going to explain it to you," she said distantly, and turned away from him.

☾

Paul had found it difficult to adjust to his new schedule. He had been dragging in the afternoons. At a certain time of day, no matter where he was, it seemed to him of utmost importance to get back to his tent and sleep.

The problem was, sometimes he wasn't anywhere near his tent. Finally, the inevitable happened that day. It was around three in the warm afternoon, and he was coaching Linette and Debbie through a second round of juggling, when he began to yawn prodigiously.

"Hey, are you tired?" Debbie asked, observing the obvious.

"A little," he confessed, trying to cover his gaping mouth.

"Why don't you go and take a nap?" Linette suggested. "You can lie down on the hammock."

"No—that's okay—" Paul's body began to go on automatic pilot. "I think I'd better go home now." He turned away, collecting his clubs. "See you later."

"Get some sleep!" Debbie yelled as they turned and ran back towards the house.

Paul stumbled towards the woods, intending a shortcut to the road. But his eyes were beginning to close. Then he spotted a hollow in the ground, plush with green moss, shaded by ferns.

Too perfect, he thought, and let his bag of juggling clubs fall. Without further ado, he curled up in the dell and fell fast asleep.

It was as though fairies had put a spell upon him, so thoroughly did he sleep. He wasn't certain how long he had been there when he heard the crack of a twig quite near him.

He slowly opened his eyes, but didn't move from his spot. Suddenly he heard voices close to him.

"Let me see, please, let me see!" a girl's voice begged in a whisper.

"Shhh! No! Not till we get to the cave!"

Then there was more cracking of twigs, and he heard, faintly, a rustle of plastic bag.

"Oh... my ... gosh... that is so gorgeous," was a hushed voice.

"Twelve bucks." Paul recognized Taren's voice.

"No way!"

"Yes. Mine, all mine. But if you like, you can borrow it after I've worn it a few times."

"That is such a killer dress. Feel the material! How did you get it?"

"Well, Mom was looking for swimsuits for the boys, so I just started looking through the sales racks. And I found it! Then I just waited for her to go into a dressing room to try something on, and rushed up to the counter and paid for it with my babysitting money! See, it's so little it folds into a nice packet. It fit right in my purse."

"Your legs will look great in that." Paul wasn't sure who the other girl was, but he was sure it was one of Colonel Durham's daughters.

"You bet. Now I just need to find decent shoes."

There was a rustle of plastic, and then silence. A few minutes later Paul heard the two girls making their stealthy way back up through the woods.

He waited until they had passed him, and lifting his head gingerly, saw them going into the house.

After a long while, he rolled over and crept out of the woody hollow where he had unintentionally hidden. Following the trail carefully, he found it wound down the side of the cliff leading to the beach. Suddenly he came upon a dark opening in the side of the rock.

Casting a glance behind him, he went into the cave, blinking in the dim light. There were a few bicycles and a large wooden trunk of rough boards. It had a padlock on it.

He put a hand to the padlock, and realized it hadn't been closed properly. Giving it a slight jerk, he opened it and slid it out of the ring.

He carefully raised the lid, and saw a jumble of dresses in a variety of colors. Folded on a plastic bag in one corner was a short brown tank dress of a suede material. They were all quite different from the dresses that the girls usually wore. Like night and day.

For a few moments he looked at the dresses, not moving, thinking. Then slowly he replaced the lid and the lock, closing it properly.

I'm taking a risk, he thought. But Colonel Durham had said he could.

Quietly he left the little cave and retraced his steps back to the spot where he had been napping, where his juggling bag still lay. He stood there in the woods, wondering what to do next.

Then he heard the screen door bang closed, and a girl came out of the house. He didn't move.

She started to wander down towards the bay, her golden hair falling around her pensive round face. He recognized her—Melanie, the quiet smiling one.

When she was almost upon him, she looked up and saw him.

"You're still here, Paul," she said.

"I am."

"What are you doing?"

He indicated the dell. "I fell asleep here, and just woke up not too long ago."

"Oh." She looked toward the bay through the woods, still pensive, and then looked back at him. Seeing his serious face, she smiled.

When she smiled, her eyes crinkled into half moons. He couldn't help smiling back at the young girl, her face as open as the sunshine. She reminded him of his youngest sister.

"Can I ask you something about Mary?" she said, walking towards the bay.

"Of course," he said, swinging his bag over his shoulders and falling into step beside her.

☾

"Meeting," Rachel said. The girls dressing in the cave by the light of the camping lamp stopped and looked at her.

Rachel, who had gotten into an old dress of her mother's, a sleeveless white sheath, said, "We've got to make some rules. In order to keep our secret." Given how Prisca had behaved this morning, Rachel was not entirely sure this conversation would go well. But she forged ahead. "Agreed?"

"Agreed," Miriam said, and Cheryl and the twins nodded. The other girls gave their assent.

"When we go out, we have to be careful how we behave, just so that nothing carries over into our lives the next day. For instance, smoking," she looked at Prisca, who had been sharing a smoke with Alan in the boat last night. Prisca had also been quite familiarly nestled up against him, which, Miriam had informed Rachel, had incensed Pete. "Smoke gets into clothes. And hair. And skin. It has a smell."

"A stink," Debbie volunteered, wrinkling her nose. Some of the sisters giggled.

"A smell," repeated Rachel, "which could tip off the parents, hmm?" The other girls considered. "Plus if you were to acquire a habit, just how are you going to satisfy that nicotine craving in the middle of the day? Running off in the minivan to spend your babysitting money on a pack of ciggies?"

"Mom and Dad would ask questions, and if they found out, all of us would be in trouble," Cheryl spoke up, a bit self-righteously. Prisca scowled at her.

"All righty then!" she snapped.

"Same with alcohol," Rachel said. "It has a smell. If you have any, you'd better brush your teeth at least three times before we go upstairs. Plus, if you take too much, you'll have a hangover the next day. You want to run that risk?"

All the girls shook their heads no. *Good, that part was easy,* Rachel thought to herself. Lucky her sisters were inexperienced with drinking anyway.

"Third thing," she said briskly. "A buddy system. We can't have anyone falling overboard, drowning, getting drunk, whatever. We have to watch out for each other, at all times, or we're going to be sorry. Can you live with that?"

This was the most ham-handed she had yet been, and she waited, a bit anxious, to see how her sisters would take it. She knew that some of the older girls were yearning to get alone with a particular guy, and this would put a crimp in their style. All the same, Rachel didn't see any way around it. *I don't mind us being risky, but not stupid,* she repeated to herself.

"Yeah, that sounds fair," Brittany spoke up. The older girls were a bit silent. Cheryl said, "Who partners with who?"

"The same partners all the time," Rachel said, forging ahead. "So you have to make sure you stick with your partner, even when you divide up into different boats, okay? You stick with your buddy, and your buddy sticks with you."

She took a breath. "Cheryl, you and Brittany. Tammy with Liddy, Becca with Taren. Miriam with Linette. Melanie with Debbie. Prisca and me."

It had taken her two days to come up with the combinations, and she prayed they would accept them without question. She had tried to split up natural rivals, had given the younger kids into the hands of the more sensible sisters, and had taken the most volatile of the group—Prisca—for herself. She didn't trust anyone else to keep Prisca in line.

"All right," Tammy said grudgingly, and Miriam said, "I got the best bud," and high-fived Linette, who perked up immediately. Debbie edged over towards Melanie, who looked relieved.

"Can we use handcuffs?" Becca asked innocently, and Taren yelped.

"Yes, for *you,*" Taren shot back.

"If necessary," a smile played around Rachel's lips. "Okay. That's it. Let's get going."

"Alan said he was going to get his neighbor to come on over with his boat," Prisca announced, wiggling into her dress.

"How old is he? The neighbor?" Taren asked.

"Nineteen. And he's not a Christian. At least, he doesn't go to church. But he has a red speedboat," Prisca boasted. Rachel downed a tiny sigh within herself. No more time with Taylor, she foresaw. Tonight, she would be guard-dogging her younger sister aboard a red speedboat.

Well, maybe that's all right, she resigned herself. Give Cheryl a chance to talk to Taylor. He's a fairly decent guy. Despite his nighttime rebellion, he was the sort of guy who would straighten out eventually, probably go for baptism to become a full member of the church. The kind of guy who would interest Cheryl.

The neighbor was named Kirk, and he turned out to be a lean, hawk-like sort of guy, not really good-looking, with a fierce haircut and a beady eye. She figured out he was a local hick, but decided to tolerate him.

She and Prisca were alone with him in the speedboat, and Prisca was chattering and flirting outrageously. Rachel only stepped into the conversation to break her sister's momentum. She was a bit embarrassed for Prisca, but Kirk seemed to find Prisca amusing and not really interesting. Rachel could tell Kirk was more interested in herself.

To pass the time, she kept looking out at the other boats. The buddy system meant that Alan and Keith had full boats—five and six total, respectively, while Cheryl (with Brittany) had Taylor all to herself. It was awfully lopsided. *What we need,* she thought, *are six boats. If only we had our own boat.*

"Whatch you thinking?" Kirk asked her. Prisca had run out of things to say and was sitting breathless, looking out at the water.

Rachel decided to alter her thoughts. "I wish I knew how to drive a boat," she said, lowering her lashes.

"Want to learn? 'Seasy. I'll show you. Move over here."

Rachel wondered if he was going to use this as an attempt to put his arms around her, but Kirk was apparently not so fast. He sat back and named the parts of the boat—the throttle, the clutch, the steering—she paid attention and started to learn.

Pretty soon she was cautiously applying pressure on the gas and chugging gently over waves. "That's it," Kirk said over the engine. "Give her more power."

Rachel did, and was enthralled at the response of the engine and the speed. Soon she was slicing through the waves while Prisca yelped and clutched the side.

"You're a natural!" Kirk yelled delightedly. When she finally stopped, breathless, she grinned, momentarily breaking her reserve.

"Thank you," she said.

"Man, you're a bit of a wild thing after all, you are," he said appreciatively. She knew he was right, but chose not to respond, merely smiled. She saw out of the corner of her eye that Prisca was insanely jealous. Perhaps this partnership was going to be more trouble than it was worth.

CRACK!

As soon as he heard the sound, Paul knew that something bad had happened. Swiftly catching all the other clubs in his hands, he stared at the one he had dropped, and the rock protruding from the ground which had split it from top to bottom.

Trying to suppress his frustration, he sat down, wiping the sweat from his brow. He picked up the broken club and tried to put the pieces back together. It was damaged, badly.

What made it worse was that these were the hand-carved wooden clubs he had borrowed from a friend, since they fit in with the Colonial period more than his plastic ones. Well, there was nothing to do now except pick up the pieces and try to do what he could to fix them. It was going to take time, and money. And it had to be done before the festival started tomorrow.

Gloomily he got to his feet, stashed the rest of the clubs safely into the tent, wrapped the broken pieces in a cloth and put them into his juggling bag. He was supposed to go teach Debbie and Linette soon, but he would have to get this club fixed first. He slung the bag over his shoulder, and headed into town dejectedly.

I should have been paying more careful attention to my juggling, he chastised himself as he jogged along. *Guess I have too much on my mind.*

While he was making some progress on the logistics of being an invisible bodyguard during the girls' midnight escapades, he felt he wasn't making very much progress towards his final goal. Maybe Debbie and Linette were beginning to trust him, but he was sure that Rachel disliked him and the other girls barely registered his existence when he was at the Durham house during the day. He wasn't sure that Melanie and Sallie's other daughters didn't think he was some kind of pagan.

Eventually, Paul found the hardware store and went inside.

"Can I help you?" a cheerful older blond lady whose nametag read "Dolo" asked as soon as he walked in.

"Uh—sure. I need to repair these," he said, pulling the clubs out of his bag.

Dolo examined the clubs with a professional eye. "Some wood glue will do the trick," she said. "And some clamps. Aisles 2 and 5."

The wood glue wasn't much, but the clamps he needed to fix the club turned out to be expensive. With a sinking heart, he shelled out more of his food money to pay for them.

As Dolo rang up his bill, she remarked, "Night job getting you down?"

He looked at her, a bit startled. "Sort of," he said cautiously, fingering his miraculous medal.

She chuckled. "You just really look tired. If you don't mind me asking, are you Catholic?"

"Trying to be," he said.

She grinned back. "Have you been to the church on Plain Street?" she jerked a finger behind her. "It's not far from here. Sure beats hitchhiking into Baltimore if you're looking for a daily Mass."

"Really? I'll check it out!" Shouldering his juggling clubs, he added, "Thanks!"

"No problem, kid: keep the faith."

As he exited the hardware store, he checked the clock on the bank and saw he was late for his lessons with Debbie and Linette. *At least I'm becoming friends with them.* He raised his pace to a jog. *Maybe if I just continue to be open and friendly with them it will influence their older sisters.* To save time getting to the Durhams' house, he cut through the development off of Plain Street.

In the meantime, I just have to make sure none of them get hurt, he thought. *Man, now I feel like I'm juggling those girls on a high-wire.* He suddenly felt cold in his chest remembering the club he had so recently dropped. *What if you drop one of the girls? And there's no safety net? They could get hurt. Damaged. Permanently.*

Paul halted, panting, wondering if he had been foolish to get so involved with this situation.

He realized that he had stopped in front of a large brick building whose pedestrian shape made it look like an office building. But a sign on the front said: OUR LADY SEAT OF WISDOM ROMAN CATHOLIC MISSION.

Just where Dolo had said it would be. And the sign said there was a morning Mass here three times a week.

Dropping to his knees, he prayed with more intensity than he usually did. *Help me not to drop them. Any of them.*

Then he got to his feet, crossed himself, turned, and started running again.

Apparently God still saw fit to answer some of Rachel's prayers—if it was God who answered them—because the next night, Pete showed up driving a trim blue boat. Pete had told Miriam a couple nights ago that he was seriously considering buying a used boat, and it turned out that his parents had helped him buy this one. Pete's parents seemed to be more laid back than most of the parents in their midnight-outing group.

He had been hanging out with Miriam, having recovered from being slighted by Prisca, and Rachel approved. Anyone could see Miriam was sensible and fun to be with, even if she was on the heavier side. And Pete, who was a tall, gawky sort of guy, seemed to appreciate her personality.

That night, Rachel and Prisca were in Alan's boat with Melanie and Debbie. Despite Rachel's fears that she was going to have to endure Kirk's attentions, Prisca had turned her short attention span elsewhere. Now Rich, Alan's friend, a senior with muscles and short brown hair, was the object of her affection. And Tammy, surprising everyone, had professed a liking for Kirk's buzz haircut. She and Liddy were passengers in Kirk's red boat that night. The other girls remained with their usual partners.

Rachel settled herself on the ample seat of Alan's boat and sighed. The headache that had been nagging her all day had finally started to dissipate.

"The boat seems really slow tonight," Debbie said after they got started.

"Yeah? Well, I'm carrying the most weight," Alan said, looking over at her. "There's six of us here."

"Your boat is *always* slow, every time I ride in it," Debbie complained. "Why do you carry so much stuff around in it?"

Rachel looked around. It was true that part of Alan's boat was covered in canvas, and there were always lumpy objects beneath it.

"My parents insist on storing all their junk here," Alan said, irritated. "That's why."

Rachel shot Debbie a warning look. "How're your juggling lessons going, Debbie?"

"Very good. I like Paul," Debbie said.

"We all know that," Prisca said. "You're the only one who does."

"I like him too," Melanie said. "Even if he is a Catholic."

Rachel leaned back against the side. "You were talking with him a lot the other day," she observed.

"I was asking him why he prays to Mary. He told me that Christ is like the sun, and Mary is like the moon. Because the sun gives out its own light, and the moon just reflects the sun's light. So he honors Mary because she reflects God's glory."

"So Mary is like the moon," Prisca repeated, nodding. Suddenly her eyes widened, and she clutched Rachel's arm, crying in a choked voice. "Like—a moon goddess! It's Babylonian Mystery Religion! Aaahh!"

Rachel burst out laughing, and then had to explain the joke to the guys. It didn't seem quite as funny to them.

"But I don't think it's pagan at all," Melanie said. "It looks weird, you know, but once Paul explained it, I could sort of understand, even if I didn't quite agree. It was kind of a nice idea. He's very good at explaining things."

"Proof! Proof! He's convinced Melanie! He *is* an agent of Satan!" Prisca hissed in Rachel's ear.

"He knows a *lot* about the Bible," Debbie said. "He's read parts of it that I bet even our assistant pastor hasn't read."

"More proof!"

"A Bible scholar," Rich commented, and Rachel smiled at his mock appreciation. "Is he going to be a pastor?"

"You can't be a pastor if you're Catholic," Debbie said. "Not unless you become a priest. Paul said he doesn't feel called to become a priest."

"You asked him about that?"

"Oh sure. I ask him everything. He tells me everything."

Prisca leaned forward. "Did you ask him if he likes any of us?"

"Yes."

Heads turned. "What did he say?" Rachel asked, despite herself.

"He said something about gold and jewels. I think he was saying we were all very nice," Debbie cocked her head, and winked devilishly. "But, he said Rachel is like the Queen of Sheba."

"Oooh!" Prisca said. Rachel colored.

"So he thinks I'm high and mighty?" she asked. "I could have guessed that."

"No, not like that. I asked him if he liked you, and he said he couldn't think of liking you any more than he could like the Queen of Sheba."

Rachel pursed her lips. "Backhanded compliment," she murmured to Prisca. "Did you ask him if he liked anyone else?"

"I was going to, but then he threw all the clubs at me at once, and I had to work hard to not drop them, and I did anyway, and then he laughed at me." Debbie bounced on her seat. "Alan, can you take us to the island?"

Rachel had planted the seeds in the other girls' minds gradually. She held her breath. Alan looked at Debbie. "You mean the big island? The private one?"

"Yes. Can't we just go and look around?"

Alan shrugged. "Hmm. Okay."

Rachel let out her breath and edged towards the front of the boat.

It seemed forever as Alan's boat cruised slowly towards the far side of the island. Then he drifted nearer, until they could see the house and the empty heliport. It was a dark night tonight, with a thin moon.

"I don't want to go on their docks," Alan mused. "Maybe we can go to one of the beaches and tie up under the trees."

"What about there?" Rachel pointed to the stone quay with the pillars. "You could drift up there and tie up under the trees to one side. That's out of sight."

"Good idea," he said.

Soon the boat was actually bobbing up and down in the waves beside the quay. Alan cut the engine, and Rachel stared, amazed at the enchanted land, now barely three feet from her.

She stood up unsteadily in the boat. "Do you want me to get out and tie us up?" she asked, clearing her throat.

"Sure. Go ahead," Alan said, and she put out a hand onto the stone, almost expecting it to dissolve into mist under her touch. But that was silly. It was solid, and she hopped onto the land and stood up, breathing hard.

"Toss me the rope," she said to Melanie, who groped around and threw out the rope.

Rachel gave a hand to her sisters before allowing herself to drink in the enchantment of it. When Alan and Rich were on land as well, the group of them stood on the edge of the quay, looking up at the ancient trees towering overhead, lush with swaying leaves.

"It's a magical place," Debbie said, hushed.

"Yeah," Rich said. "It almost seems like it."

Tentatively they walked forward. The quay was a stone portico, about a hundred feet wide by a hundred feet long. The pavement stones were irregularly shaped, with moss growing between the cracks, but the surface was smooth with no unexpected steps.

"It's like—a midnight dance floor," Prisca said, her voice barely a whisper.

"Oooh!" Debbie said. Then, "We should have a dance here! Rachel, we should."

She had foreseen it long ago, but did not mind seeming to give the credit to others. "That's a wonderful idea," Rachel said softly.

seven

After midnight, the princesses arose from their beds, put on splendid dresses, and hurried out of their room through the secret door, invisibly followed by the soldier. . .

— *Grimm*

Paul breathed. The early morning light was dim around him as he stood on the shore of the bay, breathing, hands pushed together against his chest. The cool air hummed with the activities of insects and awakening birds. Breathing, he listened, he centered himself, and began his aikido exercises with an invocation to the Holy Spirit.

Full stretch. Up. Over. Pushing down, with both hands, he made a big grab of the space before him in the air, and as though it were a huge ball, pressed it down to the ground, "as though bringing your swollen ego down to the earth," his aikido master used to say. Reach up again, he seized the nothingness and pushed it down. And centered himself again.

Now stance work—his knees bent, his body forward, he lunged. *Stance. Lunge. Stance again.* His war injury was a barely perceptible ache. *Good! Center. Center. Center.*

He knelt on the ground in the seiza position and, spreading and touching his fingers and thumbs to form the ceremonial triangle, he pressed his palms and forehead to the ground, seeking humility and discipline.

Discipline. Time to work on his joints. He sat up and methodically began to pull his wrists backwards against the joints until they hurt. The nikyo discipline increased his resistance to pain. He worked harder than usual on these, to ready his hands for the stress of juggling heavy clubs all day.

Then he leapt to his feet and stretched wide, making an expansive scooping motion with his arms while filling his lungs with air, then pushing the air out with a corresponding thrust of his arms. *Take it in, release it.* After a few minutes of this, he exhaled completely from his gut and centered himself. All his movements would begin from his center, his *hara*. He was prepared.

Now he was ready to move. He began the agility exercises, stepping forward, twisting about, stepping back, the basic building blocks of all action. When he felt ready, he leapt forward and twisted about in a flip. Landing on his feet, he reached for the repaired juggling club and tossed it into the air. The twirl of the heavy, well-balanced instrument was a pleasure in and of itself, and he caught it, stilled it in an instant, and then tossed it again. His breathing regular, his mind alert, and his body prepared, he started into the routine he was practicing for the festival. Today was the first day.

He had hung out his juggling clothes—the black pants, loose white shirt, diamond-patched vest, and black mask—on a nearby branch. For shoes, he wore ninja shoes—lightweight, soft, black leather with flexible soles. Now he took off the black shirt and pants he had been wearing and changed into his costume. There was fruit and bread left over from yesterday's meal, and he ate it for breakfast with a protein bar. By the time he was finished, the fire he had built earlier was burning brightly, and the water in his camping pot had boiled. Realizing he still had ample time, he made himself some tea and sat against a tree to drink it.

The Durham girls...he swirled the tealeaves in his cup and frowned. They were becoming almost as much a trouble to him as they were to Colonel Durham. He was beginning to think that the girls' late night escapades were not so much the problem as they were the symptom of other deeper issues.

One big difficulty was that Colonel Durham didn't seem particularly affectionate with his daughters. *You have to show your daughters that you love them or they'll start looking for someone who will,* Paul's dad had always said.

Paul wondered if part of the reason Colonel Durham was so reserved was that six of the girls were his stepdaughters. *Maybe he just feels awkward trying to be close to them? And he withholds affection from his biological daughters as well, so as not to play favorites?*

Paul tapped his fingers on his mug. There was something else that bothered him, but it was hard to express. He could find a lot of admirable aspects to the Durhams' plain lifestyle. They were unpretentious people who had money but had chosen to live simply. Apparently the parents were happy, but he wasn't sure this way of life was keeping the girls contented. The Durhams didn't have a television, but he also noticed that they didn't have many books, particularly storybooks. Except for Cheryl, who was mostly reading Christian romance novels, he had never seen the older girls reading anything. It didn't seem as if they had much of an imaginative or intellectual life. From what he could tell, they spent most of their time doing housework, serving other church members, sewing plain dresses, or being bored.

They need something good to love besides 'being good,' he thought to himself. *Or else, they'll find something to love that's not good.*

☾

Rachel had to plan her dress excursions carefully, interspersing them with legitimate errands. Between going to the grocery store and the eye doctor's, she had made a furtive dash into a clothing store and scoured the sales racks in vain. After going to the pharmacy, she had tried another store. No luck. And she had even stopped at the Salvation Army, to paw hopefully through the ripped prom dresses and dated bridesmaids frocks. In despair she had bought for twenty dollars a 1940's navy blue dress with a short swishy skirt, but it was years away from the svelte, sleek black dress she was dreaming about. As it was, she had taken too much time and would have to rush.

Now she stood in the library, jingling her car keys, having come to pick up Cheryl and the younger girls. They were still in the stacks, choosing their Christian paperback novels with care. Rachel stalked from side to side, antsy, and was shushed by a cross librarian, who pointed at her keys. Guiltily irritated, Rachel thrust them into the pocket of her blue denim dress and looked at the summertime reading display.

One book leaning against a model sailboat caught her eye—*The Wind and the Willows.* That was the book Paul had mentioned, wasn't it? She vaguely recalled seeing a silly Disney movie about weasels and racecars by that name.

She picked it up and paged through it. Yes, it was a book about talking animals, the sort of thing that held no interest for her. She fanned the pages and came across an illustration of a huge man with goat's feet and horns on his head, holding a set of pipes. He was looking down upon several cute, fuzzy animals, with an expression of love. The title bar above said *The Piper at the Gates of Dawn.*

The figure was vaguely familiar—yes, it was Pan, one of the Greek gods. *This must be the pagan part,* she thought to herself. The part that had made one of the Bayside Christian Academy teachers warn her students against the book. Intrigued, Rachel creased the page and started scanning and reading.

All this he saw, for one moment breathless and intense, vivid on the morning sky; and still, as he looked, he lived; and still, as he lived, he wondered.

'Rat!' he found breath to whisper, shaking. 'Are you afraid?'

'Afraid?' murmured the Rat, his eyes shining with unutterable love. 'Afraid? Of *Him*? O, never, never! And yet—and yet—O, Mole, I am afraid!'

Chilled by the unexpected, she closed the book. *Here I am, reading children's literature for a naughty thrill*, she thought to herself. Feeling foolish and tawdry, she set it back on the shelf and studied it warily.

Maybe she should read it. It was obviously a children's book, with the fuzzballs and all. And she was an adult, almost, too big for things like this. But Paul had read it.

The thought sat in her mind, and she set the book back on the shelf, then abruptly picked it up again and slid it under her arm. *What the heck*, she thought. If it turned out to be boring and stupid, she could always bring it out when the girls were alone and read aloud parts for laughs. As she set it down on the counter, she looked again at the cover, which showed two animals rowing a boat down the river. There was a bright blue and black butterfly in the corner.

Then inspiration struck. That was what she wanted, she decided. A dress like that, blue and black. A bit of sparkle winking here and there. Yes, that would be a dress for the moonlight. But there was no question of her ever finding a dress like that. She would have to make one.

And the fabric store was an easier place to go without arousing parental suspicion than most dress stores. Yes, that would be her strategy.

Almost pleased, she leaned against the book counter, still waiting, but now planning. At last Cheryl came out of the stacks, staggering beneath a pile of romance novels. Rachel added her one book to the pile and hurried out to the car to wait for the girls to finish checking out.

When she reached it, she noticed that the family cell phone was blinking. She must have spent too long a time at the stores, including the extra errands she had made. Quickly she dialed voicemail and listened to the message.

It was her father. "Where are you?" his voice demanded. "This is the third time I've called and no one has answered the phone. I need you to get over here, pronto, to pick up these files and mail them out for me! Don't you remember?"

Rachel cursed. She had forgotten all about that errand, which her father had told her about at the breakfast table. Her father's message went on. "Please try and be less scatterbrained! I hope I'll be seeing you soon."

Rachel turned off the cell phone abruptly. It was after five now. The post office would be closed. It was no use. Tears sprung to her eyes. *Serves Dad right for treating me as his errand boy,* part of her said rebelliously, but another part of her insisted, *I should have remembered. I shouldn't have forgotten. At least, I should have brought the cell phone into the stores with me.*

It used to be so much easier to please her dad, she thought. Back when Mom was alive, back when she was the oldest of a smaller family. She remembered her dad boasting to his friends about how capable she was, just because she had learned to set the table when she was five. She used to run to him when he came home, eager to tell him what she had accomplished, and he had always seemed interested and happy. And even after Mom had died when she was a young teenager, he used to be so grateful to come home and find the table set and dinner made. But now, he was always preoccupied and distant, and coldly judgmental when she failed—

Why bother pleasing someone like that? she told herself angrily. *I'm not even going to try.*

That night Taren wore her brown suede dress, to the envy of all the girls. However, as Prisca admitted, not all of them could have fit into a dress like that. And now that Taren and Rachel had their own dresses, there were two more dresses to go around.

Rachel, in her navy blue skimmer, took it upon herself that night to find something to suit Melanie. She had noticed that Melanie, alone, always wore the print cotton bridesmaid's dress from Sallie and Dad's wedding. "Let's try something more grown-up," she suggested, and gave Melanie the white sheath dress to put on, and her younger sister obeyed.

"I really like wearing dresses with sleeves," Melanie objected. "I'm always cold."

"Oh, come on. Try this one once. Just for me," Rachel coaxed. When Melanie stood awkwardly in front of her in the slim white dress, Rachel adjusted her shoulders and said, "We've got to do something with your hair."

"Do we?" Melanie asked, fingering her tousled long honey-blond hair. "I like it down."

"Yes, but you look so young!" Rachel explained.

"Well, I *am* young."

"Let's just try it this way, for once," Rachel begged. She longed to see her younger stepsister sparkling and vibrant and attractive, and Melanie reluctantly agreed to the makeover.

Rachel piled Melanie's hair on top of her head and skewered it with bobby pins. Then she wound a scarf around it. "That's just for the boat," she informed Melanie, "so that it won't blow all over the place. There! I wish you could see yourself. How do you feel?"

"Cold," Melanie confessed, hugging her bare arms and trying to smile.

"Oh, get her a sweater and stop fussing with her," Tammy said, irritably. "She's always complaining about being cold."

"I'll choose a sweater," Rachel said, and found a white one with lacy knit sleeves. "Maybe not the best match in the sunlight, but in the moonlight— perfect!"

Melanie put on the sweater, but she still shivered. Rachel shepherded her down to the beach. "The boys will be here soon."

The boats arrived, and Rachel was impatient to get going immediately. But not all the girls were ready, and the guys liked to stand on the beach and chat, so she indulged them while the boats bobbed up and down in the water beneath the willows.

As soon as she could politely do so, she suggested they leave. All the girls were agreed that tonight they would all go to the island.

"Just so long as no one's home," Taylor said dubiously.

"We can check," Rachel said lightly. "No one seemed to mind us being there last night."

"But that was only one boat. If someone was there, they might not care about that. But what are they going to think when they see three boats?" Taylor objected.

Rachel was glad she had left him to Cheryl—he was being a stick-in-the-mud. "Taylor," Rachel said playfully, "can't you live it up a little every once in a while?"

He grumbled, but when the other guys started teasing him, he relented, and the party got into the boats.

In the sloshing of the boarding, Alan's boat bumped against Keith's, splashing Prisca, who exclaimed. "There goes my mascara!"

"I just stepped on someone's foot," Debbie informed them in the darkness of the boat beneath the trees.

"Do you hear anyone complaining?" Rachel said, a little sharply.

"No. That's why I said something. And I can't find any place to sit. There's no room back here."

"Just move a bit of that canvas and sit squished next to me," Rachel said, situating herself.

Alan turned on the engine and the boat slowly motored out into the bay.

The moon was at a half. Rachel breathed a deep sigh. Perhaps by the next full moon, she would have made the midnight butterfly dress, as she thought of it fondly. She looked over at her sister Melanie. The transformation she had hoped for had not occurred. Melanie wasn't sparkling—in fact, she looked deadened in the pale light, gray and colorless, shivering in the thin short dress, somehow less than her buoyant self. She actually would have looked better in the print bridesmaid's dress she usually wore.

Rachel felt a twinge of disappointment. Perhaps Melanie was too much a child of the sunshine, she decided. She wasn't at home in the night.

Like I am, she thought to herself. *The night is almost my real self.*

Prisca also seemed to be more herself at nighttime. The strong colors of night makeup highlighted Prisca's already dark coloring, and made her eyes darker, her lips redder. Right now, she was wearing a red knit tank dress, which looked good on her, accentuated her full figure. But there was something about Prisca that bothered Rachel. She was almost too jumpy and eager, too unsubtle. Rich seemed to be able to tell. Like most of the church guys, Rachel noted, he seemed to hang around Prisca but seemed uncomfortable being close to her. There was an air of volatility about her that seemed to make him nervous.

Debbie was wearing a purple striped dress that Rachel had scouted out for her at Goodwill. She still seemed like a child let out to be with the grownups. Even now, she was swinging her thin brown legs carelessly.

"I wonder whose foot I stepped on," she said. "No one said 'ouch.'"

Rachel rolled her eyes. "Are you still going on about that?" she said.

Debbie ignored her. "Was it yours, Rich?"

Rich started and said, "No, I don't think so."

"I was waiting to apologize," Debbie said. "But no one said anything. I thought I really hurt someone because it was when I jumped onto the boat."

"Maybe it was my foot, but since you're such a weenie I didn't feel it," Prisca said with some irritation.

"No," said Debbie decidedly, "It wasn't you. It was a big foot."

"Then it must have been mine," Rachel said.

"You do *not* have big feet," Prisca interjected.

Rachel held up one of her size nine feet and pointed the toes. "Does that look big enough for you, Debbie?"

"No, it wasn't yours. I stepped on the toes. I thought it was a guy's foot," Debbie said. "It was very strange."

"Shut up," Prisca said abruptly. "Alan, why are you stopping?"

Alan had cut the engine. He looked at the island. "Is there someone there?" he asked uncertainly.

"Ohh—" Rachel got up, along with the others. The boat rocked, and Rich and Prisca sat back down. "No, I don't think so," she said, after scrutinizing the heliport in the shadows.

"Were all those boats there last night?" he asked, pointing to the docks.

Worried, they all looked at the docks.

"Yes," Prisca said suddenly. "There's five boats there, just like last night. I counted."

"Okay, just checking," Alan said, and the engine roared to life. They soared towards the quay and soon they were docked beside it. Once again, Rachel got out first and tied up the boat. Rich jumped onto the quay and helped the other girls out.

"This is going to be perfect," Prisca said, taking Rich's hand and swinging onto the quay, leaning against him. "Oh my gosh! I almost fell! Sorry!"

Prisca had a small CD player with her, along with a few of her "contraband," as she called them—CDs of pop music—that she listened to turned down low, underneath her pillow at home.

Now she cranked the CD player as loud as it would go. "What shall I put on first?" She pulled out a CD of dance songs and slid it into the dinky machine and pushed 'play.'

"That's like, a state of the art sound system you've got there," Alan cracked, getting out of the boat.

"Do you have something better?" Prisca asked anxiously.

"Not here."

"Are you having a dance here or something?" Rich asked, getting the prize for the most clueless remark of the evening, so far.

"Duh! Of course!" And Prisca grabbed his arms. "Come on, dance with me." She and Debbie started to bop around, and Rich, at first embarrassed, fell in step.

"You want to?" Alan cast a glance at Rachel, who grinned.

"Of course!"

And he took her hand, and they started dancing. Despite the tinny sound and low volume, it was just enough music to dance by.

The roar of the other boats coming to join them temporarily superseded the music. Tammy and Liddy leapt from their boat, convulsed with laughter, and jumped right into the dance. Cheryl came a bit more gingerly, but consented to dance when Taylor took her hand. Brittany struck her usual poker face and started doing the monster mash, which the young girls quickly picked up. Soon everyone was dancing.

It was glorious. The guys broke out some bottles of beer and bags of potato chips. Taren had managed to snag two six packs of soda from the family pantry, so the girls passed out sodas. They were careful to put all the bottles back on board the boat, Rachel reminding the guys that even a single smashed beer bottle would give them away. They played through all the songs on one CD and then restarted it to dance some more.

Rachel drank in the music as much as the beverages, throwing herself into the dance. As she swayed to the beat, she felt her own beauty like a barely-visible shadow, growing, blooming.

She and Prisca were dancing together when Prisca suddenly stopped, staring. "Who's that guy?" she said.

As if by some scent in the air, everyone on the portico froze in place, while the music from the CD played on and on. All of them were staring at the figure of a young man coming slowly down the steps from the big house.

eight

They went by boat across the water to a splendid castle in the middle of the lake, where they danced all the night long . . .   —— Grimm

Rachel's heart was thumping against her chest. All she could think was, *shoot.* She didn't want to look at Alan, because she was sure his face was as white as chalk. Something had to be done, and done quickly.

She tried to size up the young man as he came slowly down the steps. He had blond hair, gently chiseled features, eyes shadowed by the moonlight. He wore a white shirt and khaki pants with a casually studied flair.

He reached the bottom step, and stood still, watching them. Prisca sidled to the CD player, hunted for the off button, and pushed it. The music vanished, and the air was filled only with the moaning duet of wind and waves.

"What are you doing here?" he asked, and his voice came across the portico clearly, a low, resonant voice. Rachel felt a prickle in her spine.

She stepped forward, her legs trembling. "I'm sorry—" she faltered. "We didn't think anyone was—we're sorry for disturbing you."

The young man studied her with shaded eyes. She could feel herself being looked at, and flushed.

"We just wanted to go someplace private to dance," she said, "and we didn't think anyone was here. Are you—are you—the caretaker?"

"I'm one of the owners," he said, his voice felicitous with amusement. "This is my parents' place."

"Oh," said Rachel, and felt more blood rush to her face. "We're sorry. This is only the second time we've come here. We can leave right away if you want."

Unexpectedly, he sat down on the steps and put his hands on his knees. "No, no, not at all. Go on with your dancing. I wasn't expecting to find anyone here, but I don't mind."

He waved his hands. "Go on, go on."

Prisca hesitantly turned on the music, but no one seemed to feel like dancing any more. Rachel took a long, slow look around at her fellows, and approached the figure sitting on the steps. She walked up three steps and across a length of pavement to reach the foot of the stairs, where the young man sat.

She said. "That's very nice of you to let us stay."

He looked up at her, his eyes tilting out of the shadow. They were blue, sharp blue. "Thank you. I like to be nice."

"I'm Rachel Durham," she said, since there was not much else she could think of saying.

"I'm Michael Comus," he said, and extended his hand to her. She took it gingerly, unused to shaking hands with men, and found her hand enveloped in a warm, firm squeeze, then released. There were blond hairs on the back of his hands, and the fingers were quite long.

"Where are you from, Rachel?" he asked, stretching back and moving over to make room for her. She gingerly sat down beside him, tucking her skirt under her knees.

"My sisters and I live across the bay, on the other side of this island."

"Sisters?" his gaze traveled over the crowded portico. "Are *all* these girls your sisters?"

"Yes," she said. "I have five natural sisters, and my father married a woman with six girls, so they're all my sisters."

"Twelve girls," he marveled, and looked at her. "You must be Catholics."

"Oh! No, we're Christians."

A slight smile came over his face. "Your father isn't the Colonel Durham who's on the board of Bayside Christian Church?"

"He is," Rachel said, nodding and pushing back her hair.

"My father knows him," Michael said. "How old are you?"

"Eighteen. How old are you?"

"Twenty-four."

"Oh," she was surprised.

"Do I look younger?" he asked, amused.

"I can't tell ages very well," she said. He looked neither old nor young, almost timeless. She noticed his forehead was fairly high, and his eyes were set deeply in his face, giving him an aristocratic, intense look.

"Do you—spend a lot of time here?" she asked.

He smiled. "Actually, not very much at all, not any more. When I was a kid, I came here more often. Now, there's not much to do."

"Did you just come back tonight?"

"Today, actually. I needed some down time, and I was bored, so I came here, expecting to be even more bored. I was watching a movie with the lights off when I heard the motorboats, so I came down to investigate."

"I'm sorry we were trespassing," she said, after a pause.

He raised his eyebrows at her. "Why did you?"

"Well—" she flushed, and explained, "every time I went down to the bay, I would see this island and wonder what was on it. Then when we were out boating with our guy friends, I persuaded them to stop on the quay, just to see what it was like. My younger sisters wanted to have a dance party, which is why we came back here tonight."

"I see," he said meditatively. "So this island was a temptation for you?"

"Yes," she admitted. "An extremely persistent temptation."

He raised his blond brows. "Far be it from me to discourage you from giving in to temptation, Miss Durham."

A smile touched her lips, unsure as to whether he was joking or not. He smiled at her.

"How do you know my father?" she asked.

He stretched. "My father is on the chamber of commerce, and they've had some run-ins with that church, and with your father. He's one of those fundamentalist types, isn't he?"

"Yes," she said, with a bit of a sigh.

He pursued, "Your family must be quite strict."

"You could say that."

"But yet they let you girls—even the young ones—go boating on the Bay after midnight?" Michael looked at her with knitted brows and an ironic grin on his face.

Rachel had to smile. "Well, now, they don't exactly—"

He finished for her, "—they don't exactly know you're out here? Are they away?"

"No. We've just—we just have a way of getting out of the house that they don't know about."

She told him about the discovery of the secret staircase, and their expeditions out in the night. He listened attentively.

After she finished, he shook his head. "You girls have a lot of courage, going out on your own like this. Shows more spirit than I'd have expected, the way you were raised."

"Thanks," she said, unsure of what to say, but her face felt warm.

He looked at her. "You're welcome to come to this quay any time you like and dance at night."

"Really?" she asked.

"Really," he said, smiling. "I'm all for encouraging your spirit of adventure."

"That's very nice of you," she said.

"Rachel," he said, looking at her keenly. "I am a very nice man."

He looked up, and Rachel saw Prisca and Tammy hovering on the edge of the landing, looking at them uncertainly.

"Please, introduce me," he said, rising.

"Oh—certainly—" she got up, realizing how much time had gone by. She quickly said, "Michael, these are my sisters, Prisca and Tammy."

"One from each parent, I can tell," Michael said, shaking their hands. The younger girls were also unused to handshakes, and Rachel saw Prisca clutching her hand nervously after Michael had released it.

Michael was apparently well brought up, and used to small talk. He chatted in a friendly way with the two sisters, found out their ages and interests, and charmed them. Rachel introduced Debbie and Linette, who had come up next, their curiosity overcoming any residual shyness. It took the next thirty minutes for Michael to meet them all, the guys included.

"Is he mad at us?" Alan asked Rachel in a low voice while Michael talked with Miriam and Brittany.

She shook her head. "I think he was bored here alone. He said he was glad to have the company."

"Doggone lucky for us."

Rachel had to agree.

The party broke up around three, and Michael saw them off. Before she got in the boat, he took Rachel's hand suddenly and said, "I'm serious. I'd like you all to come back again. Can you come tomorrow night?" It was a polite gesture—he was just helping her into the boat—but she still felt a rush of warmth.

"Sure, I think so," Rachel said, casting a glance around at everyone, who nodded.

"Good. I'll look forward to it."

When they were roaring away from the island, Prisca sidled up to Rachel and said, "Well! *That* was luck!"

"No kidding," Rachel said, still marveling at it.

"And he's handsome too," Prisca breathed in her ear. Rachel, who had already observed this, felt no need to reply.

Yes, luck had been with them, she thought. *For sure.*

The next day, Rachel was languid. The day was muggy, and hot, and she was tired and out of sorts. She couldn't imagine a more stark contrast with the excitement of last night. Michael had told them to come back. Maybe he would dance with her. She felt certain he was an excellent dancer.

As she stood in the kitchen, cleaning up the dishes, she thought again of the midnight butterfly dress. More than ever, she needed to make it. The problem was getting the material. "Shiny material calls too much attention to the body," the pastor's wife had earnestly said at a woman's day retreat some time ago. "As Christians we're not meant to be paying that much attention to the body. And should we really be spending money on worldly excesses?" Ever since that time, Sallie had shoed her daughters away from the "formal occasion" section of the fabric store, so much so that Prisca had dubbed it the "sin" aisle. *I don't care,* thought Rachel. *I'm going there and getting it anyway.*

The problem was, she didn't know when Sallie was going to let her out of the house. Sallie was on the warpath, upset that the house was not cleaned, and irritable from having discovered three of her daughters still in bed after nine o'clock.

"I don't understand it!" she complained to Cheryl, who was moping around the kitchen, pouring cereal and rubbing her eyes. "All this sleeping in! Tammy and Taren are still lazing around upstairs and it's going on ten! Well, take advantage of the fact that it's summertime. I don't want to see this in the fall."

"I told you, Mom, they were up too late last night," Cheryl said. "We've been reading those missionary books you got us for Christmas."

"You girls have to start getting to bed earlier," Sallie said. "Linette has been cranky this entire week. Maybe I'll just have to get up at midnight and turn off your lights."

"I'll make sure the lights are off," Cheryl said quickly.

"I hope so," she said, and heaved a sigh. "No, Jabez, no. We don't pull hair." She pulled the toddler off his older brother, Robbie, who had started yelling. "Rachel, could you take him?"

Rachel had already mechanically gone for Jabez, disentangling the pudgy hand from the handful of Robbie's hair. She picked up the toddler by his overall straps and swung him into her arms. He punched her shoulders excitedly. Absentmindedly she sat him on the counter and gave him a cookie.

"Cheryl, after you've cleaned the kitchen, we need to get out the canning jars I have downstairs," Sallie said. "I want you girls to bring them up and put them through the dishwasher, okay? Rachel, no more cookies for him, please." Rachel took away the cookie. "Cheryl, while you're at it, could you—Jabez! Please! Be quiet!—Rachel, could you—?"

Rachel took the wailing boy out of the room into the living room. She felt dead tired, and collapsed on the couch.

"Okay, Jabez, let's play 'Rachel goes to sleep.' Here, lie down with me and pretend to go to sleep." The toddler tucked his big head under her chin, and she could just see, through her half-closed eyes, his cheeks puffed out in a smile. "Aww, sleepy Jabez. Sleepy...." she coaxed, knowing he would only tolerate this game for about fifteen seconds.

Then he sat up and pounded her on the chest. "Oh! Waking-up Jabez! Awake!" she breathed. "Now sleepy again! Sleeeepy...." He lay down again obediently, and then sat up a second later with a shout. "Awake! Oh, boy, Jabez. Now we sleep ... Sleepy Rachel..."

She played with him in this manner, all the while falling into a half-doze. Sleepy Rachel ...

Jabez eventually tired of the game, and scrambled off her to go play on the piano. She was able to tune out the pounding of the keys, and when that ceased, she tumbled into a deeper layer of sleep.

Sleep was like night entering into the day, and she had tantalizing visions of dances in the moonlight, in that other world where she was more alive than ...

She stirred in her sleep and then abruptly woke up, feeling herself watched.

Paul was standing in the doorway of the living room. She blinked at him. "Hi," he said, uncomfortably. "I'm sorry. I didn't mean to wake you up."

"Oh!" she said stiffly, sitting up. "No, that's okay. I must have dozed off."

He shifted his weight to his other foot. "The girls told me you might be in here, but I didn't realize you were sleeping."

"I didn't realize it either," she yawned, covering her mouth absently. "What's up?"

"That's a very nice dress you're wearing, by the way."

Rachel pulled the skirt of her plain denim dress straight in some annoyance. "Huh. Thanks."

"Um. I actually came to ask you a favor." He wasn't looking her in the face. She curled her lip in amusement.

"Sure," she said, stifling yet another annoying yawn. "Sit down?"

"Thanks." He sat on the footstool instead of the chair. "It's like this. Your younger sisters are really doing great at the juggling, and I asked them if they wanted to be part of my routine at the fair. I asked your—stepmother—" his eyes flew to her face at the word, and she nodded, "if it was all right, and she said, fine. The problem is, they need costumes. For tumbling in. And she didn't think she'd have time to help them make any. The girls said you're the best seamstress in the house. So I was wondering if you'd make them some costumes."

She considered. "Well, sure, I could. What sort of costume?"

"Well, mine is mostly black and white with a multicolored vest. For the girls I thought maybe something simple—like black pirate pants and white tunics, and sashes. The big thing is they need pants to wear when they tumble. I told your stepmother it's okay with me if she wants them to wear dresses on top of that. But I don't know how complicated that would be."

Rachel was already fitting this request into her already-in-process schemes. "Hmm. Black material. Like satin, maybe?"

"Oh, sure. Whatever you can find. Whatever is cheap and durable. I said I could pay for the costumes. Would you want me to pay you to make them?"

"Oh, never mind about that. I'm sure Dad will give money for the costumes. They're for the girls, after all. How soon do you want them?"

"Well—as soon as you can. Maybe two days? Is that too soon?"

"Not if I can get the fabric today," Rachel said, tossing back her hair. "I'll ask Sallie if I can take the car."

"That would be great."

"Do you want to come with me to pick something out?" she asked, looking him in the face.

"No, no that's okay. I trust your judgment. I actually have to go juggle in an hour. The fair opens at noon." He seemed flushed. *What's up with him today?*

"Do you need a ride there?" She asked only to see what he would do.

"No. That's okay. It's not far to walk."

"Okay." She thought of something, and said, "Maybe I can bring the fabric by the fair and you can see if you like it."

"Sure, if you want. Just ask for me at the gate, and they'll let you in."

"All righty then." She got up.

"Thank you. I appreciate it." He fleetingly met her gaze, then turned and walked out.

She couldn't help chuckling to herself. *I suspect*, she thought, *that something is up with Corporal Paul Fester.* Maybe Debbie had started some mischief. "Rachel likes you," she could picture Debbie saying.

Or maybe, of his own initiative, he liked her. She was amused, but not surprised. Guys were like that. Sad. He didn't have a chance.

nine

The next morning the princesses were tired and their shoes were worn out as before. But the soldier knew he had more time before he had to make his report to the king.

— *Grimm*

Paul was juggling.

Bap bap bap bap, bapbap bap bap

The rhythm of juggling was broken only by his occasional toss under his knee or over his back. He was sweating in the hot sun, but concentrated.

Bapbap bap bap, bapbap bap bap

He really wanted to step back into the shade, but that put him a bit closer to the craft booth behind him than he felt was comfortable. There was a ring of day-care children watching him, and he broke his rhythm to wipe his hand swiftly across his brow, making a face as he did so. The grown ups chuckled.

Bap bap! He caught the clubs and bowed. The kids clapped and then an adult said, "Okay, let's go see what's over here," and the day-care group moved reluctantly on. Paul took a moment to pull out a handkerchief and wiped his brow more thoroughly, then took a drink from his water bottle. Hot, hot work. There weren't many tips in his basket so far today, but that didn't bother him.

What *was* bothering him was Rachel. He wasn't exactly sure how to put the feeling into words. *Maybe because I've never had to deal with girls like her before. I've usually just tried to stay out of their way.*

And if Rachel Durham found out what I was up to, I doubt she would be happy with me. He couldn't help feeling like something of a sneak.

Plus I'm still not sure whether what I'm doing is a good idea or not…

Sitting down on a wooden crate that he had staked out as his own, he pulled out his flute, and began to play slowly, recovering his breath. The music absorbed him for a while. Passersby might not have recognized the tune, but it was an old hymn to the Virgin Mary. If singing was praying twice, maybe this melody would serve as double the prayers.

Rachel entered the fabric store with the sense of treading onto forbidden ground. At the same time she felt a delicious pleasure: she was one step closer to the midnight butterfly dress.

As she made her way down the "sin" aisle, Rachel thought smugly, *Well, Mrs. Pearson, today I have a perfectly legitimate excuse to be in the formal fabric section, thank you. I have to look at black materials and find a good price.*

Rachel studied the rows of black silky material judiciously. She had already picked out a simple clown costume pattern from the books in the back, while browsing the evening gown sections for inspiration. Fortunately, she knew her own body sizes so well she didn't need a pattern. Just this fall she had sewn a Renaissance dress for a play on John Hus that included an irritating and complicated closely fit bodice. Modern clothes were decidedly less complicated.

A quick search of the black fabrics (which were on clearance, since it was summer) revealed that satin was the cheapest fabric. Three yards would make two pairs of clown pants for the girls, but Rachel shamelessly bought six, plus a few lengths of white cotton for tunic-dresses. She began exploring the evening fabrics again for special fabric for the sashes—and for her dress.

As she wandered, she remembered how the pastor's wife had warmly complimented her Renaissance dress after the play, and Rachel had tasted the hypocrisy. Why was it fine to wear a fancy dress for a show less than an hour long, but wrong to wear a modern version of the same dress to a dance for the same amount of time? *Maybe anything Christian that happened in the past is fine,* she thought, *but today we're just so immoral that it's bad.*

If so, I was born in the wrong time period. And with the wrong talent.

A bit depressed, she found a bolt of glitzy material with rainbow-colored diamonds on it and tossed it in the cart. Then, rousing herself, she began to go through the remaining fabric with the discretion of a connoisseur. She couldn't waste this chance.

The bodice had to be of just the right fabric, in order for it to be the perfect dress. On the first try, she found nothing, and was disappointed. Methodically, she began to go through the bolts again, adjusting the image in her mind to fit the reality of the choices before her.

Then, she saw it. A bolt with not much left on it, wedged between two other inferior fabrics. She seized it and ran her fingers over it. It had to be silk. She checked the top label. Yes, a silk blend.

It was a knit material, woven into a tube, black and blue and silver running all together into a shimmering blend of subtlety and glamour.

Her breath caught in her throat. Yes, this was it. She checked the price. Thirty-four dollars a yard! But she didn't need a yard. Anxiously, she measured from her chest to her navel. Maybe fifteen inches. She could work it carefully, make it just to size, and she could make it. Why, maybe she could add a satin band at the top—that would make it even less. Yes, she could do it… Thirty-four divided by two was … seventeen dollars. Mathematics was a wonderful thing. She could add this material to the order for the juggling outfits and her dad would never be the wiser.

Triumphantly, she brought the bolt to the cutting counter and asked for a tape measure so that she could narrow it down to the exact inch. Finding out the fabric was twenty-five percent off was merely the icing on the cake.

Paul looked up from his flute playing and saw her coming towards him. She was swinging a yellow plastic shopping bag gaily, her dark brown hair falling carelessly around her face and into her eyes. He knew she was conscious of attracting attention, and relishing it. But he also knew she was not seeking *his* attentions. There was the same mocking half-smile on her tanned face. But she lacked her usual bored swagger. Obviously she was up to something, something that had to do with her midnight excursions.

He switched to a happy dance tune as she sauntered up. As she paused beside him, he finished with a flourish and bowed to his audience.

She watched him with interest as he passed his basket. As his onlookers wandered off, she said, "Do you make much money doing this?"

"Enough to live on," he said, unable to meet her eyes. He hated being divided, keeping secrets.

"Is this how you're going to live, then?" she asked, as though in response to his thoughts.

He shrugged, "Until I finish medical school and my residency."

She laughed, apparently thinking he was making a joke. "I bought your fabric," she said, swinging up the bag expectantly. She showed him black shiny material. "For the pants," she said. "I'll make them kind of puffy, with elastic at the knees. Okay?"

"That works," he said.

Then she pulled out white material that looked like something to make curtains. "This is cotton," she informed him. "Because I figured they might get hot. I can make big blousy tunics, with round collars and full sleeves with elastic at the wrists. The tunics will go about halfway down to their knees, and the pants will come out under them. Okay?"

"Sure," he said. He couldn't picture this at all, but it was clear that she could, and that was what mattered.

"And this," she said, pulling out a length of glittering fabric decorated with harlequin diamonds in a variety of colors, "is for sashes, but I could probably make some hats out of it too, if you wanted. If I have time."

He fingered the shining material, and smiled. "That is neat stuff," he said. "That'll work just fine."

"Good!" She seemed pleased too. "I put it on my dad's credit card. It wasn't much." She told him the total, and he agreed.

"Thanks a lot!" he said. "I hope it's not too much work for you."

"Oh, no. It'll be fun." She flashed a smile at him. "See you." And off she went.

And of course, she had a gorgeous smile, with those glinting green-blue eyes. It was good to see her a bit more animated. But all the same, whether she realized it or not, she had begun a dangerous dance. *And maybe I have too,* he thought.

Feeling a tightness in his chest, he picked up his flute again and blew out a long sustained note. The wisest way out of this mess would also be the longer road, and the more precarious one. He wondered how it would turn out.

☾

When Rachel set foot on the island quay that night, she felt the same tingle in her spine she had felt when she first saw Michael. She didn't know what that meant, but she knew it made her feel aware and alert. A not entirely pleasant feeling but mixed with anticipation of pleasure.

On the way over, Alan and Prisca and Rachel had talked eagerly and enthusiastically about the previous night's close call, but now that they were back on the island, Alan seemed uncertain. He shoved his hands in his pockets and looked around.

"Hey, there's tables over there," he said, pointing to a corner of the portico near the edge of the waterside forest.

The girls looked in surprise. "You're right," Rachel said, going over to them. There were several light metal tables and chairs. "Almost as though he was expecting us."

"Well, he's expecting us," Prisca huffed. "He said so himself."

"Then where is the guy?" Alan asked.

Kirk's boat pulled up to the quay and Tammy got out. The other two boats were coming in. Rachel, distracted, looked back at the steps leading up to the house, and saw a movement.

"I think he's coming down," she said.

I wonder if he'll invite us up to the house, she thought to herself, and felt that same thrill of tense anticipation.

But Michael didn't invite them to go up to the house. He came down carrying a boom box. "I brought my own," he said nonchalantly. "Thought I'd give your valiant little CD player a rest."

The boom box was stacked with nine CDs and an iPod shuffle. The music played and some of the girls danced. But Rachel sat with Michael at one of the tables, and talked. Alan and Prisca sat with them a while, as well, but Rachel and Michael did most of the talking.

Actually, he asked questions and she told him more about herself. About her family, about her mother dying and her father remarrying. About their school, and their family. About what she planned to do with her life.

"Not much," she said ruefully. "I can sew. I can file. I guess I can get a job as the church assistant secretary, if I wanted it."

"Which you don't," Michael supplied.

She laughed. "No way," she said. "Dad and I butt heads about the church enough as it is. Being in closer quarters might either ruin the church or result in murder."

"You're a smart girl. Why don't you go to college?"

"Dad and Sallie are willing to send me to the Bible college outside Baltimore, but I'm not sure I want to go. It'll just be more school. I'll still be living at home, still doing the same old stuff."

"And you don't want to do that."

She paused. "No, not really."

"What do you want to do, Rachel?" he probed.

She clasped her hands on her knee and looked up at the stars. "I really don't know," she confessed.

"Do you want to be an actress?"

She laughed. "Not particularly. Why? Do you think I'd make a good one?"

"You have to ask? Fishing for a compliment?"

"No," and she giggled at him. "When I was little, I wanted to be a nurse."

"Then why not be a nurse?"

"I don't know," she sighed.

"Because your parents are trying to live your life for you?" he pursued. "My mom and dad tried to do that for me. I didn't let them. Now they let me have my own way."

"What did your mom and dad want you to do?" she asked.

"Two entirely different things. My mom and dad never agree on anything, especially me. My mom wanted me to be a lawyer. My dad wanted me to go into investments, like him."

"And what did you end up doing?"

He put his hands behind his head and leaned back. "What I wanted to do."

"And what's that?"

"What I'm doing right now."

"Which is…?"

"Taking a break. Following my own star. Finding my own pleasure where it finds me."

"Hmm," she nodded. She was confused, but she guessed it was meant to be poetic.

He fixed on her with his blue eyes. "It's your life, Rachel. Not someone else's. Not your parents'. Not God's. You do what you want to do, and let the rest of the cosmos deal with it."

Obviously, he's not a Christian, she thought. She attempted to be tolerant.

"The rest of the cosmos," Prisca giggled, hearing the last line.

"I'm serious," Michael said. "Christians preach a lot about guilt. Do you girls get that a lot from your parents?"

"Oh yeah," Prisca said.

"In a way," Rachel said. "More from our church."

Prisca rolled her eyes, agreeing. "You'd think they ran our lives for us," she said.

"Why not just tell them all to chuck it and leave you alone?" Michael asked.

Prisca and Rachel exchanged glances.

"Maybe someday," Rachel said. "But not now. Not while we all live at home."

"Right now, you just … behave like good girls during the day and go wild during the night?" Michael guessed.

The sisters laughed. "You could put it that way," Rachel agreed.

"What about you, Alan?" Michael asked the young man, who had been a mostly silent listener.

"Ah, my parents don't care much what I do during the week," he said. "Just so long as I go to church with them on Sundays."

"Parents are always easier on boys," Prisca said. "It's not fair. We're watched like hawks!"

"Except at night," Michael smiled.

"I actually feel sorry for my dad, sometimes," Rachel mused.

"Don't waste your time," Michael said. "I bet he never feels sorry for you."

"You're right," Prisca said. "He just orders us around like we're his army regiment."

Michael was nodding, as though this was what he expected, but Rachel felt that this was unfair. She tried to think of something to say in defense of her father, but decided after a moment that she would rather not talk about this any longer. What she really wanted was to dance with Michael, but she didn't dare be so bold.

"So—where are *your* parents?" she asked.

"Mom's in Europe and Dad's in Bermuda," he said, looking out at the bay. "They're both in between vacations."

"Your family goes on vacations separately?" Prisca asked.

"It keeps everyone happy," Michael said. "Mom had skin cancer, so she wants to stay away from the tropics. Dad hates the damp weather."

"And you?" Rachel asked.

"I'm happy in any climate so long as I don't have to share it with them." He spoke lightly, as though it were a joke. Rachel didn't want to inquire further.

He turned to look at her. "Actually, I'm having a few friends come down and meet me here for fishing. You might enjoy meeting them. It's a shame there won't be enough to round out the party. I noticed your group is short on men."

"Yes," Prisca said. "There's never enough guys for all of us to dance with."

"But there's more than enough girls for each guy," Michael said, glancing at Alan, who guffawed. "But I can see that for you, this is a problem. Especially if you all like to dance. Maybe sometime I can find a solution."

"Oh, that would be so great!" Prisca said breathlessly. "You are so nice!"

He smiled at her, and his eyes took on that odd glint. "As I told Rachel, I am a nice man."

"Maybe on my birthday," Prisca said, artlessly.

"When is your birthday?" Michael asked.

"Two more weeks," she sighed.

"How old will you be, then?"

"Sixteen."

"Sixteen candles!" he said. "That's a special occasion. I'll have to see what I can do for you, Prisca."

Prisca flashed an eager smile at Rachel, who colored at her sister's transparency. Apparently, Michael thought it was charming. Rachel was just embarrassed.

"We should go in a few minutes," she said, feeling that the hour was getting later than it should.

"So soon?" Michael asked.

Rachel couldn't help being struck by how sad he looked to see them go. *We must really add something to his life,* she thought. And that was a weird thought, given his privileged position.

ten

*So the soldier kept his silence and the princesses
did not guess that they had been seen.*

—— *Grimm*

aul didn't reach his campsite until early in the morning, and when
he did, he was still restless.

His immediate instinct was to dislike and distrust Michael Comus, but
he preferred to give people the benefit of the doubt. He wasn't surprised that
the man had allowed a covey of curvaceous teenaged girls to use his private
grounds for their dance parties, but he had a feeling Michael was going to
start charging a toll eventually. For some reason that thought hadn't occurred
to Rachel, and it bothered Paul.

Maybe she just doesn't realize, he thought as he paced on the beach,
stepping through the wavelets in his bare feet, *that guys are rarely spontaneous
when it comes to girls. There's generally a reason for everything they do.*

On the other hand, girls, he had noticed, typically do generous or kind
things for guys on impulse without any ulterior motive. This could confuse
inexperienced guys, who believed, by default, that any attention given to
them by a girl was surely premeditated and significant.

*Heck, if I'd known that about girls, I'd have had a much easier time in high
school and college,* he thought wryly. *But I had to figure that out by trial and
error. Maybe Rachel doesn't know. Or maybe her dad hasn't had time to tell her.*

Someone had to tell her, and soon. This whole thing was getting more
and more dangerous, and he still hadn't had an opportunity to convince the
girls to tell their dad what they were doing. And they were even less likely to
be open to that now, especially if they found out Paul knew their secret. *I'll
have to try finding some indirect way of addressing the issue with them.* But how
that was to be done, Paul had no idea.

He shook his head, still not weary but worn out inside. At last, he
managed to get himself to go back into his tent and lie down.

Rachel slept late as she dared, then stumbled to the sewing room to begin the project for Paul. She threaded the sewing machine with black thread and rapidly cut out two pairs of simple pants. The rest of the black satin she carefully folded back into the bag, along with the slim packet of expensive bodice material, and secreted it in a corner of the sewing room. Her sisters all knew about her dress plans, so the only person who might find it was Sallie. And Sallie rarely, if ever, tried to clean up or sort through the jumble of fabric and half-finished projects. Her father, who was allergic to sewing machines, never darkened the door of the room.

By the time she was threading elastic through the pant legs and waistband of the second pair, she heard Paul arrive for the girls' lesson. But Linette and Debbie, who were sleepy and grouchy, had missed their chores and had to make them up. Sallie explained this to Paul, who said he could come back.

"It's a hot day. If you like, you can go swimming off our beach while you're waiting," she said.

"Thanks," Rachel heard Paul reply, relief in his voice. "I think I'll take you up on that."

The elastic on the last leg was too tight: Rachel re-did it, then cut the garment from the sewing machine with a satisfied sigh. Folding them over her arms, she went downstairs to scout out Paul.

She paused beside the open door of the downstairs bathroom, seeing her limp navy blue swimsuit hanging abandoned in the corner of the towel rack. It *was* a hot day. A swim sounded lovely right now.

Rachel slipped into the bathroom and changed into her swimsuit. She put her t-shirt and skirt back on, picked up the satin pants, and went carelessly out the door to the woods that led to the beach.

Once in the woods, she looked down from the cliff to the water. At first, she didn't see Paul, only his juggling bag lying on the beach, next to his discarded shirt. She peered through the brush this way and that. Then she happened to look towards the swimming rock, and saw him.

At first all she saw was his head, bobbing in the water, and his arm. He was walking in the deep water towards the rock so that only his head was above water, and holding something above his head, a silver wand. His flute. He was attempting to keep it dry, with mixed success.

She watched, amused, as he attempted to climb onto the wet, slippery rock with one hand, trying to hold the flute aloft and dry in the other. He fell off several times, sometimes spectacularly. At last, he managed to clamber onto the rock with the flute in his teeth, the instrument glistening with water. She smothered a laugh. He sat on the rock, pulled his knees to his chest, and attempted vainly to find something dry to wipe his flute on. A handkerchief he pulled from the pocket of his shorts was wet. He tried rubbing it against his bare chest, but that was also wet.

Finally, he rubbed it through his hair and shook the water out of it. Then he crossed his legs and hunched over his instrument, putting it to his lips. His back was partly to her, and she could see the muscles in his arms and fingers working. A wild trill came from the rock, through the air, and pierced her heart.

It was a fierce, untamed melody; unlike the mellow or cheerful piping she had heard from him before now. It was years away from the practiced, strained flute music of the school band, or the tame cooing of the worship choir's wind section at church. She hung on it as the music stabbed at her again and again, like a hawk beating its wings against her breast. His tanned skin glistened in the sun, his fingers flew more rapidly than she could follow them, and the song seemed to possess him and change him from the ordinary bland "good boy" to someone from a different reality, a denizen of faery or Olympus or some other alternate world she had never heard of.

Pan, she thought, *he's like Pan, in that book. The Wind in the Willows.*

After an unbelievable interval, Paul lifted his head to look at the horizon, and the music ceased. Rachel stood quietly, aware of nothing but the water and wind and the echo of music.

Softly, she made her way down to the shore, wondering if he would play again. She slipped into the willow grove, where the guys docked their boats. *I'll be a siren and sneak up on him*, she thought.

Noiselessly she slid into the water and swam slowly towards him. His back was still towards her. He lowered his head and the music began again.

She let herself drift up against the rock, and leaned against it. It had started to warm from the sun, and she let her crossed arms rest on that warmth. The water pushed her rhythmically against it, and she waited, listening. The melody now was less fierce, more inviting, but still wild and unpredictable.

When he finished, he raised his head to the horizon again. *I'll startle him if I say anything*, she thought, but instead he turned his head and smiled at her, squinting in the sunlight.

"Hello mermaid," he said.

She grinned. He had guessed her thought. "Hello," she said. "I heard your song, and I came."

"Ah," he said, "I must be improving."

He turned and looked at the horizon. "This is a wonderful rock," he said.

"I love it," she responded.

"Am I taking your place?"

"No, I'm fine here," she said. "The water's warm." She kicked out her legs luxuriously.

"Do you come here often, mermaid?"

"Not as often as I would like."

He nodded. "Do you ever swim at night?"

"Sometimes I have," she said carelessly.

"I hope you never swim alone at night, mermaid."

"If I really was a mermaid, Pan, I would swim wherever and whenever I chose," she said.

He looked at her curiously. "What did you call me?"

"Pan. Like in the book. *The Wind in the Willows.* I'm reading it."

"Really?" Now she had surprised him, and she smiled.

"You play the flute like him," she said.

He toyed with his instrument. "But the great god Pan is dead," he said at last. "To invite him now is to invite death."

"Death? Why?"

"Well, according to the legend, he died every year with the harvest of the grain, and rose again in spring. He was one of the corn gods, the god of shepherds." He was silent, then added, "And of course, he prefigured Christ."

"Jesus was a corn dog? I mean, corn god?" she pursued, laughing at her gaffe.

"No, He was the true Good Shepherd, the reality behind the fairy tale," Paul said.

"Hmm," Rachel said, feeling the water with her fingers. "Why did you say that to invite Pan was to invite death?"

"I was quoting someone from my theology class in college. What it means is, we can't invoke the pagan gods any more, even the ones that were close to reality. Because Christ has come, and all pagan gods have shrunk into dead tales or demons."

"So you're saying I shouldn't call you Pan?"

He smiled at her, winsomely. "Just call me a faun, if you like, mermaid. They were mythical creatures who resembled Pan, and played the pipes."

"Yes, like in Narnia," Rachel murmured. Dad had read her that book, long ago. "All right, faun."

Paul looked at her again, his lips half-parted. Then he said, "Since we're talking in this fanciful fashion, mermaid, may I tell you a story?"

"Sure," she said, bobbing in the water.

"It's not a happy story," he said, warning. He put his flute to his mouth and blew a short *ffift!* then rubbed it.

"I promise not to cry," she said.

"Don't promise that," he said, and set his flute down. "Once upon a time, there were men and women in the world."

"Just as there are now."

"Just as now. And there was a devil, as there is also now, and he desired to destroy the happiness of man and woman. So he created a twisted looking glass. This looking-glass was not a mirror, but a piece of glass so invisible that a man could look through it and not realize he was seeing a twisted reality. And it reflected a bit, like a mirror, so that a man could see himself, or what he thought was himself."

"Go on," Rachel said.

"Now, this glass was made particularly for men, and the devil made sure that men looked through it whenever they chanced to look at women. And this glass changed the women."

"It made them ugly," Rachel said, thinking she had heard this story before.

"No, not really. That's actually a lot harder to do than you might think. What the mirror did was more insidious. It reduced them."

"Reduced them?"

"So that, to a man looking through the glass, the woman appeared to be an object, a pretty plaything put there for his pleasure. Now, the man might know that the woman had brains, or talents, or any number of other gifts, but when he looked through the mirror, he saw her only as a toy. And the devil made every effort to push that glass before a man's eyes when he was as young as possible. So that most men were so used to looking through the glass that, even when it wasn't there, the images they saw in the glass dictated their reality."

"Hmph," was all Rachel could think of to say.

Paul kicked the water with his toe. "There was a further trick to the devil's glass. The glass taught men to sort all women they saw into two types—worthwhile, and not worthwhile. Or 'good' and 'bad,' as some men took to calling them. Good toys and bad toys. And so this was the way they had of speaking about women among themselves. And as you can imagine, the women couldn't help overhearing these conversations. And even though most of the women hadn't glanced through the mirror, they couldn't help thinking of themselves in this manner. As toys. Good toys or bad toys."

"What was the difference between the good toys and the bad toys?" Rachel said, scraping at the rock with her fingernail.

"Nothing," Paul said.

"What do you mean, nothing?"

"Nothing essential," Paul said. "Once you've decided to see a person as a toy, the degrees between the toys are close to non-existent. But for practical purposes as far as the deluded man was concerned, there was a difference."

"Which was?" Rachel asked.

"Time," Paul said slowly. "Only time. You spend more time with a good toy. Lots of time. You date her, you take her out, you pay her compliments. You might even marry her. But in the end, she's just a toy."

"And the bad toys?" she asked after a moment.

His face had a rigid, hard look on it. "You don't waste your time. You play with them, but not for long. Maybe not even twenty-four hours. And then you don't care if you ever see her again. Remember," he said, "From this twisted point of view, a smart man doesn't waste his time on bad toys."

"But what about Christian men?" she objected.

"Christian men were taught to look through this mirror, too. Sometimes they attached more importance to the 'good' versus 'bad' distinction. You have to make sure you marry a 'good' toy. Because a Christian man doesn't waste his time on 'bad' toys. Oh, maybe a Christian man might glance at a 'bad' toy—say, in the pages of a sports magazine or on a web page. But a good Christian doesn't waste his time on 'bad' toys. You want a good toy—just one. Or at any rate, only one at a time."

His voice was bitter. She was breathing hard, staring at him.

"But it's not fair!"

"Of course it's not."

"I don't believe all men are like this."

He met her eyes. "They're not, but don't underestimate the power of the looking glass. Many, many women do. They think they're being brave. But they're only naïve. Naïve girls who think they're being bold are girls who are going to get hurt. And maybe hurt beyond repair."

He looked away. "You see, there's no place in a deluded man's world for an old toy, or an ugly toy, or a toy who doesn't have the right figure, or whose body doesn't work the way it should—a handicapped toy, a toy who's fallen ill. If the toy was once a good toy, you might hang around—after all, she was once a good toy. And you can feast on the memories, and keep an eye on other good toys from the sidelines or glance at the bad toys in the magazines—but a 'smart' man doesn't let himself get stuck with a broken toy. Particularly a toy who's been used and is in need of repair."

She wiped her eyes, angry. "Why are you telling me this? I know all of this already. I know everything you're saying."

Now he turned and looked at her, his voice unexpectedly husky. "You do?"

"Yes," her face was red with shame. "It's what happens to girls who aren't careful. Who think too much about their bodies. I've been warned all my life about what happens to girls—who become like you said. Who become bad toys."

His face twitched, as if he were in pain. He said softly, "Don't say that. Don't you understand? The whole point is, it's all a lie. You're not a toy at all."

But she was too upset to listen to him. Pushing away from the rock, she swam back to the shore, and sprinted back onto the beach. Snatching up her clothes, she hurried up the path back to the house, not once looking back. For some reason, she had a panicked idea that he was following her, but when she glanced back as she reached the top of the cliff, she saw he was still sitting on the rock, his flute in between his hands, his head bowed.

Who does he think he is?

Who is he? Pagan or Christian? Man or god? Good or bad?

He didn't seem to fit onto any side of the scale, and Rachel decided, as she got dressed, that it was in her best interest to pretend that this conversation had never happened.

It was almost midnight. Paul straightened his scapular, then pulled on his black hood over a black shirt. He was already wearing the black pants and fitted shoes that completed the outfit. It was time to go.

Paul had learned a lot about stealth and tracking in the military, which was an asset to him now. And in college, he and his friends had done war games in the woods near the campus, involving nighttime reconnaissance, and to that end, he had acquired a black outfit that resembled a ninja costume—the same black pants and fitted shoes he wore for juggling, and a black shirt and hood. He had brought it along on vacation because it was comfortable and light, and one never knew when one might need a ninja outfit.

Though I didn't think I'd be wearing it every night, he thought, as he started weaving through the trees to the Durham's property. There was no moon tonight. At least his job would be a bit easier, but it still wouldn't solve his problem.

It was difficult to stand in the shadows and watch. In the beginning, he had kept himself occupied with the logistical problems of tracking and following the girls, of getting on and off a boat unseen. But now those problems were mostly solved—each time the boats were docked, they were in deep shadows, and he merely had to wait for the odd moment to get on or off. And the routine for the evening was rapidly fixing itself in concrete—every night from now on, he guessed that the girls would be getting on the boats, going to the island, and having their dance.

The island itself brought up contradictory feelings in him. It was indeed a place of enchantment. The nights had been particularly beautiful lately, and the island was itself extremely lovely. The willow trees, pines, and oaks provided ample cover for him, as well as a fitting background to the pageant of girls dancing in the moonlight.

And the girls were very beautiful, all of them in their individual ways, and if he had nothing else to do but watch them dance, this was going to get frustrating. Already it had become a bit difficult for him to actually watch them dance, particularly the ones who chose to wear the skimpier outfits.

But his way to salvation was through beauty, and he kept forcing himself to appreciate their beauty without reducing them to objects. Sometimes that meant looking away from the girls up at the beauty of the waning moon, or the frothy leaves of the willows, or the stars. The wonders of nature were not his personal treasures, he told himself. And neither were the girls. In particular, not the girls.

Now he left the campsite stealthily and wove his way down the bayside, across the remainder of the campsite, through a stretch of woods, across three private lots (fortunately the beaches weren't clearly in view of the houses) to the Durhams' grounds. The far edge of the Durham property was woods, mostly willows and vines. He had cut a path for himself through the brush so he didn't have to make much noise. Eventually he reached the willow tree that overhung the deep water where the boys docked their boats. He slid behind the trunk into a little hollow that was conveniently shadowed and waited.

Eventually, he heard the sound of the girls' voices from the bike cave above, and then, one by one, they started to make their way down the bank to the beach, giggling and sliding. The younger girls were usually ready the quickest—Debbie, Linette, Brittany, and Melanie came down together in bare feet, holding their sandals by their straps. Debbie started splashing around in the water, and Brittany picked up stones and started to shy them across the bay water, seeing how many times she could make them skip.

"I wish we could just go swimming," Linette said wistfully. "Do we have to go to the island every night? It's so boring."

"Yes, this used to be an adventure, but now it's all about chasing boys," Debbie agreed. "There's no boys our ages on the island. They're all in high school or older."

"Doesn't make a difference to Becca and Liddy," Brittany observed, letting another stone fly expertly over the waves.

"They're silly," Debbie said loftily. "I'm smarter than them, and I'm only eleven. I hope I don't get so dumb when I'm a teenager."

Brittany's stone skipped five times and she shouted, "Score!"

"Shhh!" Becca hissed, skittering down the sandy slope in a floral dress. "We're still home, remember?" On level ground, she dabbed at her hair with her hands. "It's too windy tonight."

Paul became aware that Rachel was coming down the bank now, slender and sylphlike in her navy blue dress, and he felt unusually self-conscious. He hadn't seen her since she had left him abruptly at the swimming rock that morning. She was back to her usual air of cool indifference, and he wondered if anything he had said to her had affected her. Most likely not. Her angry exit still stung in his memory.

Now she clapped her hands. "Come on kids, look alive," she said easily. "We're going to a party tonight."

"But we go to a party every night," Debbie said resentfully, sloshing water on her dress.

Rachel set her hands on her hips and swayed. "Yes. Aren't we lucky?"

"I wish we could do something else," Debbie said frankly. "All we can do is dance or talk. It's boring."

"I'll ask Michael for some paper so that you can draw," Rachel said, and the other girls snickered. Rachel punched Debbie's arm gently. "Come on, isn't it better than staying home?"

She looked at the older girls, and said, in a general sort of way, "I noticed that everyone seemed to be ignoring Kirk yesterday. Why was that?"

"He's such a hick," Taren said. "He always smells like gasoline."

"That's because he works at the auto body shop," Brittany said. "He fixes cars all day. He can't help it."

"You only want us to be nice to him because he has a boat," Tammy said.

"And because that's only fair to him," Rachel raised an eyebrow. "He's given us a ride every time we've needed one."

"I wish we had our own boats," Taren fretted. "Then we wouldn't have this problem."

"Well, until then, we have to deal with the situation at hand," Rachel said coolly, shaking her head. "And I'd hate to see Kirk stop coming because he feels you all are giving him the cold shoulder now that we know—this rich guy."

"Hey, the boats are coming!" Liddy called, from the middle of the cliff path. Paul heard cries of panic from the girls above in the cave, who were still dressing. He could hear the boat motors coming closer, and soon the water splashed below him as the boats pulled into their temporary dock.

The girls crowded around, greeting the guys, and Paul waited until he heard them leave the boats. Fortunately the girls were never all ready when the boats arrived, so necessarily the boys left the boats to go on the beach and hang out for a while. That was when Paul made his move.

He peered around the tree to ensure the boats were deserted, and stealthily crept through the shadows to the biggest one, Alan's boat, and slipped beneath the canvas covering part of the back. There were mostly deck chairs and old boat parts beneath the canvas, and he had found a place for himself amidst the jumble. He crouched into a small ball and waited once more.

Soon the parties started clambering into the boats, finding their way in the darkness and settling themselves.

"So how are you tonight, Alan?" Rachel asked. Paul saw her long legs, quite noticeable in her short skirt, slant down in his direction, and adjusted his position so that he wouldn't be staring at them.

"Pretty good. Hot day."

"I'm glad the wind picked up," Rachel said lazily. "Hey Rich."

"Hi Rachel." Rich's voice came in. Paul heard his heavy footfalls dropping on the boat, and his brawny legs stretched out next to hers.

Debbie clambered over the canvas, landing for a moment on Paul's back, and scrambled into her seat. Melanie edged around beside her.

"Prisca!" Rachel's voice had impatience in it.

"I'm coming! Gee whiz!" And there were two light footfalls, and Prisca landed in the boat. "Gosh I'm so hot!"

Alan started the engine, and they were off.

Paul found it difficult to hear any conversation that went on while the boat was moving, as his ears were so close to the floor of the boat and its motor. He focused on keeping still, and out of Debbie's sight. Lately she had been surreptitiously lifting up a flap of the canvas, trying to catch a glimpse of him. He hoped he was too far back to be seen.

When they reached the island and docked, Paul heard Michael come out to greet the party, as he usually did. Paul listened for the other boats, and counted them as they docked. It was only after about ten minutes had gone by that he edged out from beneath the canvas. The night was dark, and Michael had put floodlights on the portico. Fortunately, the boats were out of the range of the lights.

eleven

*When one prince said, "The boat is heavy tonight,"
the youngest princess said, "It seems light to me."*
— *Grimm*

Rachel was pensive that night as they landed on the island, despite her outward cheer. It was windy. Michael was standing on the quay, waiting to greet them. She saw him toss something into the bay as they landed, and she was surprised. She hadn't considered him a smoker.

But she didn't smell anything like tobacco smoke when he came up and greeted them. Perhaps the wind blew the scent away. He greeted Rachel first, and the other girls and their friends. Then he said, "Some of my friends came down. I'd like you to meet them."

Rachel saw three guys sitting in chairs, beers at their elbows. They all got up to greet the group, then sat back down. Mark, Brad, and Dillon were their names, but Rachel quickly forgot them. They were moderately good-looking guys, well dressed, obviously from the same set that Michael belonged to.

If Rachel wasn't particularly interested in talking to them, Prisca was, and Rachel resigned herself to sitting at her sister's elbow, trading banter with the three new guys. They seemed older—well, they *were* older than the guys from church. Rachel felt distinctly that Prisca was getting ahead of herself. After all, she was only fifteen. Prisca giggled and chattered and peppered the three guys with questions. Rachel felt compelled to leash her in a few times. She wished Michael would come and sit down with them, but he seemed to be talking with Alan and the other guys.

After a while, he walked up to the group, Alan and Rich on his heels. "Rachel, you want to come for a walk with us?" he asked. "I'm going to show your friends around the island."

"Sure," said Rachel, glad for the break, discreetly seizing Prisca by the elbow. "We'll both come." She had been seeing the wisdom in the buddy system more with each passing minute.

"Aw, do any of you guys want to come with us?" Prisca wheedled to the threesome. Dillon, a dark-haired handsome guy, said he would come, but the other two said they were too comfortable to move.

Rachel took a sweeping glance around the party. The twins were dancing with Kirk and Keith. Miriam and Linette were sitting on the quay with Pete. Liddy and Becca were pawing through a stack of CDs. Melanie and Debbie were walking by the oak trees on the border of the dance floor. Cheryl and Taylor were sitting at a table having a tête-à-tête while Brittany sat on the far end, looking slightly bored, flipping a bottle cap with her thumb.

Rachel ambled slowly after the party, which had started to file through the woods. Prisca, who had worn heels, was picking her way up the path with squeals, and Dillon gallantly offered her a hand.

Michael led them up a woody path and said, "Come over this way. There's an overlook where you can see over the island's south shore. It's the highest point outside of the house balconies."

He led them past the heliport to a stone wall, and Rachel looked down over the twinkling lights of the bay. She could make out her own home among the shadows of the trees.

"Hey! I can see the swimming rock!" Prisca exclaimed, pointing.

Rachel saw the rock where she and Paul had talked earlier that day. Recalling that conversation this morning about mermaids and toys, she felt an odd, disjointed quality—a collision of two worlds that had very little to do with each other.

"I can't see it," Dillon was saying.

"There!" Prisca said, leaning closer to him and guiding him with her arm. "Are you blind? Can't you see it?"

"Where?" Dillon squinted his eyes, obviously trying to get a rise out of her.

"There! There! There!" Prisca squealed, pulling Dillon's arm over her shoulder. Rachel, in embarrassment, turned away on the pretext of walking further up the wall. Her walk brought her closer to Michael, who turned and smiled at her. She sighed and rolled her eyes at her younger sister.

"She drives me nuts sometimes," she murmured to Michael.

Michael cast an appraising glance at Prisca, who was giggling as Dillon continued to fake long-distance blindness.

"She wants it," he said knowingly, and winked at Rachel. Then, perhaps sensing her disquiet, he took her arm. "I remember what you told me about your Underground Railroad hidden staircase," he said. "I think this property had one too."

"Really?" she asked, intrigued.

"Yes. Not this house—the house is new. But there used to be an older house here, a smaller one. You might have solved a little mystery for us. We too have a puzzlingly small artificial cave. Want to see it?"

"Sure," she said, intrigued.

"All right." He beckoned to Prisca and Dillon. "Come on." They followed him along with Alan and Rich.

Now he ducked into the woods and began following a path downhill. It wound among the trees and over a ridge, then abruptly sank down into a valley tucked into the hillside. Rachel and the others found themselves in a small hollow, sheltered from the island winds by a huge rock, which formed the side of a hollow. A tree grew against the rock, an ancient knotted tree with a smooth bare trunk rising seven feet into the air before twisting over into branches reaching over the rock and up desperately to the open air. The other side of the hollow jutted underneath the cleft, forming a shallow cave. Michael stepped aside, put a hand into a shadowed cavity, clicked something, and pulled out a powerful flashlight. The visitors gasped as he swept the bright light over the cave. It went into the rock that formed the foundation for the house, which was somewhere on top of the hill above them. There were rocks and logs dragged into positions for seating.

"This used to be my smugglers' cave when I was a kid," Michael said. "My friends and I made seats here over the years. It was a good place to go when we wanted to get away from the elders. My parents might have known about it, but they never came down here, so far as I could tell. It's my private spot."

"Cool," Rachel breathed. She sat down gingerly on a log and looked around. There was an eeriness about the cave that did suggest hidden secrets, and a funny smell.

Prisca squirmed. "That tree gives me the creeps," she said. "Why's it such a funny shape?"

Michael pointed at the old wood. "It's just trying to grow and reach the sunlight like any other tree," he said. "It just has to get around that big rock."

Prisca touched it. "Why's its trunk so smooth?"

Michael shrugged. "People tend to grab it for a handhold, or lean against it, so the bark gradually wore away." He laughed. "When we were kids, we used to try to capture one of my friend's sisters and tie her up against the tree."

"That wasn't nice!" Prisca accused slightly shocked, but laughing.

"It was just a stupid kids' game," Michael said, protesting with a grin. "We always let her go, obviously. There's no bones buried here or anything."

Rachel shivered involuntarily.

☾

Paul was apprehensive. Rachel and Prisca had walked off with Michael some time ago, and that worried him. However, Alan and Rich, who had struck him as fairly solid guys, were with them, so he had stayed with the larger party.

He didn't like the look of Michael's buddies who had remained behind, drinking. He noticed the one man kept casting glances at Debbie and Melanie, who were dawdling about on the edges of the portico. Debbie was so pretty that she was often mistaken as older than her eleven years. Paul leaned against the curved trunk of the oak tree, pulling his wrists backwards in his joint exercises, and watching both parties.

Still, his thoughts kept drifting back to Rachel and Prisca as he did his nikyo. He was feeling uneasy. His wrists were unexpectedly sore tonight, and he chafed them, wondering and turning the strange fears over in his mind.

His attention was focused again as he realized that Debbie was approaching the glade where he was hidden. She lifted up the thin curtain of willow branches that shaded the covered area, and stepped inside.

Debbie began to look around the trunks of the big oak and willow trees a few yards away from his, and Paul guessed what she was doing. He reached for the branch above him and silently pulled himself up. The massive limbs of the oak didn't quiver as he settled himself on his new perch.

"What are you doing under here?" Melanie asked, the faithful buddy following right behind her stepsister. She pushed aside the branches timidly and stepped inside the partially-shaded clearing.

"Oh, just looking around," Debbie said mysteriously.

"For what?"

"Oh, for something that hides in the woods, watching us. Maybe a wood spirit. Doesn't this seem like the sort of place where you'd find one?"

Melanie shivered. "That sounds so pagan."

"Oh, you Fendelmans always think things are pagan."

"Well, a lot of things *are* pagan," Melanie said reasonably, glancing behind her. "I don't like the music they're playing." Paul agreed with her. The rest of the girls were all on the dance floor now, and the song, which Paul had heard before, was among the more crass popular tunes of the summer.

"Come on and explore with me," Debbie said invitingly. "I'm sick of dancing."

"No thanks," Melanie said. "I just wish I could go home and go to bed. I don't like coming here."

The song ended, and a faster song started at once, and the dancers picked up their pace. Tammy was dancing with one of Michael's pals now. All the other guys were dancing as well. The party was heating up.

Just then, a figure lurched in their direction. He ducked beneath the overhanging willow branches and blinked at them. "Hey there." Paul recognized one of the drinkers and lightly leapt to the ground, still in the shadows.

"Hi, Mark." Instantly, Debbie adopted the chilly air of an utterly bored socialite.

"Either of you girls want to dance with me?"

"No," Debbie said distantly.

"Aw, come on. You have to have some fun too. What about you?" the man looked at thirteen-year-old Melanie, who flushed.

"I don't think so—" she faltered.

"You'll enjoy it." And he reached and grabbed her hand and drew her out to the dance floor, where the music chattered faster than a racing pulse. Paul tensed, reining in his desire to spring out and stop the man. Was this the time to intervene?

Debbie sucked in her breath angrily as Mark started to dance with her stepsister. Paul leaned around the trunk and watched Melanie, conflicted. Mark was whipping her around in a frenzied disco-type dance, and Paul couldn't tell if she were laughing or simply terrified. Debbie's eyes were fixed on her stepsister, and she was clenching her fists.

At last, the relentless screaming song reeled towards its end. Paul endured it, feeling for Melanie, who was looking more and more dizzy and helpless. In an attempt at a grand finale, Mark slung her around, but, being slightly tipsy, he misjudged his timing and lost hold of her. Melanie careened away from him, flying straight towards the oak tree.

Paul lost no time. He darted forward as Melanie was hurtled towards the trunk, and lightly caught and redirected her momentum to the mossy ground on the other side of the tree. Then he vanished back into the shadows in one fluid motion. Melanie stumbled to the ground, caught herself, and got to her feet, trembling. Paul was sure that Debbie had seen him, and he didn't think that Melanie had—although she would have felt his touch.

Some others on the dance floor had seen Melanie go flying into the trees and were running towards them. Mark staggered along with them, disoriented.

Debbie flew on him, her eyes flashing. "You stay away from my sister!" she yelled. "She didn't want to dance with you, and you shouldn't have made her!"

Mark retreated as Tammy strode forward. "What's going on?"

"Mark made Melanie dance with him, and almost threw her into that tree!" Debbie pointed.

The other girls, particularly Melanie's biological sisters, were incensed. Mark found himself edging away in embarrassment, and Melanie found herself being surrounded by comforting sisters.

"Poor Melanie," Taren hugged her sister. "Are you all right, baby?"

"I think so," Melanie said, still bemused. She glanced towards the oak tree uncertainly.

"That Mark is a jerk," Brittany said.

"I'll say," Debbie said. "He just barged on in here."

"Look, you two," Miriam said authoritatively. "Stick with Pete and me, okay? Or one of the older girls. You shouldn't be off by yourself. We're supposed to stick together." She wrapped a strong arm around Melanie and the other around Debbie. "Come on. Let's go get some soda for you two."

"I'll be there in a minute," Debbie said, disengaging herself from her big sister. "I think I dropped something back there."

She walked back into the shadowed glade and hovered by the oak tree. After giving one more searching glance around, she said in a low voice, "You're the best, Paul." Then she turned away with a toss of her black hair over her narrow shoulders.

Paul restrained himself from answering her back, but he couldn't help grinning.

After Rachel and the rest had finished looking at what might have been a hiding place for escaped slaves, Michael set the flashlight in a convenient niche so that the light bounced off the ceiling of the cave and gave the hollow a gentle, indirect glow.

"I still come here occasionally to chill out, and I keep some refreshment here. The stone keeps things cool," he said, and pulled out a case of wine coolers. He offered one to Rachel and Prisca, who accepted. The other guys also helped themselves, and they all sat down and relaxed and talked. Rachel still didn't like the feeling she got in the cave, historical or not, and tried to calm herself. She started to wonder what the other girls were doing down on the portico, and began to feel as though she should go back.

Then she noticed Michael had taken out a cigarette and was offering it to Dillon. He offered another one to Alan, who took it hesitantly and looked at it.

"It's weed, isn't it?" he asked.

"Ever tried it?"

"No."

"Want to?"

Alan looked at Rich, and the two of them looked uncomfortable. "No thanks."

"No problem," Michael took the cigarette back and tucked it away in some hidden recess. He glanced at Rachel. She shook her head. "Not for us."

"I know," Michael said. "I'm not rushing you girls."

Rachel looked at him, critical, and he met her gaze candidly.

"It's not an addictive drug. I don't mess up people's lives. I'm not a dealer. I'm not trying to get anyone hooked to ease my own guilt. I have friends who happen to enjoy the stuff—" Here he nodded to Dillon, who had lit his up and was breathing it in. "—so I make it available to my guests. Discreetly. I use a mix that's very mild. It's probably safer than regular cigarettes, which are chock full of nicotine, highly addictive." He added, sitting back, "What's so ironic is that it's cannabis that's illegal, and you can get nicotine in any grocery store in America."

Rachel dropped her gaze, feeling herself accused of being small-minded and legalistic. But then again, she had no direct experience with marijuana. Michael and his set were from such a different world—maybe people in that world were freer to discover their own rules, and, unbound by legalities, had discovered something genuine that the rest of the populace had yet to be enlightened about. Not that she was about to smoke a joint, but she was willing to be a bit open-minded.

Then she looked at Prisca, and saw such a look of trusting belief and acceptance in Michael's words that she immediately pulled back. Give Prisca another minute and she would start begging to try some weed herself.

"Michael," she said timidly. "I'm not trying to be rude, but we really should get back soon. My parents are starting to complain that we're too tired in the morning."

Michael rose immediately. "No problem. I understand. Let me bring you girls back." The other guys got up, but Dillon remained where he was.

"Mind if I finish?" he asked.

"Go ahead. I'll come back after I've seen the girls off," Michael said.

He took Rachel's hand and started to lead them back up the way they had come. Going up was much harder, and they found talking too difficult while they climbed. Prisca had taken off her heels in the cave but still required Rich's assistance to get up.

Rachel took a deep breath of fresh night wind and felt the fog clear from her brain. She hadn't liked the cave at all, for some instinctive reason she couldn't lay her hands on. All she knew was that she was glad to have left. The music from the portico below helped soothe her spirits.

As they hurried down the stone steps back to the portico, she started to feel that she should say something to Michael—she wasn't sure what, but something. Something about how she felt strongly that drug use was wrong, illegal or no, and that it *was* wrong for her younger sister. That Prisca wasn't old enough or smart enough to realize what she was doing. All that talk she had heard in church about standing up for what was right—being "the salt of the earth"—was starting to work on her conscience now. Not that she wanted to make a scene, but some of her sisters were so impressionable—

She was just formulating the opening words in her mind when they reached the portico. "Michael," she began.

He looked at her and held out his hand, which he had dropped during the walk down. "Care to dance with me?"

He had never asked her before. Emotion rushed over her even as she tried to quell it. "Sure," she said, straining to not sound eager. Or at any rate, as eager as Prisca.

His hand held hers, raised it a little higher, and drew her across the floor, and curled in and she found herself whirled into his arms, held lightly, so that she was still free. His right arm held her up, firmly, while he pushed her away and twirled her back in perfect rhythm. Rachel didn't know the first thing about ballroom dancing (couple dancing was not looked upon smilingly at Bayside Christian Academy) but she knew some folk dancing. Enough to keep from tripping. And of course she had watched her share of Fred Astaire movies, enough to know how it looked.

None of this prepared her for the actual experience of dancing with Michael, for the strong wizardry in his touch and the delicacy of his moving her. She was both held and not held, and it was a rush, a complete rush. Before, she had intellectually recognized that she found him physically attractive, but now she was swept away.

All too soon, the song was over, and he let her go. She stood there, a bit out of breath, trying not to look as foolish as she felt.

"Thank you," she gasped.

He smiled, and picked up her hand. "I know sometimes I make you uncomfortable, Rachel, but you know I don't mean to." His eyes were sincere, and almost a bit sad.

"That's all right," she said, attempting to cover herself with the remnants of her self-possession. "It's a new experience. It's—exciting."

"I'm glad," he said, and let go of her hand. "I hope you'll come again tomorrow."

Tomorrow. Usually she had let the girls have at least one night for everyone to catch up on their sleep, but—but—

"All right," she said. "Tomorrow."

"I'll be waiting for you," he dropped his voice low, and she thrilled.

At that point, she had to turn away under the pretense of calling to her sisters that it was time to go.

Of course she couldn't say anything about it on the way home, because Rich and Alan were there, and she couldn't help thinking that Alan was a tiny bit threatened by Michael. She told herself that she had to remind Prisca to pay more attention to him and Rich. If they were to lose their boat chauffeurs, the girls would indeed be sunk.

But she didn't feel inclined to talk much to either guy herself on the way home. Melanie, who had been looking lost and pale all night, fell asleep, leaning against Debbie. Debbie grimaced under her weight. Rachel looked at the shore and fretted to be home. Not that she wanted to be home, but she wanted time to speed up, go faster, and get her to tomorrow night quickly. And Alan's boat seemed to be more sluggish than usual. She glared at the humps of canvas-covered objects that they were forced to share the boat with and pushed one with her toe. It was an odd shape.

"What do your parents keep in here that makes the boat so slow?" she asked, before she thought.

She wished she could have bitten her tongue off before she said it. Alan tightened his lips. "I don't know," he said, and his voice was testy. "I keep asking them to put the stuff in storage, but it keeps staying here, slowing me down."

"Not that much, it doesn't," Debbie said immediately, and Melanie, who seemed to have woken up said, "I can't tell the boat is going that much slower."

Rachel looked at them both, astonished. But before she could say anything, Rich said, "How much further should we go in before you want us to cut the engine, Rachel?"

Tonight, she was anxious to move on, and she could tell the two guys were tired too. "Oh, go all the way in," she said. "It's so late it doesn't matter."

twelve

And again the princesses slipped through the secret door, and the soldier followed them off the boats onto the magic island as before.

— Grimm

Rachel's costumes were amazing, Paul thought to himself, surveying his two apprentice jugglers in their new garb. She had turned out the costumes in record time—two white blouse-tunics with short gathered collars, two pairs of black satin bouffant pants, and colorful vests that kept the tunics in place and didn't get in the way of the girls' somersaults.

"Ready?" he asked, and Linette and Debbie, for once, momentarily serious, nodded. They had black teardrops under their eyes and a touch of red on their lips, making them look like twins. He was surprised that Debbie hadn't tried to ask him about what had happened last night: perhaps she was just nervous about this first public performance.

He started juggling, and after a moment, passed Debbie a club. She passed it right back to him and he passed to Linette. She fumbled and he said, encouragingly, "Keep going," and she recovered, picked it up and tossed it back. He started his passes again, and soon they had a three-way fountain. The crowd of festival-goers around them, including Sallie Durham and the two boys, clapped in appreciation. After they finished, the girls grabbed the clubs and curtsied while he bowed. The applause was bigger than he usually got, and the contributions greatly increased.

And he wasn't surprised. The two girls were cute, and fairly skilled. Children always get more attention than adults, and girls more so than boys. But he didn't mind in the least. He was proud of his two pupils.

So was Sallie, who beamed at them, holding Jabez on her hip. "I'll come back for the girls at three," she called to Paul after the first set was done, and he gave her thumbs up.

118

As for Linette and Debbie, they couldn't get enough of performing, particularly Debbie, who had a natural flair for gathering attention. By the time they broke for lunch, Paul's basket was full of coins and bills the girls gleefully divided among them.

"Wow, we could become rich this way!" Linette cried, impressed at the morning's takings.

"We could," Paul agreed. "We made as much this morning as I made all last week. See how poor I was before I took you two on."

"Well, we'll stay with you until we perfect our skills, and then we'll go out on our own," said Debbie, lifting her chin. Her eyes danced, baiting him.

"No! Don't leave me—Oh, all right, go ahead. Throw your teacher in the ditch. One night as I'm crawling along the highway, I'll look up at a billboard and see your pictures there in lights, looking down at me, and I'll say, 'I taught them everything I knew.' And then I'll keel over and die. A broken man, but a happy one." Paul sighed and hung his head.

Debbie punched him in delight. "You know, I wish we could do this on the—" she stopped, and looked at Linette.

Paul dropped his eyes. "The island?"

"You know, don't you?" Linette whispered.

"I know."

Debbie said, "I figured it out when I stepped on your foot a few nights ago. Why do you come?"

"To watch out for you."

"Like you watched out for Melanie and me last night. That was great."

"Glad I happened to be around."

"I'm glad you're there," Debbie said, her voice still low. "But I don't think Rachel would be if she knew. She'd probably think you were spying on us or something."

"Yeah," Linette said positively. "So we can't let on that we know you're there."

"I knew you were with us every time we went to the island," Debbie bragged. "That's why I'm not afraid. Even of Michael. He's a chameleon."

"A what?" Paul asked.

"A chameleon. He changes his skin. He just pretends to be nice. I don't like him. But Rachel's in love with him."

Caught unawares, Paul stared at his hands, his hands that until that moment had seemed very capable. All the reflex training in the world couldn't keep you from being outmaneuvered by life.

"Did Dad ask you to protect us?" Debbie asked, and Paul was startled again at how intuitive she was. "I think it's a great idea."

"Your dad wants to protect you," Paul said. "Have you girls ever considered telling him what you're up to?"

Debbie stared at him. "He'd never let us go back," she said.

"You're probably right."

"I don't care if he knows," Linette said with a yawn. "I'm tired."

"But we promised our sisters we wouldn't tell," Debbie said seriously. "Not unless we all agree to tell Dad."

Paul kept back a sigh. It would be so easy to put pressure on Debbie to tell, but his goal required that he not do even that. Instead, he said, "Why don't you talk to your sisters then?"

Debbie looked at him as though he were crazy. "Why don't you catch this?" she demanded, and tossed two clubs at him.

"Two clubs are easy!" he said, quickly reaching and grabbing them and tossing them up.

"What about four?" she shot back, tossing more at him.

"Six!" Linette threw her own clubs into the mix.

"Hey!" he protested as both girls dissolved into giggles.

"Well, hello there!" a familiar voice called. "You must be the new juggling troupe I've heard so much about!" Colonel Durham was grinning at them as he approached. He was still in his shirt and tie from his office job.

The girls jumped to their feet, a bit guiltily. Debbie shouted, "Dad!" and gave him a quick hug. He patted her head a little absently.

"I've been hearing about you already," he told Paul. "People at the gate were talking about the juggling girls."

"I knew they would be great," Paul said simply.

"Good insight," Colonel Durham said. And looking at the girls, he added, "And good work, you two!"

He tousled Linette's hair and said, "I want to talk to your teacher for a moment. How about you two girls run off and get me two cones of cotton candy?"

"Sure!" the girls raced off. "We can buy it ourselves—we've got money!" Debbie yelled over her shoulder, and he chuckled.

"You've done wonders with those two," he said. "Channeled a lot of their restless energy. Think you can do that with the older girls?"

"They won't juggle," Paul said positively. "I can tell you that much."

"I suppose you're right. I wanted to ask you how things were going with your—mission."

Paul met his eyes and was silent for a moment. "It's…going."

"Is that all you can tell me?"

He nodded. "I'm sorry. I wish I could say more. I hope you're praying."

The older man sighed in frustration. "I am. But you know, prayer is never enough for me. I keep thinking I need to do something, when I guess I should be letting go and letting God."

Paul thought rapidly. "Actually, there are some things you can do," he said slowly.

"What?"

"Just positive things you can do for the girls. To build their trust in you. Well, like showing them more affection—like you just did with Debbie and Linette. And—how about this—would you mind if I ask my dad? See if he has any advice? I can let you know what he says later. Is that okay?" He saw the two girls approaching with the cotton candy.

"That sounds fine."

"Great."

"Daddy, here's your cotton candy," Debbie said proudly. "I got you green and purple."

"And I got you orange and yellow," Linette said.

"Why thank you," Colonel Durham said, taking the cones. Debbie looked at him expectantly.

"Daddy," Debbie said. "Cotton candy's not good for your blood pressure, right?"

"Or for yours, most likely," Colonel Durham said. "You're right. You can have it."

"Hooray!" Debbie cheered, and took a mouthful of hers. But Linette's face fell.

"I picked out these colors because I thought you would like them," she objected.

Colonel Durham looked uncomfortable for a moment, and Paul said quickly, "Actually, I've never tasted orange and yellow cotton candy. Can I have some?"

"Okay," Linette said slowly.

Colonel Durham said awkwardly, "How about this, Paul. I'll split it with you. I'm very fond of lemon."

"That's why I picked it," she muttered, but she looked a bit less put out.

Paul picked out a handful of cotton candy, and ate it. "It's quite good," he said.

Colonel Durham agreed. "Thank you, Linette. I think I'll eat this on my way back," he said.

"Don't you want to see us juggle?" Debbie demanded.

"Of course!" Colonel Durham caught himself. He sat down. "Go ahead, impress me!"

So the girls and Paul picked up their clubs and did their routine. When they were finished, Colonel Durham clapped heartily.

"I barely recognize you," he said. "You're real jugglers."

"You better pray we keep doing well," Debbie said. "When you pray."

"I will, and I'll stop by again," Colonel Durham promised, turning to go. Then he paused and kissed her on the forehead and patted Linette's cheek. "You two are doing a splendid job."

The girls grinned, and Paul said, "Okay, back to work." He was glad Colonel Durham had stopped by. *He has a chance of keeping these two*, he thought to himself. *If only he can learn, somehow, to connect with the others.*

And Paul was convinced that Colonel Durham's connecting with Rachel would be the key. But now, that looked like it would be harder than ever.

Rachel chewed her lip and fretted. This morning, she had some free time to work on her dress, but problems were cropping up again. She had wanted to make spaghetti straps out of the black satin, but the cheap fabric buckled and rebelled. It refused to be made into such a tiny tube. She groaned and decided to try narrow tab straps to hold up the bodice. She had already pieced together a lining from the black satin and inserted a black zipper. Now she tenderly unwrapped the tiny package of her precious expensive silk bodice material.

Fine material was a joy to work with, and she hand-sewed the glittering silver knit onto the bodice with fervor. The skirt would take her a bit longer, but the bodice would soon be done.

While she pierced the fabric with the needle and drew it out again repetitiously, her mind turned over and over what she had come to call the Boat Problem.

Now that they had started going to the island, the girls' center of gravity had shifted subtly from the church guys, as they called them, and their boats as the source of entertainment, to the island. The boats owned by the guys had gone from being the main attraction to a mere conveyance. Rachel recognized this, and saw that unless the sisters could convince the guys that they were still valued friends, the sisters were in danger of losing the boats, and with that, the island.

Of course, she reasoned, if that happened, perhaps Michael might offer to come and get them in some of his own boats. But he had never offered, and she couldn't help feeling that if he did, the girls would become too dependent upon him and his hospitality.

In a special meeting with the older girls, Rachel had tried to convey the importance of keeping Rich, Alan, Keith, Pete, Kirk, and Taylor as friends. Miriam, who was good friends with Pete, didn't object, and neither did Cheryl, who was by now falling hard for Taylor, but the other girls took some convincing. The twins were intrigued by the friends of Michael and were beginning to wish the other guys, particularly Keith, would just go away.

"Not Keith—he has a boat," Rachel had said hastily.

"Okay, then *you* dance with him sometime," Tammy had said, hands on her hips. "He's such a clingy person. He's really getting to be boring."

Rachel sensed that if she did that, it might cause more problems. Before she had met Michael, she had paid more attention to the other guys, and had sensed that several of them were hanging around, waiting for her to notice them. *Now that I'm hooked on this other man, they can hardly be happy,* she thought bleakly.

She resolved to spend more time with their guy friends, and during the next few nights on the island, she had tried to spread herself among them, being cheerful and attentive, listening to them and sympathizing. Of course, this meant she had less time to give to Michael, and that pained her. Michael, however, seemed to understand, or at least not be offended, and she was grateful for that.

But what she really wanted was to have time alone with Michael, more time to get to know him. There was so much that was mysterious about him, and she wanted to learn more about him.

"Rachel!" Sallie's voice broke into her thoughts, and she pricked herself with the needle. Hastily she put her finger in her mouth and rolled the bodice into a soft ball and thrust it back into the plastic bag with the remnants of the jugglers' costumes. "Yes?"

Sallie was coming upstairs. "Could you take the boys down to the water to play? They're driving me crazy and the girls and I are trying to bake bread."

Rachel thrust the bag back into its hiding place and hurried downstairs, feeling her usual sulkiness at being interrupted.

Downstairs it was sweltering. *I don't know why Sallie insists on baking bread in this heat,* she thought to herself. A pity Miriam and Cheryl had to endure it.

Miriam was sweating profusely while working on kneading rolls on the kitchen table, and Cheryl looked peeved as well. Jabez and Robbie had flour all over their shirts. Apparently they had been "helping." She ducked through the kitchen, took each of her brothers by one hand and led them outside. The sun was hot outside, but at least there was the bay breeze.

She led them down the gentle slope to the beach that was visible from the house. The water wasn't so deep on that side, and the tides were gentle, so the babies usually played there. She pulled off their damp and sticky floured shirts and let them run around in shorts and diapers. Then she threw herself down in the crook of a massive tree root to brood and watch them. She looked across the water to the island. From this vantage point, she could see the house and the balcony. The portico where their nighttime dances were held wasn't visible.

"Are you looking over there?" Becca asked, coming up beside her. Her younger sister had been working in the garden, and her denim skirt was dirty. "I heard you sigh." Even though she was still only fourteen, Becca typically acted much older. Maybe she was just copying Prisca.

Rachel looked at her and winked, then sighed again for effect.

"I wonder what it's like inside that house," she murmured. "I wonder if we'll ever see the inside."

"He's never invited us in," Becca said, in the same low voice.

"Odd, isn't it? And he's so polite," Rachel said. She cast a glance over the lawn, just to check. It was technically breaking her own rules to be talking like this, and she wanted to be prudent.

"He's such a gentleman," Becca said. "I broke one of my high heels the other night, and he offered to have it repaired for me, so Sallie and Dad wouldn't find out."

"You didn't let him," Rachel said, worried.

"No! Of course not. But it was sweet of him to offer," Becca sighed. "I wish we could go there now."

"Yes," Rachel said. "Then we wouldn't have to hide any more, would we?"

"Did you know that we'll be short a boat tonight?" Becca asked.

Rachel looked quickly at her. "No. Why?"

"Kirk's having to move in with his grandmother in West Virginia and help take care of her. He said goodbye to us last night when he dropped us off."

"Why didn't you tell me?" Rachel demanded, her insides sinking. "Darn it."

Becca shrugged. "Well, he was getting to be a little tiresome. At least Tammy said he was. She's interested in Dillon, now that Prisca's dropped him."

"Tell Tammy to leave him alone—he's a pothead," Rachel said, a bit brusquely. "Darn Kirk! Why couldn't he have told us sooner?"

"I know. It's so annoying." Becca ran her hands through her overlong bangs with a roll of her eyes.

Feeling that she was being selfish, Rachel backtracked. "Well, I would have liked to say goodbye to him, at least. He was a nice guy, even if he was a little coarse." Internally she considered. One less boat, true. But also, one less guy for her to worry about keeping content. Hence, possibly more time to spend with Michael...?

"The juggling troupe is back," Becca shot a glance over her shoulder. "Egads, they're headed this way."

"Look normal," Rachel murmured, and Becca stifled a giggle.

"Paul must be sweating in that suit," she said. "I can't believe he dresses like that."

Rachel looked at the trio. Linette and Debbie were cavorting on the lawn, turning cartwheels. Paul was racing beside them, and suddenly turned a complete flip and a handspring.

"Those black pants show off his legs, though," Rachel said reflectively.

Becca laughed. "Yes, he has a nice body. Too bad he's such a geek."

"Shush," Rachel said sharply, a little taken aback at her younger sister. Plus, the trio was coming within earshot.

"Rachel," Debbie cried, leaping over the tree roots and grabbing a branch above her. "Can I wear my juggling costume in the water or will it get ruined?"

"Yes, can we?" Linette chorused, coming up beside her and swinging on the branch too. Now that they were a theatrical act, the two girls were constantly mimicking each other, seeing how alike they could be.

Rachel looked at them critically. "The white blouses might be okay, but I wouldn't risk it. The satin might get stained. I say go back and get in your swimsuits first, and then go swimming."

The girls whined, but reluctantly swung down and started towards the house. Paul remained behind. He was sweating, and had taken off his harlequin vest. In his full-sleeved white shirt and black pants, he looked more like a buccaneer than a jester.

"Hello ladies," he said, nodding to them.

"How was the juggling today?" Rachel asked, perfunctorily.

"Good, thank you," he said. "My earnings have increased significantly since I hired your sisters."

"I hope you give them a fair cut."

"We split three ways," Paul said. "Chances are, they can do this next year on their own, if they keep up their practicing."

"A whole new career," Becca marveled, arching a mocking eyebrow at Rachel.

Paul inclined his head. "And you have me to thank for it."

"Oh, thank *you!*" cried Becca.

They were both hoping he would go away, but instead he sat down on the tree roots a few feet from them.

"I'm trying to be downwind. I'm afraid I must really stink from the sweat," Paul said apologetically.

"No, not at all," Rachel said automatically. Becca gave a tiny sigh.

Rachel looked at the little boys, who were involved in poking sticks into the wet sand at the edge of the water. "It's a hot day today," she commented.

"Yes. I wanted to tell you that your costumes are very comfortable for the girls, though," Paul said. "I still can't get over how good they are."

"Thanks," Rachel said.

"I wanted to ask you: have you ever thought of being a clothing designer?"

The girls laughed, but Rachel saw that Paul was apparently serious.

"I don't think so," she said, lowering her lashes.

"Well, you really are good," he persisted.

"Thank you," she said.

"Why not consider it?"

"There's no way I would be allowed to." This guy was frightfully naïve.

"Why not?" Paul looked from one to the other.

"It's an evil profession!" Becca thundered. "A snare to the godly!" Rachel recognized that her sister was imitating a popular preacher whose audio series had made the round in their church.

"Oh, come on," Paul said, rubbing his curly hair. "You girls don't really believe that, do you?"

"St. Paul says that women should adorn themselves with proper conduct, with modesty, and self control, not with braided hair and gold ornaments or pearls or fine clothes, but rather, as befits women who profess reverence for God, with good deeds," Becca informed him. "First Timothy two, verses nine and ten. Our Sunday school girls' group is studying that passage." She added self-righteously. "And that is why I never braid my hair."

Paul shook his head. "Oh, come on. I never thought he meant that women couldn't wear beautiful clothing. The inside is more important than the outside, obviously, but that doesn't mean you can't be concerned with your personal appearance."

"I've got it," Becca said, snapping her fingers. "Rachel, you could be a Christian clothing designer. You know, make Mennonite calico dresses and little caps, and eighteenth-century Quaker dresses with high collars—Sallie would love that. I bet Dad would set you up doing that."

Rachel couldn't control her snickers. "Don't you dare mention it to him. If Paul tells him I should be a clothing designer, he'll consider it a word from God and start the company for me."

"Yes! And you could work from home—from right upstairs in the sewing room! And you could hire all of us!" Becca went on. They both convulsed with giggles.

Paul looked from one to the other. "That's not what I meant," he said. "I mean, why can't you go to a regular design school and learn the trade, and then work in the regular fashion industry?"

Rachel shook her head. He was dense. "There's no way. Dad would never pay for me to go to some school staffed with heathens and homosexuals. So save your breath."

"I think you might be selling him short," Paul said, after a pause.

Rachel felt a flicker of anger. "I know my father," she said. "Maybe you were in the military with him, but I've lived with him all my life. You don't know him the way I do."

Paul persisted. "Can't you tell him how you feel, what you really want to do? Don't you think he'll listen?"

Rachel stared at Paul incredulously.

Becca stated, "You must be crazy."

Rachel said, "No, he's not crazy." She rubbed her forehead. "Paul, can you talk that way with your father?"

"Sure," Paul was earnest. His brown eyes were big and round, like a perturbed puppy dog's.

"Well, you're a son, not a daughter. And your father is probably very different from my father," Rachel said. "It's not like that in our house."

"You mean, if you were to tell him what you really thought and what you really wanted, he wouldn't listen?"

"He couldn't listen. It doesn't even occur to him. If I did that, he would take it as defiance. And he'd probably throw me out of the house." Rachel said evenly.

"So you don't tell him what you really think, or what you really feel?"

Becca snorted and shook her head. "Are you kidding? If Rachel were to ever do that, I wouldn't want to be around to see it."

Rachel did not laugh. She responded quietly, "I do everything I can to avoid that kind of confrontation. He's happier thinking that I'm living the way he would want me to live, and thinking the way he would want me to think."

"And are you? And do you?"

Rachel couldn't help laughing at him this time. "You can't handle this, can you? Would you rather see me rebel? Show up at the dinner table in a miniskirt and start cursing everyone out?"

"Is that what you really want to do?"

"That's certainly what I've felt like doing, some times."

"But that wouldn't be your real self, would it? After you get beyond the anger? What is it that you really want to do?"

"I don't know," she said distantly.

Paul looked down at his hands. "I guess I could never pretend to live out something I didn't really believe in," he said finally. "I would feel like a hypocrite."

Burning inside, Rachel kept her voice calm. "And so maybe we are hypocrites. What else can we do?"

Paul was silent, and then he spoke, with effort. "You could start to believe in what you're living."

Becca rolled her eyes. But Rachel merely stared at him.

"You don't know us. You don't understand our life," she said coldly, and added, "You should shut up now."

Paul looked at the ground, silent. Then he picked up his colored vest, which he had left on the ground, and walked away.

"What a jerk," Becca said beneath her breath.

Despite the chill in her heart, Rachel shook her head. "He just doesn't understand."

thirteen

 And again the princesses danced with their princes all through the night, until the morning was nigh.

—— Grimm

Paul swam with the younger girls at the Durhams, then hiked back to his campsite and fell fast asleep for about two hours. He roused himself before evening, walked to town, bought a sandwich for dinner, and found a pay phone outside the deli. Using a phone card, he called home.

His younger sister answered the phone and said, "Hey, you're not dead. Everyone's been wondering how you've been doing."

"I'm doing great, Annie. How's everybody?"

"Oh, you know, doing the summer thing. Working jobs. Wishing we were on vacation."

"Hey, is Dad there?"

"Yeah. Right here."

"Dad?"

"Paul! I was just thinking about you this morning. How's the life of a wandering juggler?"

"Oh, doing great. Very interesting. Actually, it's the interesting part I wanted to talk to you about. I wanted to ask you for some parenting advice. Not for myself. Remember that colonel I mentioned to you? I've gotten to know him a bit down here, and he's having some problems re-connecting with his daughters now that he's back from his tour. I know you and my sisters always seemed to get along great despite your military absences, so I was wondering if you'd divulge any of your secrets to me, so I could pass them on to him."

His father was surprised, and started with the usual disclaimer that he hadn't been a perfect parent, and only could speak from his experience, but then went on to give some thoughts. Paul, who had his journal with him, scribbled down notes. They talked for a long time, and when he hung up, Paul felt he had at least a few things to suggest to Colonel Durham.

Rachel was faced with a problem that night. Linette didn't wake up. When the others stole out of their beds and grabbed their things, Linette lay in bed, her blond hair across the pillow, snoring.

Debbie tried to shake her awake, but she just rolled over and went to sleep again, complaining, not ever really coming up to consciousness.

"She's had a hard day juggling," Miriam said.

"I've had a hard day juggling too," Debbie yawned, complaining. "Can't we all stay home tonight and sleep?"

"No," Rachel said. "I want to go." She glanced at the others, who nodded. This was a problem they hadn't planned on.

"Debbie, stay here with her," Miriam said.

"No!" Debbie objected abruptly. "I'm not going to stay here!"

Rachel looked at Cheryl, who shook her head no. Rachel didn't bother to ask.

"Okay," she said. "We'll leave her here."

Everyone looked shocked, a bit dismayed.

"Oh, come on!" Rachel hissed. "We're leaving her alone in her own bed, for Pete's sake! She'll be safe!"

Maybe not the best decision, but the substance of leadership was quick decisions. You couldn't always hope to make wise ones.

"Things are crowded tonight," Michael observed when he met them at the quay.

"We're short a boat now," Rachel said, taking his hand to get out. "Kirk had to move to West Virginia."

"That's too bad," Michael said in surprise. "I didn't know he was leaving."

"We didn't either," Prisca said dismally. "Typical local manners. He just told us last night." She shrugged as she walked over to the tables. "I won't miss him much."

"Really? And why not?" Michael asked.

"Well, he was always kind of an outsider."

Rachel again felt she had to intervene. "I still liked him," she said. "He was very laid back. Nothing bothered him." *Not even being unabashedly dropped by both Prisca and Tammy in favor of rich men.* She had come to realize that Kirk was a self-secure person, despite his rough edges.

"Did you think he was an outsider?" Michael asked, pulling out a chair for Rachel.

"Oh, sort of."

"Why?"

"I don't know," she mused, even though she did know. Kirk was from a lower-class family, while everyone from their set was upper-middle-class or higher. There must be a diplomatic way to say this. "He was just different from the rest of us. He went to public school, he worked at a gas station, he didn't go to our church. Plus he wasn't a..." She stopped abruptly, ashamed, suddenly realizing that Michael himself was most likely not a Christian.

But Michael seemed to deduce what she was going to say. "He wasn't a Christian, like the rest of you? And why would you exclude someone who wasn't part of your church?" he asked.

"It's not that," Prisca said, barging in. "It's not as though we believe that only members of our church will be saved. You just have to be a Christian."

"Oh! But he wasn't a Christian."

"Well, no. He said he believed in God, but didn't think he believed in Jesus," Prisca said.

"And so you excluded him?"

"No, we didn't try to."

"But it kept him on the outside."

"I guess so. But it wasn't his fault or anything," Prisca assured him.

Rachel listened to these exchanges, burning with mortification. "Michael, we're not trying to say we would exclude you because you don't believe," she managed to say.

"Oh, I know. But I'm just pointing out to you that, like it or not, your beliefs affect your behavior. You all knew that Kirk was not a Christian, so you never drew him into your 'inner circle.'"

Rachel was perplexed. "I don't know," she said at last, "like Prisca just said, we didn't want to exclude him."

"No. It just 'happened' that way," Michael said, his eyes dancing again. Then he paused, "Let me ask you this. Would you date someone who wasn't a believer?"

"Daddy wouldn't let us," Prisca said instantly.

"But would you?"

"Probably not," Prisca said. "I want to have a lot in common with the man I marry, and I'm a Christian, so I'll probably only date Christians because that's the sort of man I want to marry." Rachel was mildly surprised to hear Prisca say this, but Prisca always seemed to be changing her mind with her emotions.

"And you, Rachel?" he pressed her.

She couldn't meet his eyes. "I don't know if it makes a difference to me or not," she said.

He didn't pursue the matter, but then unexpectedly asked her to dance with him.

This was the second dance, and it was as magical as the first one had been. She would have melted in his arms, but after the dance, he released her again, with aggravating coolness.

He went on to adopt a teasing mood, and said everything with a nonchalance that made Rachel look at him twice to find out if he was bantering with her or not. What became frustrating was that he seemed to be set on flustering her. Which, she knew he knew, he was easily capable of doing.

"Are you upset with me?" she demanded at last as he handed her a wine cooler.

But all he said, with a mild smile, was, "I told you when I met you, Rachel, that I am a nice man."

"Michael is always nice," Prisca said to Michael's crony Brad, who had joined them at the table by the bay.

"But I may not remain nice," Michael cocked his head to Rachel. "I saw you beside the bay today with another man."

"Another man?" Rachel asked.

"Another man," Michael said solemnly. "I had my binoculars, and I could see you both."

She stared at him in incredulity. *Whatever could he mean?* Then, blankly, "Paul?"

"Is that his name?"

"Oh!" She was relieved. "*Him?* He's just a friend. Of my sisters. My *younger* sisters. He teaches them how to juggle."

"So he's just a 'friend,'" Michael pronounced.

"If you want to call him that."

"Is he your lover?"

"No!" She looked fiercely at Prisca, who was snorting and laughing. Clearly, Michael was out to get her hackles up tonight.

"She's blushing," Brad observed.

"That's because it was an embarrassing question—oh, be quiet, Prisca." Rachel touched her cheeks, surprised at herself. "What does that have to do with anything?"

"So, Rachel is more broadminded than I thought," Michael's lip twitched, his eyes dancing. "Not just 'one wife for life' for you, is it?"

"No! I mean, yes. One husband," Rachel glared at her sister, unable to meet Michael's eyes.

"Have you kissed him?"

She attempted to compose and stared back at him defiantly. "No. Why are you giving me the inquisition?"

He folded his hands and put them to his lips. "Because he looks like he wants to kiss you."

This was news to Rachel. She floundered. "He's just a friend of my dad's, really. That's how we met him."

"Ah ha! So he's the suitable suitor Daddy picked out for you then?"

"No! Not at all. He's Catholic, for one thing."

Michael looked blank. "So, you're not allowed to marry unbelievers or Catholics."

"No—yes. Well, that's not how we would put it."

"But it amounts to the same thing," Michael said. "Or am I missing something?"

Rachel grew uncomfortable. She glanced at Prisca, who mouthed, "Babylonian Mystery Religion."

"So this Paul is not the clean-cut baby-faced character he first appears to be," Michael mused. "I think I'm jealous. You're obviously attracted to his darker side."

As the most recent emotion she had felt towards Paul was weary annoyance, she was about to object, when she suddenly recalled him sitting on the rock, his lean intent figure arched over his flute, his bare skin glistening with the splendor of the wild beauty of his music. There was something about him, but she wasn't sure what it was—Paul was focused on something, bent towards it, something that she couldn't see, but which reflected its brilliance on him.

It was uncanny, and these thoughts, fleeting through her mind in an instant, made her flush again.

"Yes," said Michael, observing her. "I am jealous." But she still couldn't tell if he were joking or not.

When they got up to leave, Michael took her hand, and as he led her to the boat, suddenly, as they passed through a shadow, he curled her to him and kissed her on the lips, deeply and swiftly, and then released her.

"Rachel," he said softly. "You're too beautiful to be a Christian." And, as if nothing had happened, they walked on.

She had been kissed before—in grade school, on the playground, and her sophomore year, during a turgid school romance that quickly went sour. It was not the first time, but it still rattled her. Her attempts to say any goodnights to him faltered, and she ended up stumbling onto Alan's boat, befuddled and wondering.

As they left the island, her mind cleared momentarily. He was playing with her, testing her, pushing her away and then pulling her back. It was a game, and she wasn't sure why he was playing it. Like the songs said, in many ways, he was bad for her, but she still liked him.

Perhaps, she thought, biting a strand of hair that had blown in her mouth, because he was shy of revealing his true feelings. Perhaps he was insecure. She had heard rich men sometimes were—mistrustful.

And then Paul's words, "You spend more time with a worthwhile one…you might even marry her…" came back to her again.

Furious, she looked out at the bay again and wished, she wished that Michael had kissed her a bit longer.

As they drew closer to the shore of their house, she felt herself wilting, like a balloon caving in. The thought of going back to family life and home just now was excruciating.

"Well, you were lucky," Prisca breathed in her ear. "I saw you and Michael."

Furious, she turned on her sister. "Be quiet!" she spat. "You were hardly supportive tonight!"

"There's no need to get so—" Prisca was defensive.

Rachel didn't want Alan and Rich to hear. "I said, shut up!"

She attempted to calm herself, but when they drew closer to the shore, she made out a white figure on the beach, huddled there.

Alan pulled under the willows. The girls got out, and Rachel went over to Linette. The small blond girl was wrapped in a blanket, but she was shivering. Her hair was damp and her face was tear-stained.

"I woke up in the dark, and I was all alone," she said, and her voice was quavering. "I was all alone!" she wailed.

The guys halted by the boats, uncomfortable. Rachel looked at Alan. "Good night," she said distantly. The guys melted away, back into the boats, and pulled out.

"Why did you leave me?" Linette cried. She grabbed Rachel's arm and said again, "Why did you leave me?"

"You were tired—you needed to sleep," Rachel said sharply.

"Then why didn't someone stay with me?"

"No one wanted to stay."

Linette collapsed on the beach and began to sob. Cheryl came over and hugged her. She looked up at Rachel, her features blaming and guilty all at once.

Rachel turned and looked at the retreating boats. The guys started their engines and roared off. Then she turned back to the youngest sister, attempting to formulate some pat words of comfort.

But Linette was growing more and more hysterical. "Don't you guys ever do that again!"

"We're sorry," Rachel said woodenly.

Linette wiped her eyes with her fists and croaked. "If you ever do that again, I'll go into Mom and Dad's bedroom, and I'll tell them!"

"You will NOT!" In one swift movement Rachel seized the young girl by the shoulders and squeezed, lifting her off the ground.

Cheryl gasped and Linette, first scared by the movement, began to cry even harder.

"Let her go!" Cheryl shrieked, and seized Rachel by the hair. Rachel dropped Linette, and staggered backwards. She caught herself. She had almost, almost punched Cheryl.

"Don't you touch my sister that way!" Cheryl screamed.

Rachel's insides became stone. Her voice dropped an octave, dangerous. "Cheryl. Stop."

"I will *not* let you—"

"*You will stop.*"

And Cheryl stopped.

The other girls all stood watching, silent.

Rachel put a hand down and hauled Linette to her feet. She pushed her roughly against Cheryl. "Go up to bed. All of you."

There was a swift pattering of feet hurrying up the beach to the path through the woods to the cave. Rachel didn't look at them, didn't listen.

She heard Miriam's voice, hesitant, call, "Rachel? Are you coming?"

"No!" she bellowed. "Leave me alone!"

She picked up the blanket that Linette had dropped on the beach and wrapped it around her like a cocoon. She was a butterfly, a midnight butterfly. She didn't belong to the sunlight. She belonged to the darkness. Where men spoke softly and caressed, and where she was powerful and beautiful and—

She forced down the memories of the ugliness that had just occurred. It was because she wasn't meant for the tangled day world of family but for the private and solitary meetings of the night. Hugging the darkness around her, she prayed: *Take me now. I'm not going back. I will stay in the night world forever. I will be in the darkness, beautiful. I will be one with the darkness. I—*

She was shivering, and got up to edge closer to the beach, to the faint warmth of the day-dried sand. The tide was going out. She could stay here, in the sand, and dream of the island. And maybe her dreams would become reality. Maybe she could enter that nighttime world and stay there. She was sure Michael had the power to make it happen.

Now possessed, she spun a fantasy of Michael coming in a boat to take her to the island, forever, of returning to the island alone. Of dancing. Of darkness. *Yes.*

She huddled into her dream, her eyes dancing in sleep.

She heard stealthy footsteps, heard a creeping, the rubbery sound of sand on the beach. Someone was coming.

At once she sprang up in a fury, her hair falling over her face and blinding her sight of the night visitor. "Go away! Leave me alone!"

She threw herself back down onto the sand, and heard the footsteps retreat, and the bushes rustle, and then grow silent.

She was alone with the night. As she had wished. Warmth rushed through her, and she was no longer cold.

The hour approaches, she thought. *If I say the right thing, if I dream the right dream, I will be able to walk into that enchanted world and be a midnight butterfly forever.* She felt power coursing through her, down to her fingertips.

Yes, she thought. It will happen. It will.

And she lay down, and listened to the waves, and drifted hauntingly to sleep.

fourteen

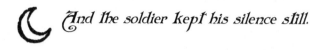 *And the soldier kept his silence still.*

— Grimm

achel woke with the taste of sand in her mouth.

She smelled it, and breathed it in, and woke up, choking.

At first, she couldn't move. It was as though all her limbs had frozen. The sand lay on her tongue, the roof of her mouth. All that was left was sand, dust, and dryness.

She rolled forward, and every joint moaned with pain. Not a sharp pain, but a dull, bruised pain. She put a hand to her face and touched grit, and dryness. Nothing was there but dust and sand.

Eyes blinked open, and sand smarted in them. It was a gray world, a fog. Neither night nor day was visible. Both had fled.

For a moment, she experienced with each of her senses all that remained of her dreams—felt sand, smelt sand, saw sand, tasted sand. And there was no sound but the dull, inanimate rush of a wind tunnel.

For a moment, she took this in, and then her spirit shrunk shrieking into naked insanity.

Sand, dust and ashes. Dust in the wind. Sand blown away. Foundationless.

She writhed, a faceless, breathless, mouthless victim.

Gripping, she only slid further on the sand. Where was something to hold onto?

God—

She flailed outwards and with a splash, found salt water.

And so she lifted her head to the cold world, her face dripping with salty water and crusted over with sand. There was sand on her lashes, and she couldn't wipe it off, because her hands, though wet, were still sandy. Once again, her body moaned with soreness, and she sobbed.

She raised her eyes to the island, and saw only the heaving gray waters of the bay. If there was a rising sun, it had shrouded itself behind heavy clouds and would not look at her.

Stiffly she pulled herself onto all fours and crept back up the beach, sickened by how wretched she felt. The blanket was a wet stiff knot that held no more comfort. Her own clothes clung to her like damp rags, a sodden sandy mass that kept the cold in instead of keeping it out.

Her tears, at least, were dissolving the sand out of her eyes and lashes. She crept about in vain for something to wipe the sand off of her. She found a piece of driftwood and attempted to scrape the sand off, but it was useless.

I'm like a crazy crone, she thought, *sitting on the beach trying frantically to clean myself.*

All of her dreams of the night rose up with the wind to yank at her sand-clotted hair and slap against her face, jeering in her ringing ears. Sand blew out of her nostrils, mixed with mucus. All enchantment had fled.

How could she ever face anyone again?

At last, staggering like a crippled woman, she scrambled up the beach, clutching at sea grass that traitorously came loose, spraying more sand on her. She was so cold.

Through the woods and into the grayness of the cave she hurried, and stripped herself of her sodden dress and pulled on the clothes she had left there—a t-shirt and denim skirt. At last she could wipe her hands clean, and then wipe her face and hair clean.

A *shower*, she thought fixedly, but even the thought of bodily comfort did not tantalize her. Would she ever get the sand out of her hair? More to the point, would she ever get the taste of the sand out of her mouth? It was still there. Her tongue was thick, and swollen.

She couldn't face her sisters. Creeping up the stairs in this devastated state was more than she could bear. Alone, cold, and ashamed, she wound her way up the bike trail to the lawn, where she realized she would have to sneak inside the house without being seen. She skulked through the woods to the garage, and sidled around the edge. She was just hurrying towards the open door to slide between the cars when she saw Paul walking up the driveway.

He was wearing his usual khaki shorts and striped shirt. When he saw her, he halted.

She couldn't hide from him. He hurried towards her.

"Rachel," he said. "Are you okay? What happened to you?"

He was looking at her anxiously; his brown eyes all puppy dog concern.

She licked her lips vainly, and attempted to speak.

"Rachel," he said in a low voice. "What happened?"

"Nothing," she said hoarsely. "I just spent the night on the beach."

"Why?"

That was a stupidity she could not confess even to herself, let alone anyone else. "What are you doing here?" she said with an effort.

He didn't respond. "Let me take you inside," he said at last. "You're shaking. I hope you don't have hypothermia."

"I don't want to wake up my parents," she said faintly.

"I understand."

He led her into the garage and made her sit down on the steps leading to the house. He opened the door cautiously, listened, then grabbed a huge towel from the stack in the mud room and threw it around her shoulders.

Then he knelt in front of her. "Let me see your feet," he directed, and she put one out aimlessly. He began rubbing it vigorously, circulating the blood, first one, and then the other.

After a few minutes, he looked up into her eyes, scanning her face for something she couldn't fathom. Then he said, "Go inside and take a shower. And then go up to bed."

He didn't say she would be okay. She wondered how much he had read in her eyes.

Mumbling thanks, she got to her feet and stumbled indoors to the bathroom and locked the door. The frightening sheet of madness had lifted, and she was coherent enough to get herself a long drink of water from the bathroom faucet.

Then she undressed, fumbled with the knobs, and got into the shower. But she couldn't stand up any longer. She sat down, put her back against the cold tiled wall, put her head between her knees, let the warm water drum down on her head and neck muscles in a hypnotic rhythm. At last the physical sensations overwhelmed her tattered psyche, and she slept.

Paul went down to the beach.

There was much he knew about, but he didn't know what had happened to Rachel on the beach last night after everyone had left, including himself. He had walked back from Alan's dock and found Rachel alone on the beach. Having heard part of the fray between the sisters, he had assumed she was cooling off. But something in her aspect frightened him. He didn't know if she was waiting for someone, or perhaps attempting to drown herself. So he had sat around and waited. But after she had driven him away with her shouting, he felt weary and thought to himself, *I'll let her sit in her pout.* And had gone back to his tent.

Still he had woken up early, anxious about her, and had gone over to the Durhams' house to make sure she was okay.

And she was not okay—one look at her had told him that. But why, he couldn't tell.

Let it go, he told himself again. *She can tell me if she wants to.* Once again, he felt conflicted, wishing that he could somehow force Rachel to open up to her father, who, in his groping way, would have thrown himself between her and whatever danger was threatening her soul if she would let him. But Paul couldn't force Rachel, or any of the girls.

He had chosen this path of standing away, of guarding but not preventing, and once again felt the frustration. It was difficult to sit in the shadows, watching the twelve sisters so naively flirting with their own destruction. He probably would have given up or given in days ago, if Debbie and Linette hadn't confided in him how much his presence reassured them. But they were young—what they needed was a strong witness of someone rejecting the whole lifestyle their older sisters were being initiated into. Was he confusing them by standing by, and not interfering? He was guessing that their instincts were good enough to figure out right from wrong, even in this tangled web, but he didn't know. He was trusting—dangling in midair on a thin trapeze of trust, a chain of girls hovering in midair—and they were all playing without any net but supernatural grace. And that could not be presumed upon.

He murmured his prayers as he moved his fingers over his rosary beads in his pocket, and paced, wearing a frustrated track in the sand. It was difficult to wait, and to trust. Only the bright figure of the Blessed Virgin Mary, that wonder of terrible trust, with her shining peaceful visage, comforted him.

After her shower, Rachel got dressed and looked at herself in the mirror. She looked better, but still drained. After a while, she hesitantly started upstairs, hoping to get to the girls' bathroom unseen for an early skin masque job. She wasn't particularly anxious to see anyone from her family.

As she rounded the corner, she met Melanie coming down the stairs. Her younger sister brightened with relief when she saw her. "Hey, Ray," she said softly. "I went outside to look for you but couldn't find you."

"I came in by way of the garage," Rachel said quietly. Then, "Want to go up to the bathroom with me?"

"Sure."

Once they were inside the large long bathroom, which was thankfully unused, Rachel locked the door, turned on the hot water in one of the two sinks, and breathed a deep sigh, starting to feel more normal.

Her younger stepsister hopped onto the counter and sat Indian-style, and started to brush the tangled honey-brown hair that hung around her gentle face. She didn't ask any questions—she just waited for Rachel to start talking when she was ready. Rachel ran her fingers under the surging water from the faucet and felt grateful for the lack of emotional pressure to tell what had happened to her. She still didn't quite understand it.

"I had a lousy night," she said at last. Melanie nodded. Rachel, remembering the feelings, blinked suddenly. "I know how Linette felt now, anyway," she managed to say.

The next moment, Melanie's arms were around her, gently hugging her. "That's all right, Ray. You don't have to say anymore."

"Thanks," Rachel whispered, wiping her eyes again. It never ceased to amaze her how someone as young as Melanie could be so comforting to talk to.

"Dad said we're having his share group over for dinner tonight," Melanie said, changing the subject when the time seemed right.

"Of course they would be coming," Rachel murmured, with a trace of her usual, normal annoyance.

Melanie's smile was barely touched with wryness. "Lord, give us the patience to endure your blessings," she said, quoting a plaque that hung in the downstairs bathroom, and Rachel had to smile.

When she had recovered, and started her daily skin therapy, Rachel said, "You know, Melanie, you're the only person in the whole family I wanted to see today. I'm glad I met you first."

"Thanks, Rachel," Melanie said softly. "I'm glad I found you, too. I was worrying about you all night and praying."

"I'm sorry I made you worry," Rachel said with a sigh. "Your prayers probably helped." Dabbing on some cleansing soap, she added, "I'm so glad we can talk like this together. Everyone else, I feel I have to be guarded in some respects, but I feel you and I can be totally honest with each other. I'm grateful."

As she plunged her face into the water, she noticed out of the corner of her eye that Melanie's face had fallen. Eyes shut, rubbing her face vigorously beneath the water, she decided it was just Melanie's usual embarrassment at being complimented. But when she emerged from the water and had patted her face dry with a towel, she noticed that her younger sister looked genuinely distressed, as if she were about to cry.

She was about to ask her what was wrong when the door handle turned. When it didn't open, there was a fury of hammering and yelling from outside the door. "Come on, it's not private property in there!" Becca yelled.

Rachel heaved a sigh, and reached over to open the door with a disdainful click. "What's your problem? Geez!" she snorted.

Recognizing Rachel, Becca retreated slightly, but seeing that her older sister appeared sane, she edged inside. "Sorry. Didn't know who it was," Becca muttered. Then added cautiously, "You feeling better, Rachel?"

"Hmph. Yes," Rachel said carelessly. She studied herself in the mirror. She was looking much better. Dear God, what kind of an impression had she made on Paul this morning? Rubbing the moisturizer into her cheeks and heaving a sigh, she resolved to go down and talk to him again, later on, to show him that she had recovered herself—that she was okay. Somehow, the thought of being indebted to Paul Fester's kindness rankled her.

Paul took a morning swim, dried himself off, and took up his rosary again. He was praying aloud as he walked up and down the beach. As he walked, distracted in his meditations, he glanced over at the island. A strong breeze was sweeping across the bay, and he could see the large house wrapped in its cloak of swaying firs. He barely made out a figure on the balcony of the house looking towards the Durham house. A flash of light coming from the figure caught his eyes. Light reflecting off of glass? Binoculars?

Suddenly self-conscious, he wondered if he was the one being scrutinized. But a rustle in the bushes above told him that Michael Comus was probably training his spyglass on a more desirable target. Rachel was coming down the track to the beach.

She had showered and dressed, and carried herself with a bit of her usual pretense of disdain, but he could make out the hollows below her eyes.

Rachel was still beautiful, even with the hairline cracks in her veneer of sophistication.

"What were you saying?" she asked, a touch of mild fascination in her words as she came up to him. "I was standing up on that cliff, watching you. You were just jabbering to yourself, the same words over and over again."

He colored, and turned his back on the island. "I'm saying the rosary in Japanese," he said.

"Really? Why?"

"My old aikido teacher was a Japanese Catholic, and he taught me. I just like the language," he laughed, a bit uncomfortable. "Plus I've been trying to calm Melanie's fears for my soul."

"What do you mean?"

"She heard me praying the rosary in English once and became disturbed because of the language I was using with Mary. I figured I don't want to rock her world, so whenever I'm over here, I just use Japanese."

"I see," Rachel pursed her lips, and he saw she was keeping back a smile. Why did she always hide her smiles? "So you were praying down here, not pacing in a cage?"

"Yes," he said, and flushed. Had she actually been watching him that long? Why? "How are you feeling?" he asked, changing the subject and beginning to walk down the shore once more. He wanted to get her away from the gaze of the man on the island. "You looked pretty bad this morning." *Like an old woman*, he thought, but he wasn't going to tell her that.

"I'm all right," she said, dropping her eyes and licking her lips. "I just spent the night on the beach, and woke up sore."

"Was that all?" he had to ask as they rounded the bend.

"I had a nightmare."

"Oh." He understood something like that, and was relieved.

"Paul—"

"Yes?"

She had an odd expression on her face. "You have a problem with me, don't you?"

He halted, wondering if she had found him out, after all. "What do you mean?" he asked at last.

"You think I'm a hypocrite."

"I think you're not living honestly," he said at last.

"What do you mean by that?" Now she was defensive, her green eyes angry and afraid.

"You said the other day when we were talking by the tree that you didn't think you could express your true feelings."

"Oh, that!" she laughed sarcastically, but he could tell she was relieved. "Well, if I could have another life, totally separate from my regular life, I would! A day life and a night life. Wouldn't you?"

"No," he said. "I would try to live honestly in every part of my life. I think what you're doing is a dangerous way to live."

"Why dangerous? You could keep all the dark things in your life away from contaminating the light parts. Or would you prefer to be totally dark?" she pursued, swinging her hips as she walked.

He halted. "You're a very strange girl, Rachel."

"Why do you say that?"

"Because you seem to see everything as a conflict. Why does there have to be a battle between your day and your night? God separated them, but there's light in both. God made the moon, you know, to beautify the night. There's got to be room for mystery. Don't draw battle lines where they're not meant to be. There's enough war in the world without them."

She was amused. "Is that what's so different about you?"

"What?"

"You're not divided. I can't make up my mind as to whether you're a pagan or a Christian. You're so strange that way." She had taken a step towards him and was studying him curiously.

"Rachel," he said with an effort, feeling self-conscious. "Trying to split your world in two, and then trying to live differently in one world than you do in the other—that's just not healthy. It can't be done for long. It can lead to —" he paused. "Well, one thing it could lead to is mental disintegration."

Rachel looked at him sharply, and flushed.

"What?" he asked. He saw that tense expression on her face again.

"Suppose—" she dropped her eyes and started walking carefully around the rocks at the edge of the water. "Suppose you'd been told all your life that you had to keep your eyes on the things of heaven, and keep away from the entanglements of the flesh, and then you grew up and realized that you were beautiful, and knew that wherever you went, you were going to keep on turning men's eyes away from heaven down to earth and—" she looked up at him, "fleshly matters. How would that make you feel?"

"Evil," he said flatly. "That's why I don't agree with looking at the world that way. Is that how you feel?"

"I'm not the only girl who feels that way," she said quietly. "Prisca scares me sometimes. I mean, I'm a bit rebellious, but she's very rebellious. Sometimes she's actually hostile about God and church and everything."

"Is that what you're worried about?" He knew she was changing the subject, but it was clear that this other matter had been on her mind as well.

"Yes. Do you know what I mean? Isn't there something a bit—strange—about her mood swings?"

He hesitated, again knowing more about the situation than she realized he knew. Prisca seemed overly excited, swinging back and forth between exhilarating highs and sour lows. And the way she threw herself in the path of strange men was disturbing.

"I've actually been wondering," he said, "if your sister might have some undiagnosed physical problems."

She stared at him. "You don't mean mental problems?"

He dug into the sand with his toe. "A good doctor would look at her holistically. Yes, there may be some psychological problems, but I'm not sure that's the whole thing. I've been sort of watching her. She doesn't eat very well. It could be that she has an undiagnosed food allergy, and her mood swings are due to blood sugar fluctuations." Feeling he was overextending himself, he looked at Rachel, who was gaping at him. "I only have a pre-med degree—I'm not even a medical student yet. But I guess I'd say my instinct is that your parents should have her checked out. Just have her tested for allergies, to begin with. And a glucose test."

"You mean that everything might be due to—" she started.

He shook his head. "No. There's a definite moral problem she's struggling with, and that won't go away just because of a medicine. But it's always more difficult to make the right choices when you're feeling lousy, and this might help her out."

Rachel lifted her face to him, and he saw she was looking at him differently. The disdain in her blue-green eyes was dissolving. "You're very observant," she said slowly.

He shrugged it off. "I probably have too much time on my hands right now," he said nonchalantly. "Have I answered your questions?"

"Partly," she said. "I'll talk to Sallie, though, about Prisca. Right away." She turned and started up the path. "Thank you," she said, over her shoulder, and with a toss of her brown hair, she hurried off.

He watched her and then turned away. She was a pretty girl, dancing with danger and hiding her secrets carefully, but she cared about her sisters deeply. He had to admire her for that.

fifteen

And the eldest princess laughed and said, "It is good for the fool that he does not know our secret."

—— Grimm

Paul found Colonel Durham in his home office that morning. "Good morning, Paul," Colonel Durham said, when Paul came into the room. "What can I do for you?"

Paul shut the door behind him and sat down in the chair across from the colonel. He swallowed hard, and tried to find the words to begin. He took a folded paper out of his pocket. "I remember that you were looking for ways you could re-connect more with your daughters. I asked my dad if he had any recommendations about raising daughters, and I wrote down a few things he said," he handed Colonel Durham a folded paper.

Colonel Durham took it. "Your father has how many daughters?"

"Five. The oldest is thirty-two, and the youngest is eighteen. They all get along with him just fine."

"I see," the man read over the paper silently for a few minutes. "Some of this I try to do already. 'Speak respectfully to them.' I always try to do that. 'Listen to them.' Well, if they would talk to me, I would listen to them." He read over the paper and frowned. "This is a lot. I'm not sure if I'd have time to do all these things. 'Take her out on a date periodically.' Paul, I have a hard time trying to get some special time with my wife, let alone all those girls. Did your father do that?"

"Yes," Paul said. "He and my mom would go on a date about once a month on their wedding anniversary day, and he'd also schedule time to take my sisters out to breakfast, or lunch, or whatever once a month too."

"But he had five and I have twelve," Colonel Durham said with a wry smile. "I'd spend half of every month on a date. Well, maybe that would help.

146

I guess I could take them out to lunch on the days I work at home… All right, I'll think about it. Thanks for taking the time to put this together."

"You're welcome sir." Paul rose.

"There is one other thing I'd like to ask you about," Colonel Durham looked at him keenly.

"Yes sir?"

"Sit down."

Paul sat again, and Colonel Durham took off his glasses and folded them. "I was up very early this morning," he began. "And I was sitting at the kitchen table when I heard you and my daughter Rachel talking in the garage. Then she snuck inside into the bathroom, and I suppose you left. I was surprised, as you can imagine, to hear you two together so early in the day."

Paul swallowed, suddenly aware of his precarious position.

"Can you tell me what was going on?"

Carefully, Paul considered before he spoke. "I was up early myself, and I came up the drive and saw Rachel right outside the garage. That was how I met her."

"What was she doing out there so early in the morning?"

He paused. "Sir, I…need to be free not to say anything about that at this point."

Colonel Durham looked at him for a long moment, then sat back and put his glasses back on, shaking his head. "Okay. I'll trust you."

"Thank you."

"But I wanted to tell you that I heard you two."

Paul's stomach churned. "Thank you, sir."

Colonel Durham sighed again. "I am continuing to pray."

"Keep it up. Please."

Sallie, concerned about how the younger girls were dragging during the day, was making them take afternoon naps. Now that they were getting extra sleep, Debbie and Linette were becoming even more proficient at their act. On Monday, they did their first three-way fountain with Paul, to great audience appreciation. After the act was over, a local reporter approached them wanting to do a story on them, and Debbie and Linette were delighted. They posed charmingly for the photographer. Paul also got a chance to highlight his own work in the article. Afterwards, one of the festival organizers stopped by to tell Paul and the girls how much their act was enjoyed, and extended an invitation for them to return next year. The girls were thrilled.

They were having a celebration with ice cream cones when they were surprised by a group of family members. Miriam and Cheryl had brought over Robbie and Jabez, and Brittany and Melanie were tagging along. Paul suggested the young girls take a break and go on some rides with their sisters, but they wouldn't hear about it unless he went with them. So he called it an early day and the jugglers packed up. Then they walked off to explore the fairgrounds in a chattering group.

Paul wasn't surprised when they happened to meet Pete and Taylor, and less surprised when the two boys joined their party. He was introduced to them, although he already knew who they were, of course. The high school boys initially seemed a bit uncomfortable around him, but Paul talked easily to them about colleges and sports, so they warmed up. He liked Pete, but Taylor was a little less friendly. It was obvious that he and Cheryl had something between them, and Paul caught them whispering furtively together when they thought no one was watching. In contrast, Pete and Miriam joked together as though they were two guys.

Debbie and Linette each took charge of one of the baby boys, and were carrying them on their shoulders, showing them all the sights that would be interesting to small boys, like the ponies and the Revolutionary War band. Not wanting to be a third wheel, Paul focused his attention on the two outwardly quiet middle girls—Brittany and Melanie. They had always struck him as the most unpretentious of all the Durham girls.

Knowing that she was a good athlete, Paul challenged Brittany to best him at one of the fair games, and Brittany took him up on it with alacrity. They let the rest of the group go on while they competed at the bean toss, the hoop throw, and several other games. Melanie applauded them both equally. Eventually the couples joined them at the games, and they spent at least an hour and too many quarters to count getting even with each other.

They ended up the day at the picnic tables, eating popcorn and hot dogs and talking, while Jabez slept in Debbie's arms, and Robbie occupied himself with the balloons they had bought him.

Eventually the guys said goodbye, and left them at the picnic table. Paul remained with the Durham girls, and they chatted a bit longer as the afternoon drew on.

"We should go home to dinner soon," Cheryl said regretfully. "That was a lot of fun, though."

"Paul," Miriam said, toying with her straw, her blue eyes snapping, "do us a favor?"

"What's that?"

"Don't mention to anyone that Taylor and Pete were with us?"

"You mean, to your parents?"

"Of course," Miriam looked uncomfortable.

"You weren't doing anything wrong. Why do you have to keep it a secret?"

"Because it would cause problems," Cheryl said. "We're not supposed to be spending one-on-one time with guys."

Paul paused. "I doubt it will come up," he said. "But why do you feel you have to sneak?"

"Because Mom and Dad don't trust us," Miriam said. She was obviously irked.

Paul was silent, the two-faced nature of the girls' relationship with their parents confronting him once again. He hated it.

"It's not so bad to have a harmless secret from them, is it?" Cheryl said uncertainly.

Paul shrugged. "It's on your conscience. Does it bother you?"

"Sometimes."

"It should."

Melanie spoke up suddenly. "What about if you have a secret from someone you love that you don't want to keep?" she asked.

The other girls became more uncomfortable. Debbie and Linette eyed Paul with worried expressions. Paul tried to look nonchalant, knowing what Melanie was asking.

"Well, if it bothers your conscience to keep it, and you don't intend to cause hurt, then in some cases you should bring the situation to light," he said.

"Even if that would hurt an awful lot of people?" Miriam demanded.

"Or just one person?" Melanie said quietly.

"Sometimes that's all right to get it out in the open," he said, meeting her sad brown eyes. He got to his feet. "Shouldn't you girls get going now?"

They packed up their things silently, and the older girls were giving him hard looks. His juggling partners were guilty and a bit fearful. He tried to keep a light tone, and helped carry Jabez back to the car. But he could hear their whispers in the background, and had no doubt that this would be a topic of much sisterly discussion later on when they were out of his earshot.

The next day, the ideas that had been swimming around in Rachel's mind gelled at last. She finished picking tomatoes, washed her hands, and went in search of Melanie as the afternoon wore on. Her favorite sister was usually the first person to hear her ideas.

She found Melanie upstairs on her lower bunk bed, dozing, and sat down beside her. "Melanie, I want to do something special for Prisca for her birthday."

"Okay," Melanie said softly. She sat up, and rubbed her eyes. "It's this Friday, isn't it?"

"Yes. Look, you know that Prisca has been having a hard time lately, with Dad and the church, and all that. I want to do something to—well, just really give her a good birthday, to let her know that we all love her. Maybe we sisters could do something special together for her. What do you think?"

Melanie started to smile. "I think that's a great idea, Ray."

"Good. I was thinking that you could help me come up with some ideas of what Prisca would really like. Like, we could each write a special card for her."

"I'll think about it," Melanie said, and put her head back down, wearily. Rachel noticed that she looked drained, and recalled that lately Melanie had been looking pale and drawn. Melanie wasn't thriving in the moonlight, Rachel saw, and felt a sting of conscience.

"I'm sorry I woke you up," she said quietly. "You need to make up your sleep."

"Yes," Melanie said, staring at the wall. Her eyes looked close to defeat.

"Mel, is something wrong?"

Her sister was silent, but her eyes blinked. They were sad half-moons now.

"Mel, something is really bothering you. I can tell. What's the matter?"

Melanie sniffed, and wiped her nose. "Please don't be mad, Rachel."

"I won't," Rachel promised, stroking her sister's hair, concerned. Melanie, who had such a heart for others, had difficulty in talking about her own emotions sometimes, afraid of hurting people's feelings.

"I—I don't like lying," Melanie said.

"Lying?" Rachel whispered. "You mean, our secret?"

Melanie nodded.

"Having a secret among all of us isn't lying, Melanie," Rachel objected.

"I know," Melanie whispered. "But every time we go, my heart gets a little heavier. I feel I'm getting closer and closer to lying." Tears ran down her face. "I don't want Mom and Dad to be mad at you. I don't want you to have to lie to them. I don't want to have to hide anything. I just want to be free and truthful, you know?"

Rachel swallowed, and kept stroking Melanie's hair. "Yes," she said at last, her heart like a knot inside her. "Melanie, I wish I could work it out," she said at last. "So that you could be happy and we all could be happy as well. I just don't know if I can."

"I know," Melanie said in a bare hush. "It's just making my heart hurt, that's all. It gets hard." She rubbed her eyes. "I have to tell you something," she said finally. "I can't keep hiding from you, at any rate, when you trust me so much."

"Go ahead, tell me," Rachel said encouragingly.

Melanie took a deep breath, and rolled over to look at her. "Paul knows our secret. He's been watching us."

Rachel blinked. "What?"

"I don't know how he found out. But I've seen him hiding on Alan's boat under the canvas and he goes with us to the island."

Rachel was silent for a moment as she took this in. "How long has he been doing this?"

"For a while." Melanie covered her eyes. "I thought you should know."

Rachel was unable to think of anything to say. A fury was rising in her, bolstered by a fresh, new fear. All this time, she had thought they were so safe.

"Are you mad?" Melanie asked, her voice quavering.

"At you? Nonsense," Rachel hugged her tightly. "I can see how hard it was for you to tell me. Now lie back down and get some sleep."

"All right," Melanie said, a half-sigh. It was clear she had needed to get this off her chest for some time. "Please don't be too angry."

"Go to sleep," Rachel whispered, tousling her hair and getting up from the bed. She didn't want to hurt Melanie. "You were right to tell me," she said with an effort, and walked downstairs, closing the attic door behind her.

Now alone, she swore beneath her breath, and stormed downstairs.

This time, she didn't bother to tell Sallie she was borrowing the car. She grabbed the keys and a stack of library books as an excuse, and went out to the car. "Tell Sallie I'm going to return these books!" she bellowed out the window to Cheryl, and threw the car into reverse before she could hear Cheryl's protests.

She drove to the fair, parked the car in the gravel lot, and hurried through the parking lot, her face flaming but her insides tight. Entering the fair with a wave at the ticket booth attendant, she made her way through the thin crowds of cheerful people in colonial costume. She was hot and more bothered than usual by the farce of it all. She worked her way among the craft and game booths until she found the place where Paul and the girls usually juggled. When she got there, Paul was there alone, playing on his flute. At that particular moment, he had no audience.

She walked up to him, cutting off his song. "Where are the girls?" she asked.

He lowered his instrument and looked up at her. "They're off getting us some lunch."

"Fine. Then come with me. We need to talk."

"All right."

He packed up his flute while she waited, seething inside. When she was certain he was following her, she walked away.

She deliberately picked a path behind the booths that led out to the field behind the festival. She walked quickly to keep well ahead of him, not desiring to make any small talk that might put him at ease.

When she had walked a good distance out into the waving grass of the field, she turned on him.

"What's the deal with your spying on us?"

She saw by his reaction that he had guessed already the reason for her fury, and that only made her angrier. "What do you have to say?" she demanded when it was clear he didn't feel the need to explain himself.

"I told Melanie that she should tell you if she felt it burdened her conscience," he said. "She's suffering, Rachel. She's been suffering for some time to keep your secret. I hope you can see that."

Breathing hard she said, "Did my father hire you to spy on us or something?"

"No."

"But you've spied. And pried. And now you know everything we've been doing." Scorn spilled over into her words. "What are you, a peeping Tom? Too afraid to show yourself? Or are you some kind of sicko? I cannot figure you out! You talk about being honest and open, and yet, here you are sneaking around, spying on us in the dark."

He was staring beyond her, red-faced.

"Why are you doing it? Is my dad behind it? He is, isn't he? I *knew* he would try something like this! You military guys! What, do you have to obey him because he's a colonel?"

"No."

"But he *did* put you up to this, didn't he?" she demanded again.

Paul was silent, and she began to be afraid. Seeing her predicament, she was very cold.

She gripped him by the arms, trying to get him to look at her. "Paul. You have got to promise me that you are never going to tell him. Do you know what will happen if you do? Do you?" her voice was getting shrill, and soon she was almost yelling in his face. "Promise me!"

"I can't."

She dropped her hands and stared at him in contemptuous disbelief. "So. You know what it will do to us. But you're going to do it anyway. So that you can be proud that you did the right thing. Oh, Paul, you're *so* holy." And she slapped him across the face.

Paul stood, his face slapped to the right, breathing hard, blinking. He hadn't moved, but Rachel suddenly became aware of how tall and muscular he was. She felt a sudden new fear creep through her, even though he had not even looked at her. His eyes were on the ground, cast down where her blow had forced them.

Her chest tightened, and she backed away. "You're going to be sorry," she said, her blood racing through her forehead. "You tell him anything, and you'll be sorry."

She stumbled, turned, and raced back to the car. Already she knew what she was going to do. Her throat was closing and her hands were quivering, but she forced herself to the task.

She drove home and walked inside, holding her hands so that no one else would see them shaking. In her mind she knew what she was going to say.

Her dad was in his home office, on the phone. She stood at the door and waited for a minute that seemed infinite. Finally he hung up. She walked into his office, shut the door behind her, and looked at her father. His face was surprised and perplexed.

"Rachel, what's wrong?" he asked.

I'm doing this for all of us, she thought. *To protect our secret.*

"Dad," she said with an effort. "I have to talk to you about something."

"What about? Sit down."

"Paul," she said, and forced her knees to bend, to sit on the chair. Finally she sat on the edge.

She hadn't planned the silence, but it was a moment before she could bring out the words. "He tried to force me to kiss him."

He leaned forward. "What?"

"He tried to force himself on me," she said again. "He didn't want me to tell you, but I had to. He's been watching me for some time. He's been watching all of us sisters. And then, this morning—I just told you what he did."

Her father sat back in the chair and she knew that she had ruined Paul. Whatever he told her dad now would seem like excuses. She had done it. Told a lie, a real lie, with intent to hurt. The tears came up into her eyes, and she tried to push them down. Darn it, she was not trying to dissemble. She was really crying.

"Does this have anything to do with you both being out so early in the morning together the other day?" her father's voice came into her mind. "I heard you come in."

The other day—the day the night-world had abandoned her on the beach. Yes, it was the night's revenge—the sand was in her mouth again. She could feel its dryness. Was it too great a price to pay?

"No," she whispered. "I mean, yes."

"Rachel, I think you and I should have a talk with Paul. Can you handle that?"

The girl who had once been Rachel Durham nodded.

"What happened to your face?" Debbie asked Paul. "It's all red."

Paul put a hand to his cheek.

"I didn't turn the other cheek in time," he said, a bad quip. "What's for lunch?"

The girls had brought back historical food for lunch—beef sandwiches and apple cider drinks. He started to eat his portion, with the mere semblance of enjoyment.

"Ready to start again?" he asked.

Debbie said, "Hey, look! It's Dad and Rachel."

Paul's stomach churned again, and he pushed aside the food and got up. Colonel Durham approached him, every inch of him full of formidable military bearing. Rachel, her arms folded, was not looking at him.

"Debbie and Linette, Rachel's here to drive you home."

"Why?" Debbie demanded. "We're only halfway done."

"Pack up and go wait in Rachel's car. Is it open, Rachel?"

Rachel, her hair blowing across her cheek, her eyes distracted, nodded.

Debbie started to object, but Paul said, "Go ahead, girls. Listen to your dad."

"Corporal Fester, I'd like you to come and talk with Rachel and me."

"Yes, sir," he said.

Paul followed them away from the fairgrounds to the car. Colonel Durham and Rachel got in the front, and he got in the back.

Colonel Durham put on the engine and the air conditioning, but didn't move the car. Instead, he turned around in the seat and looked at Paul.

"Corporal, Rachel has told me something I find quite disturbing."

Paul listened in silence to the ugly accusation. He looked at Rachel while the words came out. She was in profile, her tanned cheek smooth, her brown brows furrowed and set. Her blue-green eyes seemed to have faded. They were dead, empty.

So that was it. She had jumped ahead, taken the advantage, and tried to destroy his credibility, because of the information she now knew he had.

He heard the faint snap of the ropes that held his trapeze wire, and felt himself hurtling to the ground.

Now Rachel turned and glanced at him quickly. Maybe she expected him to speak, to lash back at her, to attempt to reveal anything, now that he was accused.

He was silent.

There was a chance—a slim chance—that there was another trapeze bar he could catch to break his fall. In order to seize it, he had to trust again, and fall, open-armed.

"Rachel, could you please leave us now and take the girls home?" Colonel Durham asked.

The girl with the secret seemed to dare him to shoot her down. But as he saw her get out of the car and walk away, her hands were clutched tightly around her.

"Corporal Fester, is what she said true?"

Paul looked in the eyes of the older man, eyes that looked tired and worn, though his warrior's jaw was set.

What could he say?

It's not true. But his word against hers: he couldn't prove it.

Tell him everything. At this point, that would destroy everything.

A voice inside was telling him what a fool he was for getting involved in this situation, with an army colonel's family, none the less. Paul's military record, his entrance into medical school—he could see it all dissolving like sand through his fingers.

But I risked all that when I said yes to this.

At last, he managed to say, "Colonel Durham, I'm not sure how to answer that. Perhaps it's best if I just stay away from your family from now on."

There was a silence while the two looked at each other.

At last, Colonel Durham looked down, his voice steady with an effort. "I agree. I guess it was a bad idea from the start. I think you should leave now."

In his mind's eye Paul saw the last trapeze bar he was groping for swing away from his outstretched hand as he continued to fall.

"Yes, sir," he said quietly. "Colonel Durham, are you going to report this to the police?"

Colonel Durham looked up abruptly, surprised. "I'm not sure."

"Ask Rachel if you should," Paul said. "Goodbye then."

He got out of the car, and walked back to the fairgrounds to pick up his juggling bag. The police could find him easily enough if they wanted him, he had no doubt of that. All the same, he felt a sudden urge to leave town.

seventeen

 And still the soldier kept his silence, telling no one what he had seen.

— Grimm

achel, are you out of your mind?"

Tammy was the first one to say something after Rachel had told them. Rachel sat on her bed, her arms wrapped fiercely around her knees.

"You lied, Rachel. You lied to Dad about him," Taren said.

The other sisters were sitting around the double bed. They were all there, except Melanie, whom Rachel had seen fit to occupy with some task downstairs. Rachel looked around, and saw horror and dismay on all their faces. Angrily, she spat back.

"There was no other way. Don't you see that what I did, I did to keep our secret?"

Miriam choked. "Yeah, but it was totally unnecessary. Up until now, there hasn't been any actual lying involved. No one's questioned us so we haven't had to lie. But this is different."

"How is it any different?" Rachel demanded, hot and flustered. She had expected more support than this. After all, she was the one who had had to lie. It hadn't exactly been easy.

"It's just different," Brittany spoke up. Her jaw was thrust out, but her eyes were sad. Cheryl stood next to her, her arms folded, her face white and strained.

"Look," Rachel kept her voice quiet with an effort. "Obviously, Dad brought Paul to meet our family in order for him to spy on us."

"Paul's not a spy," Debbie cried. The other sisters hushed her, and she subsided.

"Someone had to do something to destroy his credibility, so that Dad wouldn't trust him any more." Rachel pointed out.

There was silence.

"No," Miriam said.

"What do you mean, no?" Rachel shot back.

"You jumped the gun, Rachel. You should have consulted us. If Paul was going to tell Dad, he could have told Dad a long time ago. And we would have found Dad standing by the cave waiting for us with a Bible and an M16. But nothing has happened. Therefore, Dad doesn't know. Therefore, Paul hasn't told him. Therefore, he probably wasn't planning on telling him, until this happened."

Rachel looked around. The other sisters were nodding—even Prisca, who had been silent until now, was bobbing her head.

"He's a geeky spy, but he's an honest one," Prisca said.

"He's not a spy! He's just trying to protect us," Linette said. "That's why he's been coming with us."

"Yeah," said Debbie. "Like he protected Melanie that one time."

The others turned on the two youngest sisters.

"What! You've known about this all along!" Taren said.

"Melanie didn't tell me you two knew," Rachel said angrily.

Debbie flushed, "I'm glad Melanie told you," she said. "She hated hiding it from you."

But Linette looked angry. "Melanie could have kept our secret," she said, folding her arms.

"Secrets! Secrets! There was only supposed to be *one* secret, one that we sisters shared," Rachel said, glowering at the youngest girls, who shrank down. "Then you two started keeping secrets from the rest of us. We used to be unified. If you two had told us about Paul right away, this never would have happened."

"That's true," Taren said, glaring at Linette.

"Well, he wasn't doing anything but following us and watching out for us," Debbie protested. "And he's our friend. I don't think he would want us to get in trouble. But I think he was worried when we started going to the island. I think he was being our bodyguard."

"Oh, please," said Rachel.

"He saved Mel from being thrown into the tree, that one time when Mark made her dance with him," Debbie said, and the other girls looked at her in surprise.

"Is that why she didn't get hurt?" Miriam asked. "I saw her go flying towards that tree, and I was sure she would be knocked out."

"He came out and pushed her out of the way just in time, then disappeared again," Debbie said.

Rachel flushed despite her iron will. She and Prisca had been in the cave with Michael during that episode.

"So what is Dad going to do to him?" Liddy turned back to Rachel suddenly. "Did he say?"

"I think he told Paul to stay away from our family," Rachel said.

Debbie's face crumpled and she put a pillow up to her face and sobbed. "It's not fair!"

"He didn't do anything except try to be our friend, and you—you slandered him!" Linette accused Rachel, her large brown eyes filling with tears. She threw herself on the carpet and cried.

Rachel covered her face with her hands and waited for them to shut up.

But the younger girls kept crying. Miriam leaned over to Rachel and spoke in her ear. "Listen Rachel, normally you're pretty sharp. But this time you made a big mistake."

Abruptly Rachel got up and went over to the secret door. She pushed it open and slipped inside. As the door snapped shut behind her, she heard Becca say, "Man, she is getting bizarre."

If she had a boat of her own, she would have gotten into it, revved up the engine, and driven over to the island. She stood on the beach, gripping her arms, wishing with all her might that Michael would hear her soundless call, drive up on his boat, and sweep her away. She would tell him about Paul's spying. He would agree with her, she knew. He understood about the need to preserve secrets at any cost, about preserving independence. And privacy.

I did it for freedom, she told herself fiercely. *I need that freedom.*

At last, not wanting to arouse suspicions, she stalked back to the house and started doing her chores before supper. She had a headache.

She took over preparing dinner single-handedly. When each of her sisters trickled in to do her assigned chore, she said, "Leave me alone. I'll do it," in a cold voice. And each sister readily gave her the space she desired. Only Melanie hovered on the edge of the counter for some time, but when Rachel looked up at her, she saw at once that her younger sister had heard about the lie, and was crushed. Unable to deal with this, Rachel turned her back and went on working.

She browned the ground beef, chopped onion, sliced carrots and celery and garlic. She made the broth, seasoned it with fresh spices from the herb garden. She boiled the macaroni, shredded cheese, and tore up lettuce for a salad. She stirred up a new pitcher of iced tea.

While she worked, Brittany and Melanie set the table. She heard her dad come home, but he didn't come into the kitchen. She heard Sallie come in from shopping with the baby boys, and heard Robbie and Jabez start chasing each other around the house. She heard Sallie showing her daughters some new sandals she had bought for them.

"I don't understand how you girls keep wearing out your Sunday sandals so fast," she remarked.

All of this went on around her, but her mind was engaged elsewhere. Meanwhile, she slid dirty dishes and cutting boards into the kitchen sink, wiped up the counters, scrubbed the stains from the stove while the stew cooked. She drained the macaroni. She dressed the salad and slid it onto the end of the counter, for the table setters to carry out.

Then her dad was standing in the kitchen doorway. "Rachel," he said. "I'd like to speak with you in my office."

It was as though she had a commanding officer instead of a father. "I'm cooking," she said.

"Get one of your sisters to finish it for you. I want to see you, now."

Blinking back tears, she pursed her lips and shouted, "Miriam!"

Cheryl came in. "I'll finish dinner, Rachel."

"Thanks," Rachel said distantly, and handed her the wooden paddle she had been stirring the stew with. She shouldered off her apron and hurled it onto the counter.

Down the hallway to the office, she walked, shut the door behind her, and threw herself down in a leather chair, looking out the window at the trees outside. "What?"

Her father looked at her silently. She finally looked over at him, and saw he was holding a thin stack of papers.

"I just received these from your sisters," he said.

He put on his glasses, and picked up the first one and began reading it.

"Dear Dad, Rachel is lying about Paul. I can't tell you why, but she told me that she lied about him. I don't think this is fair. Please don't believe her. Sincerely, Lydia."

He put it down, and looked at Rachel meaningfully. She couldn't move. He picked up the next one.

"Dear Dad, I don't trust what Rachel said she told you about Paul. Paul is a decent, good man, and he wouldn't do such a thing. Love, Miriam."

He read the next letter. "Dear Dad, Paul Fester is a Christian even though he is a Catholic, and I don't think he would ever do such a thing as Rachel said. In Christ, Cheryl."

Going on, he read the others, one by one, "Dear Dad. Please don't take seriously what Rachel said about Paul. I think she was ticked off at him for some other reason, and didn't realize how bad what she said must have come off. I don't think there is a need to look into this matter more closely, but I would advise you to not trust what she has said. I for one do not believe it. Sincerely, Taren."

"Dear Dad, Rachel can be really strange sometimes. I don't know why she said what she said about Paul, but I know it is not true. Love, Rebecca."

"I think Paul is honest and Rachel is lying. Don't believe her. Brittany."

"Dear Dad, Rachel has been very stressed out lately. Please try to understand her. But I don't believe what she said about Paul, and I don't think you should either. In Christ, Melanie."

"In my opinion, you shouldn't listen to what Rachel said about Paul. It's just crazy. Sincerely, Tammy."

"Dear Dad, Paul Fester is good and kind and has been a great teacher. He is also a good friend. We have never seen him do anything like what Rachel said. Please don't make him leave. We love him. Love, Debbie and Linette."

He set these aside and picked up the last one. "Dear Father, Rachel is really, really wacked out. I think what is going on here is that she has a crush on Paul. But I think he already has a girlfriend, so she made up a crazy story about him for spite or something. I wouldn't believe it if I were you. Prisca."

Finished, he looked at her quizzically. The silence stretched between them. At last, he said in a stern voice, "Rachel, it appears to me that you have some explaining to do."

She bit her lip, which was salty with tears, and wished she could push herself into the crack of the chair and disappear.

"You do realize, don't you, that Paul could be charged with sexual assault for what you said about him."

Startled, she looked at her dad. "You're not going to charge him with that, are you?"

"Would you want me to?" he asked.

She sat silently staring at the floor.

"Rachel, despite all of these," her father gestured at the letters, "I am still willing to believe your story if you are telling me the truth. But are you?"

This was the moment. Was she going to stand by her lie, or not?

Trembling, she shook her head, no.

"Then what happened between you and Paul was not as serious as you led me to believe?"

She shook her head, no, again.

"Rachel, why would you set out to destroy a young man's character like that? Do you realize the seriousness of what you said? You could ruin his military record, you could ruin his chances at medical school, you could ruin his life. Our society takes actions like those seriously. I can't believe that you would knowingly damage an innocent man's good name out of spite."

She whispered, "I wouldn't."

She tried to stifle a sob. Her father rose, picked up a box of tissues, went over to her, and handed them to her. She took one, and surprisingly, he put a gentle hand on her shoulder.

"Rachel, why would you do such a thing?"

Would she try to patch things together with another lie? She sobbed, thinking, trying to decide. At last she managed to say, "I was angry at him."

Surely her father would ask her why. And the interrogation would begin. But instead, all he said was, "I see."

She waited, and her father continued, "I think you owe that young man an apology."

Bemused, she merely nodded her head, yes.

Paul was packing.

He was still struggling over whether or not to try to get out of his commitment to juggle at the festival. But there were only a few days left before it ended, and he thought perhaps the coordinator might let him go. He would be losing out more than they would—the last week of the festival was usually the biggest. He would have made quite a bit of money.

But at any rate, he thought he should move to a campsite further away from the Durham's property.

He was still in free-fall, and he was fairly sure that his chances of recovery had smashed to the ground by now.

It hurt. With a deep sigh, he rubbed the miraculous medal on the chain around his neck, and whispered a prayer. He was weary of trusting, but he had to keep trying.

As he took down his tent, he looked over his shoulder, and saw a group of girls winding their way through the woods towards him. The Durham girls. Rachel wasn't with them.

"Hi," Miriam spoke up.

"Hi," he said, folding up the drop cloth from his tent, his face warm with shame. He saw Debbie's lip was trembling. The rest of the girls looked a bit uncomfortable, or shy. They ranged themselves along the edge of the campsite and watched him.

"Are—are you leaving?" Linette asked.

He looked over at her, a bit embarrassed himself. "I'm not sure," he said. "I have to find out if the festival coordinator will let me leave early. I'm supposed to work until the festival ends next week."

"So why are you packing up?"

"I just thought I would move to a different campsite, that's all," Paul said, with an effort to be casual. He glanced at them again.

Miriam was eyeing Cheryl, who nodded at her. Miriam cleared her throat. "Well, we just wanted to come to—express our support."

He looked at them, a bit dubious. "Support for what?"

Tammy, who had never deigned to speak to him before, tossed her golden hair and said, "Rachel told us what she accused you of. We don't agree with what she did. We told our dad so."

Taken aback, he repeated, "You told your dad?"

"We wrote him letters," Debbie said. "It was Mel's idea." Melanie, her eyes red, gave him a tiny smile.

"All of us," Prisca said. She winked at him. "I think Rachel's a bit daft, if you ask me."

Paul blinked, completely astonished by this turn of events. He turned the folded drop cloth over and over in his hands, not sure of what to do.

"So we don't want you to leave," Debbie said. She walked over to him and tugged his hand, as though she were still a small child. "Can you stay?"

"All right," he said, feeling a different kind of warmth spread over his face. In his heart, he felt his grip closing on an unexpected trapeze bar, barely in time. He had been saved. Unconsciously he felt for his miraculous medal to say thank you.

"Can we help you put your tent back up?" Linette asked.

"Uh—sure."

"We used to have a tent like that," Cheryl said. "My dad used to use one to go on his fishing trips."

"Really?" he said. The girls crowded around him, offering advice, picking things up, taking things out, and attempting to help. All in all, it took Paul much longer to set up his tent now than it had been to set it up the first time.

Taren and Liddy ran back to the Durhams' to ask if Paul could come over for supper, and when the reply came back in the positive, he found himself escorted back to the Durham house with a contingent of dark-haired and blond-haired girls. Despite the chatter and friendly banter, he felt a slight discomfort. Rachel was nowhere to be seen.

Colonel Durham met them at the door. He took Paul's hand and shook it, with a creased smile. After the girls went in, he said, "I'm sorry about the trouble you had with Rachel. She has something to say to you, but since dinner's ready, let's eat first." He held up a sheaf of papers. "I thought you might want to know I received these eleven votes of confidence in you. And you have my vote of confidence as well."

Paul hesitated. "Thank you, sir. Then—should I—?"

Colonel Durham nodded. "Carry on, soldier. Carry on."

As they sat down for dinner, Paul saw Rachel come out from the kitchen, her face red and her eyes were puffy. She slipped into a chair on the end of the table and said nothing during the meal.

Afterwards, Colonel Durham said, "Rachel prepared this delicious meal for us, so I suggest the rest of you girls return the favor and clean the kitchen together." He looked at Rachel and nodded at her meaningfully.

Paul saw Rachel blow out her breath and stand up. She abruptly got up from the table and walked out to the front hallway. Colonel Durham looked at Paul and made a slight movement of his head toward Rachel. Paul folded his napkin, and followed Rachel out of the dining room, knowing all eyes were fixed on them both.

eighteen

aul followed Rachel as she walked out to the south side of the house. He hadn't been in this section before. She went down some stone steps to a small herb garden terraced into the ground. It was a very pretty spot, with a stone bench on one side. She tossed her hair over her shoulder and sat down on the end of the bench, her arms folded, her dark lashes lowered over her eyes.

Paul sat down on the other end, and leaned forward, his hands on his knees, looking at the herb garden. It was planted in the shape of a cross, with a sand path around it. It was simple, pristine, and beautiful.

He couldn't look at Rachel. Her competence, skill, and real concern for her sisters made him genuinely admire her. He respected her. But because of this, he knew she was capable of hurting him more than the others could.

"Dad said I needed to apologize to you," she said at last, stiffly.

He watched a tiny white butterfly flit from one plant head to another.

"I'm sorry," she said.

"I forgive you."

There was silence. Finally she heaved a sigh and pushed back her hair. "So, are you going to tell him?" she asked.

Paul turned and met the blue-green eyes that were looking at him resentfully. "I think *you* should tell him," he said

"What? Tell him everything?"

He closed his eyes and nodded. When he looked at her again, she was turned away, shaking her head.

"So that's why you haven't told him? Because you want me to tell him?" she asked, her voice touched with irony.

He nodded again.

165

"You're insane."

He shrugged. "Rachel, how much longer do you think you girls can keep this up before he finds out?"

"We'll see, won't we?"

"It's...perilous."

"Perilous? Don't you mean wrong?"

He shook his head. "There's nothing wrong with taking a midnight boat ride, going to visit friends, and dancing under the moonlight."

"Some people at my church would disagree."

He shrugged. "It's not intrinsically immoral. But what's wrong is that you're doing something like this in secret. Without your parents' knowledge. It's imprudent. And going to that island is courting danger. For yourself, and especially for your younger sisters. You love them, don't you?"

"Yes," she said defensively.

"Then why don't you stop?"

She toyed with her hair for a long moment before she answered. When she did, that smile was on her lips again. "Because I don't think it's dangerous. And even if it is, isn't dying from danger better than dying of boredom?" She laughed shortly.

"You're bored?"

"Yes. Bored with always trying to be good."

"Are you sure you know what goodness is?"

She looked at him curiously. "What is it, then?"

He paused, and thoughts flew through his mind—mountains, trees swaying in the wind, his father kissing his mother, sitting around the supper table with his brothers and sisters, Mass—the beautiful statues, the lovely paintings in the church, the glory of stained-glass windows, the harmony of the liturgy, the haunting of music, the poetry of the human body—

Using phrases he had learned in theology class and read in books, he attempted to articulate what goodness was—its power, its concreteness, above all, its beauty—a tangible, hands-on beauty as well as a spirit-lifting, mind-firing beauty—theology and poetry and philosophy and mathematics and order and the romp of playfulness—new babies and bulbs shooting from the earth and creases on the hands of an elderly lady who had spent her life in service to others—

He knew he wasn't an orator, or a particularly good communicator. He spoke haltingly, rambling, then, gaining certainty from the truth of what he was saying, grew effusive, quoting the saints and poets and prophets, recalling sayings of the popes and philosophers, trying to paint a verbal portrait of what goodness was, and why loving it was so critical.

And Rachel smiled, listened to him, and looked up at the sky. He noticed it was getting dark. The moon would soon be rising.

"Paul," she said softly, and he realized he had been talking for some time without her really listening.

He felt defeated. She had grown up listening to sermons, he realized. Some of them had probably been quite sound, and quite eloquent. But they had no effect on her. Words were not going to win her heart.

He fell silent.

She rose, then turned and looked at him. "Are you still going to follow us?" she asked, a bit mocking.

"Yes."

She lowered her chin and looked up at him. "Michael wouldn't like that, if I told him."

"I suspect you're right. Are you going to tell him?"

She half-smiled, and then changed her tone. "No," she said gravely, her eyes serious. "Because of my younger sisters. They like having you with us."

He felt a surge of frustration with her, and he wanted to stop her from going. But he hadn't chosen that path.

"All right," he said, dropping his gaze to hide his disappointment. She was effectively immunized against preaching, theology, and philosophy. It might hold her interest momentarily, but it couldn't change her heart.

He wondered what there was in the world that could.

The midnight butterfly dress still wasn't done. After putting on the skirt once, Rachel had been dissatisfied with the way it looked. Normally, she wouldn't have cared, but after this much effort, she felt the dress had to be perfect. So she entered into the long process of ripping out stitches and doing the basting over again. And she had decided to alter the neckline. But Prisca's birthday was at the end of the week, and Michael had promised a special party for her. She was determined to wear it by then.

That night, trying to be classic in the 1940's navy blue dress, she strolled out of the cave, a bit nervous. She glanced around to see if Paul was skulking in the bushes. But she couldn't see any sign of him.

"What does he look like?" she asked Debbie in a low voice.

"He's all in black, with a ninja mask that covers his face," Debbie said. "He's very tricky to find. I can never find him until we're in the boat."

"I see," Rachel said thoughtfully, and decided to put all thoughts of Paul out of her mind. He had always seemed determined to be a bridge linking one cosmos with another, refusing to let the world be nicely divided between night and day. A devout Catholic who played the flute as sensually as a pagan god, a clean-cut juggler for kids by day, a ninja bodyguard by night. He didn't fit, and he wouldn't leave her alone. But at least he wasn't stopping her.

Heaving a sigh in frustration, she slid and jumped down to the beach, hearing the motors coming closer. She stood on the wet sand, holding her sandals in her hand. Now there were only four boats instead of five. At least they still had four.

The guys pulled up beneath the willows, then came out to greet the girls and hang out for a few minutes. Pete lit up a cigarette, careful to stand downwind.

Prisca danced down the slope in a short purple dress she had bought last week. "Sallie's taking me to the doctor's," she informed the guys.

"What for?" Pete asked.

"She said I needed a checkup. Tammy thinks they've finally figured out I'm a human disease." She bounced up and down. "Pete, can you give me a smoke?"

Rachel said warningly, "Pete, don't."

"Oh, you party pooper," Prisca scoffed. "It's just one."

"You'll smell," Rachel said.

"Oh, all right."

Rachel turned just in time to see a thin dark shadow slide from the trunk of the willow tree to the boats bobbing in the dark water. She abruptly turned away, and tried to forget she had seen anything.

The ride to the island was uneventful, and Michael and his friends met them at the quay as before.

"You are coming on Friday, aren't you?" he asked Rachel as he gave her a hand up.

"For Prisca's birthday? Of course," she said. "We're all looking forward to it."

"Good," he said, and drew her apart. He said in a low voice, "I'm thinking of inviting a special friend for Prisca. Tell me, do you think she prefers blond or dark-haired men?"

"I can't tell," she said, thinking. "Dark-haired, I think."

"Which do you prefer?" he asked, looking at her, his eyes smoky.

She laughed. "Now that's a loaded question."

"Is it? Or do you prefer another alternative, like brown hair?"

"I prefer nice men, if that's what you're asking," she said coyly, curling her arm around his.

"Good," he said. "Would you dance with me?"

"Sure."

They danced several times that night, and Rachel was hence more distracted than usual. She forgot about looking over her shoulder to detect Paul's presence. To tell the truth, she had forgotten he was there.

Paul sat cross-legged in the crook of his oak tree, aware that Rachel was just below him, swaying in the arms of the master of the island. He felt enormously insignificant just now. Apparently all the girls now knew he was with them, but they barely seemed to care, with the exception of Melanie, Linette, and Debbie.

He couldn't help watching as Michael crooked an arm languidly around Rachel and cupped her face in his hand. Paul caught a glimpse of her green-sapphire eyes flashing up at Michael as a smile toyed about her lips. Paul looked away as they kissed.

How much longer could this go on? he wondered. The magic of the island seemed overarching, seductively irresistible. Even if the girls were to stop coming here, would they ever stop yearning for it, for the forbidden something beyond their reach?

The problem was, he knew, that in the heart of the forbidden fruit was nothing but dust, an empty husk of life, its potential wasted, its soul shriveled into rot. But how much further would Rachel eat into this fruit before she found the bitter core? He didn't want to see that happen to her, but he felt, at times, helpless to prevent it.

He shifted his position on the knobby branches and centered his breathing again. *Trust.*

On the way home, Rachel leaned over the boat, watching Michael's figure until their wake curved around the island, hiding him from sight. Even then, she still sighed, and tried to rouse herself to enter into the talk. Now that Tammy, the other prima donna, was in the boat, Rachel didn't feel the need to always keep the conversation going. Perhaps she would just let her sophisticated stepsister be the queen bee for the evening.

But she was roused out of her reverie when she heard Tammy say, "And Keith was an absolute idiot tonight. Do you know what he did? He was smoking marijuana!"

They were all so close together that the rest of the boat was instantly silent.

"For real?" Rich asked.

"Yes!" Tammy exclaimed, full of incredulous disdain. "Dillon offered him some. Actually, he offered us all some, but we all said no. Keith said no too, but then, when we had started dancing, he went off with Dillon and had some. Pete found him and told him he was a numbskull, and Keith just started cursing him out. What an idiot. Can you believe he's such an idiot?"

There was silence. Alan said, "Keith's parents divorced a year ago. He took it hard."

"He did?" Rachel hadn't known that. Keith had always projected such a cool persona.

"He always takes things hard," Rich spoke up. "He's not a strong person."

"That's why he's had such a rough time," Alan agreed.

The girls looked at each other, and Rachel was consternated. She had never dreamed Keith Kramer, upstanding member of her dad's Bible outreach group, would smoke pot—and with a sinking feeling, she thought, *If I hadn't brought him to the island in the first place, maybe he wouldn't have tried drugs.* But she forced that feeling aside.

"We've got to help him," she said, briskly. "We're friends. We can't just stand by and let him do this."

"Well, what can you do?" Alan looked at her. "You can't stop people from taking drugs. That guy Dillon smokes dope like a freakin' chimney. Keith might not have the money for it himself, but as long as he's around these guys, he's going to be smoking. And maybe doing the harder stuff too, if they give it to him. They have that stuff, too. I've seen it."

Rachel thought. "Then we've got to get him to stop coming," she said at last. A chill swept over her. "Dang it, Tammy, if he was smoking dope, why'd you let Becca and Taren ride home with him? You should have told me."

Immediately all eyes went towards Keith's boat. Rachel saw it, behind them. Keith seemed to be driving normally.

"Oh, come on," Tammy protested. "Can't you smoke marijuana and drive a boat? I mean, people smoke cigarettes when they drive. And it's not like he's driving a car. There's nobody on the bay besides us. It's not like drunk driving, is it?"

"Oh yes it is," Rich said bluntly. "The moron. He should know better."

"We can't let him do this again," Rachel said. The silence began again. Rich shuffled his feet. "I'm friends with him," he said. "I've known him since kindergarten. I'll get him to go do something with me tomorrow night. Alan, you can take more people, can't you?"

"Sure," Alan said. "I'm getting on my dad's case about all the junk he still leaves in here."

Everyone seemed to be relieved by this decision. Rachel felt a flush of admiration for Rich, whom she barely ever talked to, and tried to think of something fitting to say to him. But all she could think of was to reach over and touch his hand. He raised his eyes and she smiled at him. He smiled back, and she thought to herself that she had overlooked someone worthwhile. A slight smart of conscience still irked her, and she looked away.

On Friday afternoon, Paul was juggling the clubs, in a single routine. Debbie and Linette were off exploring the festival, which was now at its height. Today was the busiest day yet, and the crowds had significantly increased. As Paul concentrated on doing a double-cascade fountain with the clubs, he saw a familiar face in the crowd around him. He glanced swiftly between catches and recognized Michael Comus.

The blond man, surrounded by his cronies, was watching his routine, a sardonic smile on his face.

As Paul finished with a bow, Michael approached him. Paul licked his lips as he gathered up his clubs. He recognized Michael, and he guessed that Michael had recognized him. But the problem was, Michael couldn't know that he, Paul, recognized him, Michael.

"So, a juggler," Michael said, stuffing a dollar bill in Paul's basket. "Are you new to this area?"

"Just passing through," Paul said.

"A wandering clown," Michael said, his face mild. "You're the one juggling with the Durham girls. Are you a friend of the family?"

"Sort of. I actually just met them this summer," Paul said, and added casually. "You know them?"

"Oh, to recognize, not necessarily to speak to," Michael said. "I've heard about the young juggling girls, of course. They're quite a local sensation. Picture in the paper and all that. So you trained them?"

"Yes."

"Must be a hard life, being a clown."

"It has its challenges," Paul replied.

"I'm sure," Michael said. Then he added, "I've always hated clowns, actually." He continued to smile. But his eyes were cold and empty.

"Lots of people do," Paul agreed, uncertain. "They get frightened by a man in a funny mask as a kid, and they're scarred for life."

"Yes. That must explain it," Michael mused. He squatted down and picked up one of the clubs. "You juggle these things?"

"Yes," Paul said.

"Like this?" and Michael suddenly threw the club upwards, straight at Paul's face. Paul swiftly caught it, barely in time.

"Oh, sorry," Michael smiled. "Good reflexes."

"Thanks," Paul said, reaching down and gripping the others, taking them out of the man's reach. "Enjoy the festival."

"I am." The blond man strolled back to his companions, who had been standing a bit apart. As Michael reached them, they suddenly convulsed with laughter and walked away.

In a second, Paul was back at the air terminal under the hot desert sun, hearing the soft, high whistle of destruction wafting through the air towards him.

He put away his clubs quietly.

All day Friday, Rachel and the other sisters worked hard preparing for Prisca's birthday. They had a chance to do quite a few things while Sallie took Prisca to the doctor's for her tests. Everyone pitched in to do something. Rachel even had Jabez and Robbie sit down and scrawl some birthday scribbles with crayons on pieces of folded paper.

She was so involved that she was surprised, and a bit annoyed, when her father called her into his office. When she walked in, she was taken aback to find her dad sitting at his desk, his head in his hands. When she shut the door, he lifted his head, and she was even more concerned to see that it looked as though he had been crying. But with her dad, she couldn't be completely sure. She approached him warily.

"Dad, are you okay?"

He looked up at her, and then looked down at his hand. She saw he was holding his cell phone.

"I was checking my voicemail, and deleting old messages. Then I listened to this one message. It was someone talking in a harsh, angry tone of voice. This person was berating someone for being late. I was really offended by what I heard, and I was racking my brains, trying to think of who could have called me and left such a rude, disrespectful message on my phone. Before I deleted it, I listened to it again, and I realized—" he paused. "I realized the caller was me, talking to you, on one of the days when you had the cell phone."

She remembered that day, and looked down at the carpet, silently.

"And what hit me was that the message was indicative of how I talk to you much of the time. I just heard myself, Rachel, for the first time in years."

He looked up at her, and now she guessed that he really was on the verge of tears. "Rachel, I don't blame you for not opening up to a man who has been treating you like that. Can you please forgive me?"

Embarrassed, she swung her foot on the carpet and whispered, "Of course I can, Dad."

He looked at her, and, as if in a dream, tentatively reached out his hand.

She went to him and hugged him, and he held her tightly. Just as she remembered him holding her when she was a little girl. Involuntarily she felt the tears coming, and heard him weeping as well.

"Rachel, I'm so sorry. I wish I could recall each time I've talked to you like that and ask your forgiveness."

"That's okay, Dad," she spoke at last, her voice choking her.

"I was just thinking of the time after your mother died, and how much I depended on you, and how capable you were—it's not right for me to call you scatterbrained the way I did. I've just acquired some bad attitudes, and I want to change them, Rachel."

She nodded, and wiped her eyes. Looking around, she reached for the tissue box, and handed it to him. With a grin that reminded her acutely of how he used to smile at her, he took it.

"See? You're always capable, and aware of what others need. When's the last time I told you that?"

She sniffled herself, and shrugged. "I can't remember."

His shoulders sagged again. "There's part of the problem right there. All this time, Rachel, I've been thinking it was you who were the problem, but I think a big part of it was me and my attitude towards you. I wonder when I began to get off track."

She blew her nose, and said quietly, "I think I know."

"You do? When?"

"When they made you a leader in the church," she said. "You began to get busy. And stressed out, and you weren't as home so often. Even when you came home from a military tour, you still weren't home. You gave so much time to the church. I think it was too much."

He shook his head, looking at her. "So that's how it happened."

"I knew at first it was because you were lonely, after losing Mom. So we tried not to mind. But then even after you met Sallie, you just kept on getting further and further away from us, and more involved with these other people."

She couldn't believe she was saying this to him, and that he was listening to her. Steeling herself, she went on, "You have a big family, Dad. It takes a lot of your time and energy. But you don't have that much time and energy because you're letting yourself being pulled in too many directions."

"Let me ask you this," he said slowly. "Is that why you girls resent our church so much?"

A bit startled, Rachel nevertheless nodded, "I would guess, yes, that's it."

"I see." He sat back in his chair, thinking. After a moment, he looked at her. "There was actually another reason why I called you in here."

"There was?"

"Yes," he leaned forward, a bit uncomfortable. "Today is Prisca's birthday. I'd like to get her a present and I'd like it to be something she really wants. But I'm not sure of what that is. I thought maybe you could give me some ideas."

nineteen

On the last night, the soldier put on his cloak of invisibility and prepared to follow the princesses as before.

—— Grimm

achel chewed on her fingernail, not sure of how diplomatically she could answer this question. Usually Dad got them devotional books on their birthdays. "Something that she really wants?"

He nodded, a bit flustered. "Yes."

Rachel sat up, took a deep breath, and folded her hands in her lap. "Well," she began hesitantly, "what she really, really wants is a manicure and makeup kit."

She held her breath, waiting for the speech about St. Paul and godly women and vain adornments. But instead, her father paused. She could see that he was trying to be open-minded about it.

"Okay," he said, "Where do I get a—what was it you said?"

"A manicure and makeup kit. At the drugstore, they have them on sale for twenty-five dollars, in a silver case that locks. I know that was the one she was wishing she could get." She watched her father carefully.

"Okay," he pulled out a paper and pencil and he wrote.

"Dad, are you really going to get that for her?" she asked, scarcely able to believe what she was seeing.

He glanced up at her, saw her face, and continued writing, smiling a bit jokingly. "She'd never expect to get a gift like that from me in a million years. Might be worth it, just to see the expression on her face, don't you think?"

"I'd say so," she agreed, still half-stupefied.

"Of course, I'm going to ask you to keep this a secret, if that's all right."

"Cross my heart and hope to die."

She paused, and then asked, "Dad? Can I ask you a favor?"

"What's that?"

175

"Could you keep this conversation between us a secret?"

He looked at her, taken aback. "What do you mean?"

"I mean, don't share about it with your men's group, or the pastor, or anyone," she said. "I want it to just be between us. Is that okay?"

"That's important to you?" he asked slowly.

She nodded. She hated it when the personal interactions between family members became fodder for public "sharing" with other people. "I want this to be a secret just between you and me," she said stubbornly.

A bit of understanding came into his face. "All right, Rachel," he said. "It'll stay our secret."

"Thanks," she said, and hugged him again. As she did so, she suddenly remembered her own secret, the sisters' secret, and flushed with shame. Because she wasn't ready to give that up. Not yet.

Awkwardly, she kissed her father on the forehead, squeezed his hand, and said, "I'd better get back to work, if that's all right."

"Sure. I'm going to run out and buy this thing," he said, and stood up as she walked out. "Thank you again, Rachel."

"You're welcome, Dad."

Her face red, she closed the door, feeling a sudden need to get away from him.

Prisca returned in the afternoon with Sallie, beaming with self-importance. "Guess what?" she cried to the twins and Rachel and Melanie. "I'm actually really sick!"

"No!" Tammy exclaimed, but Prisca nodded. She ticked off on her fingers. "I'm allergic to wheat. I'm allergic to dairy products. In addition, the doctor thinks I'm developing a glucose intolerance problem. He said it's a good thing they caught it now, because it might turn into diabetes."

"Oh my gosh," Taren breathed, and then her face fell. "That means you can't have any birthday cake." They had just finished the cake about half an hour ago, frosting and everything.

Prisca shrugged. "Oh, that's okay. I'm just so relieved to find out there's actually something wrong with me." She laughed. "Isn't that funny? But I knew I was always feeling sick and irritable and moody, and I never knew why, and now it turns out there was a reason."

Rachel shook her head, dumbfounded. "Then Paul was right," she said. "That's just what he guessed."

"What?" Prisca yelped. "Is that the reason Sallie made the appointment for me?"

Sallie, who had come in from putting away her purse, nodded. "It is. Paul said something to Rachel, and Rachel talked to me. Then I talked to Paul, and your dad and I thought we should have you checked out."

Rachel was still in wonder. "So Paul was right. He said he thought you should get some allergy tests and blood sugar tests. He wants to be a doctor himself, you know," she added.

Prisca was impressed. "Well, you have to invite him to my birthday party as a thank you. That is truly amazing!"

Sallie reminded her, "You have to watch what you eat from now on. I'm going to get you some spelt bread from the health food store and rice cakes. Actually, maybe you should come out shopping with me and pick out food for yourself. We have to make sure you take good care of yourself so your problem doesn't get any worse."

Prisca waved her hands. "Sure, sure. That sounds great. Man, I am just so relieved. I can't tell you—it's like having a weight off my chest. I'm going to go upstairs and change." She hurried off.

Sallie looked at the girls. "Have you already invited Paul to her birthday dinner? No? Well, make sure you do. I think we owe him a lot."

The other girls nodded their heads in agreement. Tammy looked at Taren, "Isn't there a recipe for a wheatless cake somewhere?"

"A wheatless cake? Is there such a thing?" Rachel asked.

"Actually," Sallie drummed her fingers. "There is. I made it for Valentine's Day one year. It's made with eggs and powdered chocolate. It's not half bad. Let me get the recipe."

"I'll go and tell Paul he's invited," Melanie pushed back her chair. "He and the girls are out swimming in the bay."

The family birthday party was an unparalleled success. Paul joined the family for dinner, which was London broil, Prisca's favorite. Prisca herself was radiant in the attention, unabashedly basking in it. But beside that, Rachel noted that Prisca actually seemed more peaceful. The note of tension was missing from her voice.

After dinner, Rachel and the other girls presented her with her first gift—a big basket of cards. "You can look at these on the couch while the rest of us clear the table," Rachel said. "There's one from everyone in the family. We each wrote a card to you describing what we like the most about you."

"Wow! Thanks!" Prisca said, amazed, taking the beribboned basket heaped with pastel envelopes.

"Perhaps while you do that, I could provide some background music," Paul suggested. "I brought over my flute."

"Yes, do," Rachel said, and Prisca heartily agreed.

"And I'll be doing the dishes," Dad said, getting up from his chair.

So Paul sat on a chair perched in a convenient position between dining room and kitchen and played a soft, waffling melody while Prisca sat curled up on the couch, ripping open envelopes and reading cards. The sisters heard her giggling over some of them. But others she spent a long time over, reading slowly. Apparently, she was very touched.

Dad, who had heard about the project at the last minute, had disappeared into his study a half hour before dinner and come out with a big ivory envelope, which he added to the basket. "Whose idea was this?" he had asked.

"Rachel's," Debbie had volunteered, and Dad, surprised, had beamed at his oldest daughter.

"Now that was a great idea," he said appreciatively.

They didn't talk much while doing the kitchen, since everyone preferred to listen to the flute music. Everyone, that is, except Jabez and Robbie, who were as boisterous as usual. Brittany bundled them out to the garage and played monster with them until everything was done.

When Prisca finally finished the cards, her face was wet but her eyes were full of light. "I love you all!" was all she said, and gave each of them a hug. Rachel couldn't help noticing she hesitated at hugging Dad. Instead, she said something in his ear. He smiled at her and said, "You're very welcome," and kissed her. Then he walked back to his office.

Prisca sat down at the head of the table beside Rachel. "Well!" she whispered, raising her eyebrows. "You should have read what Dad wrote! Sometimes even I get surprised!"

Rachel couldn't help grinning at the thought of how much more surprised Prisca was about to be.

About an hour later, Rachel looked out the window. The family party was winding down, and the moon was rising. Dad was sitting on the couch with Sallie, watching Prisca, who was sitting on the floor, holding the silver manicure-makeup kit like a treasure on her lap. Prisca was painting Linette's nails pale pink. Rachel was reminded of parents watching their child open her first Christmas presents. Jabez was asleep on the couch, his fat arm thrown up over his face, his cherub mouth open in tiny breaths. The other girls were watching a video on the computer with Robbie.

Paul was packing up his flute. "I'll say goodnight now," he said, and went around, shaking hands and giving Prisca a hug, as she insisted.

Rachel watched the sky darken, and felt the shimmer of excitement run through her. Not too long now, and Prisca's second party would begin. And the midnight butterfly dress was finished.

"Rachel?"

She turned, and Paul was standing there, his flute case in his hand. His dark eyes were somber.

"Good night."

"Good night," she said, and gave him a brief side hug, the sort that she gave publicly to male church members. Tonight she had started to like him again.

"Meet me in the herb garden before you go tonight?" he asked softly.

"All right," she whispered back, guarded.

She wondered what was up with him as he turned and walked out.

But accordingly, she got out of bed early, before the other girls had started to get ready. "I'm going down now. I'll see you there," she whispered to them, disappearing into the secret stairwell.

Down in the cave, she had prepared a special toilette for herself. She brushed her hair, and using the battery lamp, applied her makeup judiciously. She had already put on black nylons and a slip upstairs. Now she slid into the midnight butterfly dress with a luxurious sigh. The satin whispered over her, and like a butterfly's cocoon, transformed her from ordinary beauty to extraordinary splendor. The short cap sleeves curled back over her shoulders, embroidered sporadically with glass beads that winked in the light. She had appliquéd a piece of darker blue satin, cut from a stained dress-up dress, to the full black skirt so that it cut across her front in a graceful swathe, studded with more clear glass beads. The effect was like scattered dewdrops.

Eagerly she zipped up the back and strapped on her black sandals, which she had decorated for this occasion with glittering silver curlicues of fabric paint. Sadly, there was no full-length mirror to see herself in, but she knew, she could feel, the phantasmagoric change.

Like a glittering shadow she passed through the woods up to the lawn, feeling herself growing more graceful as she moved. A good dress, she thought, made you walk like a lady. It was nearly impossible to slouch.

She approached the gray mist of the herb garden, which Sallie had planted for her prayer times. Rachel found it convenient for private conversations, since you could neither see it from the house nor hear anything that was going on there—and vice versa. As she entered the garden, she heard the soft lowing of a flute once more, and knew that he was waiting.

He was sitting cross-legged on the bench, crouched over his flute. She saw he was all in black, a black half mask, black shirt, and his usual black pants and soft shoes that fit his feet. Once again, she thought of Pan, but said nothing. As she drew near, he ceased, and looked up at her. For a long moment, he did not speak. Then, he set down his instrument, got to his feet in one fluid moment, and took off his black mask. But she couldn't see his expression in the dimness.

"You wanted to see me?" she queried, swaying her hips slightly, a tad impatient.

"Yes," he said. "Did you make that dress, Rachel?"

She nodded. "I did."

"It makes you look—" he began, and halted. After a second, he said, in a lower voice, "I was going to say you look beautiful, but you always look beautiful. I don't know how to say that it's amazingly increased your beauty without sounding trite." He paused. "So I won't try."

"Do I look like the Queen of Sheba?" she couldn't help asking.

"But more beautiful."

"Thank you," she half-smiled, and reclined on the seat, putting one elbow on the arm of the bench. "So what do you want to tell me?"

He sat down on the ground, holding his mask in his hands. Now she saw his face was growing uneasy.

"I wanted to ask you not to go to the island tonight," he said quietly.

"But we can't not go," she said. "Michael's having a special party for Prisca."

"I know," his voice was low. "That's what worries me."

She stared at him. "You really don't trust him, do you?"

"No, I don't," he said.

"Michael is a very nice man."

"'Nice' is not the same thing as 'good,'" he said.

"What's the difference?" she said, irate. "You're not making sense."

"Rachel, please. I know you don't have much of a desire to listen to me, but I just have—a bad feeling. A very bad feeling. So I wanted to ask you to try to keep the girls here tonight."

She studied her polished nails. "I'm sorry, Paul, but that's impossible," she said.

He sighed deeply, as though he were in pain. "I knew you'd say that," he said simply. "I just thought I would ask anyway."

Perturbed, she said, "You *are* coming, aren't you?"

"Yes."

"Good." She looked up at the moon. "I should go soon."

"All right." He moved, and before she realized it, he had vanished into the shadows. Amazed, she got up and turned this way and that, but he was gone.

Unsure of what to do, she said softly, "I'll see you there." And hurried back to the cave.

The other girls were downstairs now and dressing. "Okay, the birthday girl gets first dibs on dresses," Tammy was saying.

"You can wear my brown tank dress," Taren said generously.

Prisca wavered, her hand hovering over the trunk of evening dresses. Then she plunged down and brought up a cream v-neck dress with a collar and short sleeves. It had belonged to the Durham girls' mother.

"I think I'll wear Mom's dress tonight," she said.

The sisters were a bit surprised but agreed that it would look stupendous on her. Despite her flippancy with Paul, Rachel was secretly relieved that Prisca hadn't chosen to flaunt her endowments tonight.

"Rachel, you look magnificent!" Cheryl gasped, catching sight of the dress. Rachel flushed, realizing that she would seem more dressed up than Prisca. But Prisca didn't seem to mind.

"She is gorgeous," the birthday girl declared, creasing the cream collar on her own dress. "Rachel, the dress suits you completely. Make sure you stay away from Michael tonight!"

There were titters all around, and Rachel said, "All right, let's hurry it up! We don't want to keep the guys waiting!"

After making sure that no one was dallying, she made her way down to the beach carefully (she was wearing heels tonight) to await the boats. Soon a half-dozen of the other girls joined her, including Prisca, who was preening herself in delight. When they heard the motor of a boat approaching, Prisca actually bounced up and down with anticipation.

But as the sound drew nearer, the sisters stared in dismay. Instead of three boats, there was only one, Alan's boat.

Rachel drew close to the willows as Alan pushed his boat towards the shore and tied up.

"What's going on?" she asked.

Alan jumped out of the boat and pushed aside the willows to get out on to the beach. "Girls, I'm really, really sorry," he said. "Taylor's dad is having a midnight fishing expedition, and Keith and Pete's dads are going. None of us knew about it—Pete's dad just told him at dinner. And Keith wants to go out and do something with Rich, Pete and Taylor, and I'm supposed to join them. But I know you girls have that party tonight, so I thought I would drive the boat over for you to use."

Rachel was struck by his open-handedness. "Alan, that's very trusting of you, and very generous. "

"No problem," he nodded. "I know you'll be careful with it. I cleaned all the junk out of it—I think it should hold you all. It's only supposed to hold ten people, but it's a calm night, and I don't think you'll have too much trouble. I know you know how to drive it, Rachel."

"Sure," Rachel said. "Do you need a ride back?"

"Nah. I can walk back to my house. It's not far. Besides, there'll be less people in the boat that way."

"How can we get it back to you?" Rachel asked.

"Just leave it on your beach, and I promise I'll come back and get it before sunrise."

Rachel looked at the other girls. They were clearly disappointed, but Prisca shrugged.

"We'll miss you, Alan."

"Thanks. Like I said, I'm really sorry this came up. We were all looking forward to it." He handed Rachel the keys.

"Why don't you just show me everything, just in case?"

"Okay." He and Rachel started towards the boat, but Debbie and Linette barged ahead of them and jumped in first. The rest of the girls followed.

As usual, there was some scrambling about in the dark to get places.

"Shoot! Sorry, I stepped on someone's foot," Alan's voice came through the dimness.

"It was mine," Debbie piped up.

"If that was you, why didn't you yell?" he asked in disbelief.

"I'm trying to learn to be tough," Debbie said.

Alan turned on the dashboard light and showed Rachel the controls. "And just in case," he said, "Here's the emergency gear. There are flares here—you break them to light them—and also there's an alarm. You turn it on here. That's if you're stranded, or sinking, or attacked by pirates, or whatever. It's pretty loud."

"Awesome," Rachel put her hands on the steering wheel and felt ready to go. "Thanks for setting this up for us, Alan."

"No problem. Like I said, I'm sorry about the mess-up. Save a piece of cake for me."

"I'll save you mine, since I can't eat any," Prisca informed him.

Alan scrambled back onto the shore, and the rest of the sisters got into the boat. It was congested. All the seats were full, and some sat on the floor. Alan untied the boat and gave it a heave forward, and they drifted out of the willows towards the island. After they were sufficiently away from the shore, Rachel started the motor and thought suddenly, *I wonder if Paul made it on board.* Unexpectedly alarmed, she looked over her shoulder. After a brief search, she turned back, stifling a laugh. Paul was hunched up in the back corner of the boat, a black lump, and Linette and Debbie were sitting on his back.

The other sisters apparently didn't notice or care to notice. As they chugged through the water, the boat noticeably dragging with its overload, the sisters chattered about the usual things, with eager anticipation. Rachel concentrated on driving the boat, only half listening.

When they neared the portico, the girls fell silent. The stone steps were lit with small candles, and the house itself was ablaze with light.

twenty

And the princesses disembarked and went up to the faery palace, all lit as if for a festival, and the soldier invisibly followed them.

— Grimm

achel and her sisters stared in awe. Michael and a group of men the quay, waiting for them. As Rachel pulled up, Michael stepped forward. "Throw me the rope," he said. "I'll tie up."

He was more dressed up, with a gray silk shirt and a blue jacket, his hair slicked back—all in all, he looked even more handsome than usual.

He gave a hand to Prisca, the first to step off the boat. "The birthday queen. My, you look radiant tonight."

"Thank you, Michael," Prisca said. With her hair swept softly back into a sophisticated bun at the nape of her neck, Rachel thought her younger sister looked older than her now-sixteen years.

"But where are the others?" Michael asked, helping the other sisters out of the boat. "Alan? Keith? Pete?"

"They couldn't come," Cheryl said, and told them of the last minute-change in plans.

Michael's face fell. "Well, then it doesn't work as well as I thought," he said. "I promised everyone a dance partner tonight, but seeing that the other fellows are missing, we'll be short, just as we usually are."

"That's okay," Tammy said loyally. "We're used to having fun here, and we can do the same tonight."

"I'm sure you will," Michael said, giving an arm up to Rachel. "Debbie, Linette, aren't you coming?"

"We're just fixing our nails," Debbie called up. Neither of them had moved from their 'seat,' and both were busy with nail files. "We'll come out in a minute."

"Suit yourself," Michael said, turning away. "Rachel, you look ravishing. Prisca, enchanting. Come and meet my friends."

Rachel looked around. Dillon, Mark, and Brad were still here, of course. Rachel had noted that the guests of the rich seemed to stay on indefinitely. *I can understand why,* she thought.

The new guests were introduced as fraternity brothers of Michael's. "Rachel, meet Craig and Todd. And Prisca, meet Brandon."

Brandon had a smooth, handsome face, dark hair, and large blue eyes. He was young looking, even though Rachel was sure he had to be at least twenty-five. He took Prisca's hand and shook it, flashing a movie star's grin. "Hi, Prisca."

"Hi," Prisca breathed, her acquired sophistication temporarily melting. Michael winked at Rachel.

"Let's go up to the house," he said.

He took Rachel's arm and Brandon took Prisca's arm, and Michael led them across the portico to the stone steps, which were lit with candles in paper bags. The other guys took two girls each. Casting a glance backwards, Rachel saw that the other girls had immediately paired up with their buddies. *Good,* she thought. Then she looked around at the enchantment they were entering.

As they approached the house, it seemed to stretch and broaden before them. Rachel made out a veranda that wrapped itself around the three-story house. There were numerous windows, most of them lit. As they climbed the last of the stone steps, three broad wide steps led up to the house itself, to French doors opening out on to a wide deck.

The other girls couldn't help oohing and aahing as they approached the house, but Rachel was silent, entranced by the beauty. Michael led her through the doors to a living room where a buffet table was set out. Candles flickered in silver candlesticks over a generous repast of appetizers and desserts, with a round white birthday cake in the center, studded with sixteen candles. Jazz music came softly from hidden speakers.

The girls exclaimed over the preparations, and Michael said, "First things first," and lit a wooden taper from the candles, then lit the birthday candles on the cake.

They all sang, "Happy Birthday!" and Prisca enthusiastically blew out the candles, laughing and waving away the smoke. "I'm getting so old!" she panted.

Michael cut her the first slice, put it on a paper napkin, and handed it to her. She thanked him, and then at once, all the sisters remembered.

"Oh my gosh!" Prisca gasped first. "Michael, I'm so sorry—I can't eat this. I went to the doctor's today, and he told me I have a wheat allergy and glucose intolerance."

"You're kidding," Michael said slowly, and Rachel prayed he wasn't angry.

"No, I wish I was, oh, I wish I was!" Prisca moaned. But she looked over the other food and brightened. "But there's so much here I'm sure I'll be fine. And this does look so delicious. You all will have to eat an extra piece for me. Brandon, would you start with this one?"

She went on so gaily, slicing the cake for the rest of them, and Rachel observed the cloud on Michael's brow pass.

"A wheat allergy?" he said in a low voice to Rachel. "Is that true?"

"Yes, it is," Rachel said. "She just came back from the doctor's today. She wasn't allowed to eat the birthday cake we had made her at home, but Cheryl whipped up a wheatless chocolate cake for her."

"I wish I had known," Michael said, critically appraising the food. "There's not much here she can eat."

"Oh, don't worry. I'm sure she'll be fine, like she said," Rachel assured him.

The group eagerly started on the food, and after Rachel had eaten a bit, Michael looked at her and said, "Care to dance?"

"Of course," she said, looking around. There didn't seem to be space to dance in the crowded room.

"Out here," he said, and led her out another set of French doors to a shaded stone porch that ran off in both directions. The music was louder outside, an inviting melody.

It was captivating, but Rachel was aware of the need to keep the buddy system going. Perhaps Paul's intuition was affecting her. *Where was Paul now?* she wondered as she said, "Let's see if Prisca wants to join us."

"Why not?" Michael said, a faint smile on his face. Rachel had thought that he had observed the mechanics of the buddy system early on, but it didn't seem to bother him.

Rachel approached Prisca, who was perched on the edge of a chair talking to Brandon, who seemed to be engrossed in every word she was saying. Rachel didn't particularly like the way he was looking at her younger sister, despite his good looks.

"Prisca, you want to dance with us?" she asked, and Prisca stood up, dusting potato chip crumbs daintily off her dress. "Of course!" she said, and glanced at Brandon. "If that's all right with you."

"Absolutely," he inhaled, and took her hand.

Rachel noticed that Tammy and Dillon and Taren and one of the new guys followed them out onto the porch. The twins' buddies followed them loyally and stood by the door, watching. Michael swung Rachel into the dance, and said, "By the way, that's an exquisite dress you're wearing."

"I made it," she admitted, since he wasn't likely to ask.

"Really?" he raised his eyebrows. "A girl of hidden talents." He twirled her around. "Just as I suspected."

The dance moved around them, and Rachel felt a glow of appreciation. She basked in the dance, and forgot momentarily about buddies and worries and apprehensions. Her dress swirled around her, the blue and black satin glinting, the glass beads flashing. Michael seemed to appreciate her dancing as well.

"You're exceptional," he said to her.

After a dance or two, she tired, and Michael nestled her in his arms and danced lightly, humming to her. "Want to go for a walk?" he asked softly.

Her gaze traveled to Brandon and Prisca. She noticed Brandon was leading her sister, strolling around the bend of the house, following the veranda. "Sure," she said, and instinctively followed Brandon and Prisca.

Michael didn't seem to mind. So they walked, and the music followed them. "You must have speakers all the way around the house," she remarked.

"Actually, we do. They're in the trees. It's convenient for large parties," he said.

"You can't see them at all," she said, after looking around.

"There's one right there," he said, pointing, putting his arm around her.

She couldn't see, but noticed then that he had moved his face closer to hers. The closeness was invigorating. She sighed, and he held her.

Then she became aware that Brandon and Prisca were out of sight. Again, she wondered where Paul was. "Shall we go on?" she asked, after allowing the moment to politely linger.

"Certainly."

They strolled around the corner of the deck, and Rachel noticed that there was still no sign of Prisca and Brandon.

"Rachel."

"Yes?"

"Would you dance with me again?"

"Okay."

He held her and twirled her again, then pulled her back into himself. But this time he put his face next to her and kissed her. She enjoyed the kiss, but when she tried to pull back, he kept going. It was different. She began to decline, but he put his finger under her chin, and said, "Rachel, aren't we on this road together?"

"Yes," she said, uncertain.

"Then let me take you to the next step."

He lowered his lips upon hers, but this time she turned her face away.

"What's wrong?" he asked gently.

She murmured something incoherent.

He traced her collarbone gently. "I want you to want to go forward with me, Rachel. Lovely Rachel."

"I'm not sure if I want to yet," she said.

"Is it you talking to me, Rachel?" he asked softly, "Or is it guilt? Or religion? They've taught you all the wrong things. You know that, Rachel."

"I'm not so sure about that," she murmured, trying politely to move his arm from hers. "Maybe we should go back…"

"Rachel," he said, and his voice took on another tone. "Have you been wasting my time?"

Wasting time. She looked up at him, and saw Paul as he sat on the swimming rock, the day he had told her the story about the toys, his eyes hard. *"A smart man doesn't waste his time."*

Michael's eyes were not hard, but they weren't loving, either. There was a coolness to them, a frankness. He wanted to know.

"I hope not," she muttered.

"Have you just been playing me?"

"No!" she objected.

"Then why are you pulling back from me now?"

"Because—" she stumbled, searching for words.

"You don't want to pull back, not deep inside, do you?" She couldn't move his arms. "I know you, Rachel. I see it in your eyes. You want it as much as I do."

His tone had dropped to a whisper as he lowered his head, but she raised her voice to a slightly above normal pitch.

"No, no—I don't—Paul—Please!"

"What did you say?"

"I mean, Michael," she whispered, her face red. But Michael was clutching her arms now, searching her eyes, boring into her. He no longer looked so nice.

"I meant, Michael," she said faintly, again, and tried to disentangle herself. But she was trapped now, she realized. She wasn't going to move unless he wanted her to.

He seemed to make a decision, and bent over her again. "Perhaps it's better for you if you struggle," he whispered, and she yelped and tried fruitlessly to move away from him. Then she heard an extra beat to the music—the sound of feet softly landing on the stone near her.

"Let her go," a measured voice said.

Rachel's heart leapt. Michael twisted around to see who had spoken, and then Rachel had a clear view. A masked man in black stood there, his stance defiant and ready.

"Who are you?" Michael swore.

"Let her go," Paul's voice came calmly through the mask.

"Daddy's hired bodyguard?"

"I said, let her go."

"Get off of my property."

Paul took a step forward and put a hand on Michael's shoulder. "Not until—"

Michael turned suddenly and threw a roundhouse punch at Paul's face, releasing Rachel's arms. What happened next was almost too quick for Rachel to comprehend.

She saw Paul step to the side while neatly grabbing Michael by the arm and the back of the skull, giving him a deft twist. Having missed Paul, Michael was thrown forward by the force of his own punch and landed head over heels onto the stone pavement. From Rachel's viewpoint, Paul had barely moved, and yet Michael was sprawled on his back, smarting.

But he leapt back on his feet with surprising quickness, his face red. "Someone thinks they're a ninja," Michael panted. He rose into what Rachel could recognize as a karate stance, defensive but geared up to attack.

There was a pause, and then Michael came forward, a challenging expression on his face, throwing small, rapid punches at Paul without making any contact, daring Paul to respond. Paul retreated sideways, his palms open, his fingers spread out, his eyes fixed on the center of Michael's body. It was clear he was waiting for Michael to stop feinting and make a real attack. Rachel wondered briefly why Paul didn't try to punch Michael back—some of Michael's blows were coming very close.

Then abruptly Michael leapt forward, his foot darting up at Paul's face. Apparently expecting this, Paul merely stepped backwards, blocking the kick with a quick dab of his hands. Michael continued to drive forward with incredible energy, swiftly kicking with one leg then the other, while Paul continued to bat the kicks away with his hands and forearms, his face concentrated. Michael made a half-kick at Paul's face, then swiftly bent his knee and kicked Paul in the chest. Surprised, Paul stumbled backwards, and Rachel caught her breath. Viciously Michael leapt forward, driving down his leg to stomp on his opponent.

But Paul let himself fall, and something else happened that Rachel almost didn't see. The next instant, Michael was on the ground again, his other leg caught between Paul's legs. Somehow Paul had redirected the kick and thrown him off balance again.

Paul rolled over and got to his feet neatly, but didn't attack Michael, even though the other man was still on the ground. *Why doesn't he get him now?* Rachel wondered intensely, still trying to regain her composure. She had retreated to a safe distance but couldn't take her eyes off the fight. "Get him, Paul," she whispered.

But Paul seemed to feel he didn't have to expend energy in attacking. He merely kept his eyes on his opponent, and seemed to be waiting for something.

Michael got to his feet like a tiger, his eyes flashing, breathing hard. Now he drove forward with a shout, kicking, punching and swinging in a deadly rhythm. But Paul did not retreat. Instead, he stayed close to his opponent, moving around him, tossing Michael's fast-paced punches and kicks aside as though he were juggling Michael's limbs. It barely seemed as if he were fighting, merely playing a complicated game where Michael provided the momentum. Around and around they went, Michael screaming and throwing punches and kicks, Paul merely sidestepping and tossing away his opponent's punches. Rachel, bewildered, had just begun to think that Paul really was playing around when suddenly the tableau froze. Paul had caught one of Michael's punches at the wrist and elbow and had twisted his arm over.

Now he immobilized his opponent by pressing steadily down on the back of Michael's elbow, so that Michael grunted with the sudden pain, unable to move. His face twitched, and Paul, his expression intent, began slowly to force Michael to the ground.

But just as Rachel was sure that Paul had won, Michael suddenly lurched forward, yanked his trapped elbow up and jabbed Paul in the stomach while kicking him in the leg. Paul caught his breath and fell back, stunned, and Michael was free.

With a snarl, Michael raced forward for the kill, and Rachel cried out.

Seeing him coming, Paul rolled backwards in one of his characteristic tumbles. In a flash, he had caught one of Michael's arms, put a foot in Michael's ribs, and thrown his opponent over his head. Michael landed flat on his back, his roar turning abruptly into an "oof!"

Both of them were winded, but Paul got to his feet first, a little more slowly than before. Once again, he did not attack Michael, but instead leaned forward, waiting, his hands on one of his knees, trying to catch his breath.

Michael rolled over, a mixture of rage and bewilderment on his face. Seeing Paul's unprepared stance, he seized the moment. With surprising speed, he was on his feet and closing in on Paul before Rachel understood what was happening.

But Paul was not completely caught unawares, although he had no time to block the blow. He barely ducked Michael's punch, and spun around, his arms swinging. As he twisted past Michael, one of his arms caught the man squarely in the eye. Michael fell to the ground like a stone.

"Oops," she heard Paul say.

The next thing Rachel knew, Paul was leaning over Michael, turning him over and examining him.

"I wish I hadn't done it that way," he was saying.

Rachel recovered, ran forward and seized Paul's arm.

"Why not?" she exclaimed.

"I think I gave him a black eye. He's not going to like that. Not at all."

"Who cares? He's a jerk!" She tugged him forward. "Come on! We have to find Prisca!"

It had all been a ploy on Michael's part, she realized. He and Brandon had planned to split up the sisters so that he could have his way with Rachel. And where were Brandon and her younger sister now?

Her heart in her mouth, she raced around the veranda, around the house, searching and calling for Prisca. But there was no answer and no sign of them.

Paul was close on her heels. "What do you want me to do?"

"I've got to find the others. Follow me," she said.

She hurried back to the front, where the party had been. When she and Paul reached the living room, the music was still playing, but the buffet area was deserted. Rachel's heart tightened in her chest. "Oh no," she prayed. "Please no."

Maybe Michael's net had been stretched out even further than she had imagined. All her sisters—and Debbie, Linette, and Melanie, so innocent —

"They could have gone into another part of the house," Paul was saying. "There are lights on all over the place."

"But suppose they're split up—" Rachel was thinking rapidly. She had to get all her sisters back here immediately, so she could get them home. Her eyes fell on a white plastic disk on the ceiling. "Is that a fire alarm?" She pointed.

"Yes," Paul said, catching her idea.

Quickly she seized a handful of paper napkins and thrust them in the flame of the candlesticks. The napkins caught fire quickly and Paul blew some of them out to create smoke. Rachel let the rest keep burning on the buffet and waved a handful of the smoking mass under the fire alarm. A shrill beeping pierced the air.

"Paul," she said. "Go outside and as soon as my sisters start coming out, get them down to the boat as fast as you can."

"Right," he said, and vanished into the shrubbery.

She lit more napkins and threw them on the table, then began shrieking, "Fire! Fire! The buffet's on fire!"

She was answered by footsteps thundering up steps. A door exploded open and Todd, Craig, and Tammy burst into the room.

"The napkins are on fire! The candles—!" Rachel screamed, pointing. "What can we do?"

"I'll take care of it," Todd said, and he and Craig began trying to douse the fire.

She looked at Tammy and said abruptly, "Where are the other girls?"

"Downstairs. We were all playing pool."

"Where's Prisca?"

"I don't know—I thought she was with you."

"Get the others and get down to the boat, quick."

Tammy dodged downstairs past other guys who were coming up, and shouted, "Everyone upstairs! Fire!"

Rachel seized the first girl who came up—Brittany—and said in her ear. "Get down to the boat, quick, and don't stop." Brittany obeyed, and Rachel sent Miriam, Debbie, Liddy, Becca, Cheryl, Melanie, Linette, and Taren down after her. By now the smoke was filling the room.

"Let the guys take care of the fire! Where's Prisca?" Rachel shouted again, coughing and dragging Tammy to the door.

Just then Prisca and Brandon hurried into the room, exclaiming. Rachel herded Prisca out the French doors, and pulled along Tammy, who seemed to want to linger.

"But the fire—" Tammy protested as she was yanked down the steps.

"—was an excellent diversion!" Prisca exclaimed, laughing. "Good thinking Rachel!"

"Where were you?" panted Rachel, her black skirt puffing around her as they hurried.

Prisca's laughter was almost uproarious. "In the kitchen!—Not in a bedroom—thank God! I knew what Brandon was about so I told him I was starved and asked if I could make—an omelet," Prisca gasped. "It worked! He believed me. Luckily—they had eggs there—and I was chopping onions—and talking his ear off—when the alarm went off."

"Very good," Rachel breathed as they reached the portico. "Now go!"

They sprinted across the stone pavement to the quay. Paul had Debbie and Melanie by the hands and was helping them run towards the boat. The others were getting in. They had escaped from Michael's net. They were going to make it.

Looking back, she saw several guys leaping down the steps. She thought she recognized Michael in the lead, his face a sheet of angry incredulity, and she couldn't help smiling despite her fear.

Quickly she leapt over the other scrambling girls and into the pilot's seat. Luckily, she had left the key in the engine. "Hurry up, everyone!" she begged. The last person, Tammy, got in.

"Untie the boat you idiot!" Miriam screamed, and Rachel, about to turn on the ignition, realized she had forgotten.

"I'll get it," Paul said, and jumped out of the boat to the pier where the boat was tied.

He pulled at the rope, but it wasn't coming loose, and the pursuers were nearing the end of the steps. "Michael tied it," Debbie cried, and Rachel's heart chilled.

"Start the engine!" Paul yelled, and Rachel obeyed instantly, her foot hovering over the accelerator. Paul yanked, and a loop came loose. He swiftly untangled it and unwrapped it. The first of the guys was tearing across the portico towards him. He reached for Paul, but Paul merely shrugged him aside, and the guy fell splashing into the water.

Paul tossed the rope free into the boat. "Go!" he shouted, standing up and starting to jump as Rachel hit the accelerator.

But hands seized him around the waist as he leapt forward, and caught off balance, he twisted around, and fell.

It had happened so fast that it had an air of unreality. The girls stared back, dazed, as the dock receded rapidly behind them, and Paul, back on the quay, disappeared beneath a crowd of men.

"Paul!" Debbie screamed.

Her voice was drowned in a general wail. Rachel's vision clouded, and she felt her hands trembling on the steering wheel. Viciously she forced her mind free and pushed hard on the gas.

We have to get help, she thought. *And fast.*

But the boat was still heavy and slow, and it seemed like she was caught in a limbo of immobility, surging towards a house that never got any closer. The effect was heightened by the fact that she was surrounded by weeping and commotion, including her own.

"Quiet!" she shouted at last, and the sisters subsided. She had rounded the bend towards their house, and the quay was out of sight.

"When we get to shore," she said, "everyone needs to run upstairs as fast as you can, and get Dad, and the police, and get them back over to the island quick."

"We tell them everything?" Cheryl asked, the weight of this sinking in quickly.

"We tell them everything," Rachel said, abruptly wiping her eyes. "Like we should have done before," she said. "Prisca! Come here!" Her younger sister put her head near hers. "Make sure you tell Dad everything. Make sure he knows."

Prisca quavered, "Okay," uncertainly. *She'll understand in a moment*, Rachel thought.

They were drawing near the shore, at long last. "I'm not going to dock," she said. "Buddies, stick together. Jump off into the water, get to the shore, and RUN!"

The sisters splashed into the water, the boat listing to one side as they did so. Rachel leaned the other way to steady it. They floundered to the shore, the older ones holding the hands of the younger ones. Rachel counted them all, and as soon as the eleventh one had reached the shore, she pushed her foot down on the gas and yanked the steering wheel sharply, peeling around in a spray of foam.

"Rachel! Where are you going?" she heard cries behind her, but she didn't look back. Her tears flew behind her into the wind. She was going back for Paul.

twenty-one

And the princesses saw that their secret was known and there was no point in farther concealment.

—— Grimm

aul," Michael's voice hovered in the air above him. "So that's who you are. I should have guessed."

They had torn off his mask. Paul, held down by six men, looked up, and saw a slow smile spreading across the blond man's face.

"He's the one who gave me this," Michael said to his buddies, lifting his face to the moonlight. Paul could see the beginnings of a dark bruise swelling on his cheek.

"Let's give him one of his own," Craig said, squeezing his hand into a fist. "Or do you want to do the honors?"

"No," Michael put a hand out. "We can have him arrested for trespassing and assault. There's no need to bloody him up. What we want is something more like this." And Michael punched Paul in the stomach, and his friends laughed in surprise.

"Good one, Comus," Craig said while Paul tried to recover his breath. "How about we get going with turning him over to the police?"

"But what about the girls?" Brandon asked, looking at the escaping boat. Behind them, Mark was crawling out of the water, dripping wet.

Michael shrugged. "They won't tell anyone. Their father is a strict fundamentalist Christian. He'd throw them out of the house if he even thought they were out at night. No, I think we're safe."

His eyes wandered over Paul and he smiled again. "Paul, on the other hand, is just passing through town. I saw him at the festival yesterday. He's a juggling clown."

The others chuckled. "Ooh, a ninja clown!" Craig chortled. "This is going to be great!"

"Get him up," Michael said, and Paul found himself roughly heaved to his feet. Craig and Todd still held onto his arms.

Michael reached down and nonchalantly picked up a life preserver that hung on a hook in the quay. He flipped open a pocketknife and cut the rope off the life preserver. Coiling it around his arm, he said, "Bring him up to the heliport," and tossed the life preserver aside.

Craig twisted Paul's arm behind his back painfully and moved him forward. They pushed him up the narrow stone steps that led through the woods to the flat ground where the helicopters could land. As they moved upwards through the dappled black of the forest, Paul's thoughts were on the girls. They might be almost home by now. At least they were out of danger. Even though he wasn't.

There was a big helicopter coming into view now, black and insect-like in the moonlight. For a moment, he half-believed that they were going to fly him to the mainland and hand him over to the police. But Michael abruptly turned off to the side, and started to go down into the woods. As Craig and Todd started to force him to follow, Paul knew his instincts were right— Michael had something completely different in mind.

Seizing his chance, he thrust an ankle between Todd's feet, tripping him, while yanking his arms free and pulling Craig off balance. Todd let go of him and fell, while Paul seized Craig and threw him on top of Todd. Both men crashed to the ground.

It was a fast move, and the four guys ahead of them almost had no idea what happened. Paul was just about to turn on them when two swift punches hit him on either side of his spine, directly on his kidneys. Stunned by the sharp pain, he fell to his knees, and Michael's arm tightened around his neck. Craig and Todd got back up from the ground, red-faced and angry and seized Paul's arms.

He felt a breathy chuckle in Michael's chest. "Got you there, Paul."

Michael yanked Paul's chin upwards and looked at him, breathing hard. The bruise on the blond man's eye showed clearly in the moonlight. "Strip him. And tie him up. This clown is going to provide us with our entertainment for the night."

Rachel drove fast. Alan's pudgy boat was surprisingly swift with only one person in it. She splashed over the oncoming waves with rhythmic bumps that hammered at her as her heart hammered at her chest. Soon she was approaching the island, its shadowed shores widening and engulfing her vision. The island was disrobed of its delight, but not of its dark power.

She decided that the quay was too exposed for her to return to. So instead, she piloted the boat along the shore on the opposite side, near the docks. There were overhanging trees over deep water, and she cut the engine, paddled the boat into the shadows, and got out, trembling. She was not entirely sure what she was going to do, but her anger and sense of justice wouldn't let her stay away. Remembering Paul's apprehension that something bad would happen tonight and his poignant acceptance when she refused to heed his warning, she felt even more bound to help him...*This would be a good time to pray*, she thought abstractedly, but she couldn't formulate any words, except *Help*. Hurriedly she fastened the boat to a strong branch, and plunged into the woods.

Paul shivered in his boxer shorts, his hands tied tightly behind him as they went along through the forest, going down, sharply down. He clenched his teeth as he stepped on thorns and was thrust through bracken, which scratched his bare skin. His war injury, which had been bruised in the fight with Michael, was starting to ache. It was difficult to see in the unfamiliar woods, but Michael and his cronies seemed to know where they were going.

And then Paul found himself being pushed forward around a sharp bend and then he was stumbling on level ground.

He caught himself and had barely time to take in the surroundings—a small cave with a wide opening that writhed away into shadows, lined with rough benches and log stools. And behind him a massive rock, with a twisted tree crawling up its side, branching over its top. There was an odd smell in the air, a mixture of sweetness, foulness, and dust.

Michael pushed past him and turned on a light somewhere, and the cave area was filled with an unearthly gray light. The blond man popped a pill into his mouth, opened a beer bottle, and took a drink.

"Let's get started," he said.

Craig shoved Paul's shoulders back against the tree's trunk. Michael flicked out the rope, and passed it around the tree and across Paul's chest, pulling it tight. As his shoulders were arched back against the tree, Paul's bound wrists were shoved into the small of his back, throwing him off balance. He tried to compensate by planting his bare feet on the sandy ground of the cave as best as he could while the rope was tightened and knotted. Recalling his breathing exercises, Paul began his mental preparation.

The other guys lurched passed them into the cave and threw themselves down on the rough benches. Paul saw Dillon reach greedily behind a rock, pull something out and light it.

While Craig tied his ankles to the base of the tree, Paul concentrated on centering himself. He knew that his body would get used to the discomfort of the knots if he could keep his mind from focusing on it. Plus, he sensed there was worse to come.

When Paul was tightly lashed in place, Craig sat down, but Michael remained standing in front of him, observing his prisoner with a strange smile on his face. His eyes were deadened, as usual, but with a pale flicker of interest. Paul kept his eyes on Michael's chest, waiting, watching for his adversary's next move while keeping himself upright and balanced.

"A Catholic boy," Michael murmured, putting out a hand to Paul's miraculous medal. He jerked downwards, snapping the chain, and held up the gleaming silver.

"I'm superstitious too, you see," he said softly, and hurled it over the rock into the forest.

Paul caught his breath, his neck smarting. He resumed his mental preparation, slowing his breathing, and finding his way back into calmness.

Craig twisted open a beer bottle and flicked the bottle cap at Paul, hitting his thigh. "Make him scream, Michael," he said. Some of the others chuckled in anticipation.

Paul ignored him and kept himself still and as upright as possible, his head down, watching Michael, waiting, and preparing. He saw Michael's eyes fix on his neck, and began to tense his toes in preparation, to turn the pain away from the upper part of his body.

Michael's eyes glimmered as he reached out with both hands and pinched the large nerve centers on the back of Paul's neck and pulled up. Pain ratcheted up Paul's neck and across his shoulders, but he was partially ready for it. He concentrated on working his toes, knowing that eventually the pinched nerves would adjust to the pain, and it would subside. He just had to wait. He hung from his tormentor's hands like a limp cat, flexing each of his toes in turn, keeping his breathing steady.

After a few moments, Michael dropped him and stepped back.

There was general dismay. "You didn't feel that," Michael said accusingly. "I'm disappointed."

Paul meant to keep disappointing him, as long as he could. He dropped his eyes to hide his defiance. Openly taunting Michael in this situation would not be prudent.

Michael probed along Paul's neck again, his fingers as methodical as a large spider's. He pressed Paul's collarbone, working his way up towards the shoulder. Then he began to dig his fingers into the skin on either side until he had a hold on the fragile bone, and quietly began to pull on it.

The pain was swift and screaming, followed fast by fear that the thin bone would snap. Paul writhed his wrists, found a nerve center, and dug down into it with his fingernails, so that competing pain began rushing into his hands. He wrenched his mind away from the fear and seized his self-inflicted pain and thrust it downward, away from him. *Take it, take it,* he prayed. Breathe. Breathe. Still. Still.

"You're not doing it right," Craig complained, lurching to his feet. "He's not squealing. Come on, break his collarbone! He won't need it!"

Paul disregarded the words and held on.

"He's just being obstinate," Michael said. He held the bone ten seconds longer, and then released it.

"You're losing your touch," Craig warned.

Masking his relief, Paul tried not to let himself relax entirely. He wasn't trained enough to stop from completely feeling the pain, but he had managed to stop himself from responding erratically. Once again, he sent up a grateful request for further endurance. It was not going to get any easier.

Resolved or not, Rachel floundered about in the woods, trying to find her way up towards the house. The black skirt of her dress caught on the branches, and she wrapped it around her legs, trying to move quickly as well as quietly. But her outfit was scarcely conducive to stalking. *At least it's black,* she thought to herself grimly.

At last, almost miraculously, she stumbled across a path—plank steps leading from the dock to the side of the house. Her heels made clocking noises on the stone, and they were impractical. She tore them off. In her stocking feet, she crept up to the house, trying to ignore her anxiety. She wasn't sure what she would find, or exactly what she would do when she found it.

The lights were still on, but the house was silent.

She approached cautiously, tiptoed up to the veranda and stood behind a pillar, looking in the window. There was no sound from inside, and no more music. The smoking ruins of the birthday feast were still on the table, sprayed with extinguishing foam, water dripping from the tablecloth to the carpet.

After a moment, she stepped inside the house. She opened the door to the basement and listened. There were no sounds but the hum of some appliances. After a moment, she stole downstairs. There was the abandoned pool game, with cues and balls all askew, party napkins and drinks littered around the empty room.

She searched the entire basement, then returned upstairs, opened the door to the kitchen, and tiptoed inside. There were the remains of Prisca's omelet preparations and a can of beer on the counter, but nothing else.

Finding a hallway and a staircase, she stole from room to room, opening doors onto empty rooms with increasing bewilderment. There was no sign of life. It was eerie.

It was as though Michael and his cohorts had never existed. As if, with a flick of a magic staff, they had vanished with their captive into the ground, never to be seen again.

Starting to become unnerved, she opened a bedroom sliding door and hurried out onto the small balcony. The breeze whipped her hair as she looked down at the portico where they usually danced. It was deserted. Only the branches of the willow trees swayed over the silent stones. She could see the helicopter gleaming on the heliport. Had they taken him away in a boat? She looked down at the dock, but couldn't tell if any boats were missing.

She stood on the balcony, searching over the wooded island, thinking. Her gut instinct told her that Michael was still here, though unseen. Perhaps he was watching her from some hidden corner, waiting merely for her to give up before springing his trap. She looked over her shoulder despite herself, and then steeled herself to be rational. Yes, somehow, she knew he was here, but not seeing him made her enemy seem increasingly omnipotent.

☾

Pain and humiliation. Those were their weapons. Weapons to both punish him and shut him up. Weapons to break him, and make him ashamed to go to the police, or to tell anyone about his ordeal.

His obstacle was his helplessness. Tied down and barely able to move, he was relatively unable to resist. But within those boundaries, he had to fight his enemies, with as much persistence as if he were unfettered and armed.

So far, he had managed to remain silent as he sweated and endured, even though he couldn't keep his expression fixed. Although his concentration was sustained, he was finding it hard to stay still and upright, to keep pressure off his upper body, whose muscles would otherwise start cramping from the extra-tight ropes.

His seven captors were taking turns, trying experiments and debating about what they could do next to break him. Since pain expands rapidly to fill its temporal space, Paul wasn't sure after a while if he had been tied there for minutes, an hour, or several hours.

He had to let that sense of time go, he told himself, licking his dry lips between moments. To hope for a definite ending would only make him desperate. And desperation was his biggest enemy now. *Trust. Trust*, he told himself. *From moment to moment. That's all I need.*

"I almost think he's enjoying this," Michael said, casting a sidelong glance at his prisoner.

They had tossed beer bottles at him to see him duck, and doused him with the leftovers of their drinks. His shoulders were sprinkled with broken glass where one had smashed over his head. Paul attempted to distract himself by taking an inventory of his wounds. He was bruised, he could tell, but not seriously cut. The beer still dripping down his neck continued to irritate his skin wherever it ran, and the smell mixed with his own sweat was unpleasant.

"He should enjoy his prize even more then," Craig said, with a sneer. "A free helicopter ride to the deserted field of our choice."

"Does he get his clothes back?" Dillon queried.

"At this point, no," Michael said.

"He's made you really mad, hasn't he?" Todd said.

"He knows it," Michael said. His eyes were fixed on Paul's face, but Paul was intentionally not meeting his gaze.

"Then the deserted field is going to be at least as far away as Ohio," Mark said.

"More like Minnesota," Michael said.

"Too much trouble," Craig said, flinging a bottle cap. Paul ducked again and it pinged off his neck. "I say if he's being this obstinate, let's fly over the Atlantic and see how far he can swim."

Paul knew they hadn't meant most of what they said. He recognized that if he had given them what they wanted—groveling and begging for mercy— they would have let him off by now. But the foundation of aikido was treating even adversaries with dignity. He had to extend that respect to himself as well. Besides, he was stubborn.

Breathing deeply again and making a sudden dodge against the dart of a bottle cap, he steadied himself internally.

"No clown is going to get the better of me," Michael's voice said softly.

Rachel retraced her steps downstairs to the ruined buffet, trying hard to think of what could have really happened, shoving aside the bloated image of evil in her mind. Unless Michael Comus were truly a demon, he and his cronies—and Paul—had to be visible and apparent somewhere on this island.

A shudder ran through her, and she suddenly remembered following Michael down that secret stair, to the little hollow with the twisted tree and the heavy sense of squalor....

The cave. Michael's old hiding place. That's where they must have taken Paul.

The answer was hardly reassuring. She ran to the veranda and looked out towards her home. She couldn't see or hear anyone coming. Her sisters must have told Dad by now, but perhaps something had delayed them. There was nothing for it but to go herself.

Turning back into the woods, she raced down the narrow steps back to Alan's boat, trying to think and plan as she plunged downwards. By the time she reached the boat's shrouded hiding place, she had the beginnings of a strategy. Michael was not going to win if she could help it.

After devising several inventive but obscene games for their amusements with Paul's person, Michael and his cronies appeared to give up. They all settled themselves on logs, opened new drinks, and lit up fresh joints, gazing at him with almost professional perplexity. Paul saw Michael down two more of the pills.

Paul waited wearily, feeling the sweat and beer drip off of him. Flexing his raw wrists against their ropes, he tried to drive down the swelling in his upper arms. And his wound was starting to ache from the sheer exertion. *Center, center,* he told himself. *Still yourself. Trust.*

"New game," Michael said suddenly. "Who has a pen?"

Todd did, and handed it over. Michael twiddled with it, his eyes gleaming. He said, "Each one of us has to come up with a few appropriate words and take turns inscribing them with the pen somewhere on this clown's skin. Then, we vote on the one we like best, and carve it into his flesh as a permanent reminder of this encounter."

He pulled out his knife, snapped it open, and thrust its silver point into the log he was sitting on, with another smile at his victim. Paul realized a line had been crossed.

"Oh, fun!" Dillon said, stumbling to his feet. "Give me the pen. I've got a good one."

Paul prepared himself, but winced as the man scrawled an obscene word across his chest with the sharp-tipped permanent-ink pen, driving the point in hard as he wrote. The result was greeted with howls of raucous laughter.

"Oh, gimme that, I've got one," Mark hurried up and took the pen from Dillon.

Mark wrote his message up one of Paul's arms and down the other one, snickering to himself the whole time. Paul turned his head aside so he wouldn't have to smell the guy's alcoholic breath, and attempted to let go of the pain once more. It didn't help that Mark was standing on his foot. He caught a glimpse of what Mark had written and was repulsed.

"That's a good one," Todd said appreciatively.

"F—Fiddlesticks," Craig lumbered to his feet and snatched the pen from Mark. "You're too long-winded."

He squeezed Paul's cheeks, and, squinting, wrote something across Paul's forehead, the pen slipping in the sweat. He wiped off Paul's forehead and outlined his letters again. It took him several attempts to write the one word. "Oooh!" the party exclaimed.

"We're running out of room," Brandon complained, after three other words had been written.

"We can always untie him and turn him around—there's more room behind," Craig said, with a snicker.

But no one else came forward. After a moment, the ringleader stood up.

"All right then," Michael said, pulling the blade from the log and tossing it back and forth in his hands. "We vote."

At the boat, Rachel groped in the darkness, pulled out the emergency kit, cursing her shaky hands and grabbed the flares and the matches. Then she flipped the alarm switch on the boat to "On."

A loud zooming alarm started echoing over the water and the land. Rachel sprang into the woods, struck a match, and lit the flares one by one and threw them in the air as they exploded. Then she ran in the opposite direction, hoping the noise hid her approach, making her way up the steep wooded slope towards the cave.

Paul heard the noise of the alarm first. He stretched his numbed fingers and relaxed them, praying. Someone had come. The others heard it next, and were startled.

"That can't be the police," Craig said.

"I don't think so," Michael got to his feet, snapping the knife closed and putting it into his pocket. "If it is, tell them I drove the clown back to the shore hours ago. You got me? He's gone."

He moved to the back of the cave and clicked off the light. The cave transformed from dull gray into indigo light, and after a moment, Paul saw the men, changed into dark blue shadows, slip out of the hollow one by one. But Michael stopped by Paul and pulled out a handkerchief. Methodically he folded the cloth into a triangular half and stretched it across Paul's mouth and knotted it at the back of the head. Then he thrust most of the cloth into Paul's mouth with two fingers.

"Even if it is the police, they'll never find anyone down here," Michael murmured, tightening the ends of the gag as Paul choked and worked fruitlessly with his tongue to push the wad of cloth out. "Don't think you're going to get out of your nice helicopter ride." He slid into the darkness.

With an exertion, Paul made himself slow his gulping and found that he could still take in air around the gag and through his nose, although it was difficult. Now that he couldn't breathe so easily, he found it too hard to remain firm on his feet. Unwillingly his body sank down against the ropes, which squeezed him like vises. Shuddering, he felt pain coursing through him from all different directions. He was cold, drained, and desperately thirsty. But temporarily, at least, he had a respite. Until they returned.

Rachel crouched in the bushes as the seven men ran by her, down the slope. As she had guessed, they had come from the direction of the cave.

As soon as she was sure they had all left, she crept stealthily upwards, until she reached the massive rock that hid the cave. She moved swiftly through the bracken around to the entrance. There was a rank smell coming from the cave—of spilled beer, sweat, and worse things. Listening at the entrance, she heard someone's labored breathing.

"Paul," she called in a whisper.

She felt her way around the stone and looked into the cave.

There was a pool of moonlight, cut into odd shapes by the branches of the disfigured tree. Bound to its bare trunk was a mostly naked man, his head down, his chest heaving, his arms twisted back by ropes. Catching her breath in shock and repulsion, she barely recognized her friend.

He was far from the skilled rescuer she had last seen, and even further from the splendid flute-playing god on the rock. The laughing, joking, persistent goodness that was Paul had been stretched, scarred, and humiliated.

Her stomach violently wrenched inside her, and part of her wanted to turn and run away. But if this was real, she couldn't leave him. As if in a nightmare, she took a step forward, her stocking feet crunching on broken glass, and stretched out a wavering hand to touch him. She felt the smooth, damp skin of his shoulder, crossed by tiny red cuts.

With a gasp for air that was almost a sigh, he lifted his head heavily, his brow crowned with shame, and the amount of pain reflected in his eyes was almost too much for her to bear.

Hurriedly, she came up to him and put her hands around his neck to undo the gag, looking up as she felt for the knots so that she wouldn't have to look him in the face. Her fingers pulled at the tight little knot obstinately, and at last it came loose. She worked the wad of cloth out of his mouth, damp with saliva.

"Rachel, don't stay here. Go get help," he said huskily after he got his breath. She could feel his intense shame.

"I'm not going to leave you," she said fiercely, licking the tears that were falling into her mouth. She ran her fingers over his face, attempting to wipe some of the sweat away. As she did so, she brushed his lips with the tips of her fingers, and trembled at the deep feelings that welled up within her.

Quickly, she groped around him, naked or not, trying to find the knots. Finding one buried in his ribs, she began to pull at it.

"They'll come back, and find you," he whispered, attempting to get back on his feet.

She didn't care. A loop came out, and she quickly pulled the knot apart. She started to pull the rope from his chest, but it caught again. Following it, she found another knot, and began to worry it.

"Rachel, please go." His voice was a rasp.

"Not without you," she answered stolidly.

"Rachel, *please*," Paul insisted, his voice more urgent but quieter. "I hear something."

"I'm never leaving you again," she whispered intensely, curling her fingers through the rock-hard knot and pulling it, softening it, coaxing it loose. He was almost free.

Paul seemed to stiffen, listening. "Rachel," he whispered. Then, he barked a warning, "Rachel!"

Too late, she felt fingers clamping around the back of her neck and pinching tight. She flailed and blackness swarmed over her vision and she sank down into murk.

twenty-two

*The princesses told the whole story to the king,
who realized that the soldier had indeed spoken
the truth.*

— Grimm

aul twisted towards Michael as Rachel dropped to the floor of the cave. The blond man was almost laughing as he released her neck. There still was not much margin left for Paul, but he threw himself forward against the loosened ropes and hit Michael hard with his shoulder, throwing the man off balance. Twisting himself back up, Paul waited until Michael predictably struck at him. He blocked the blow with his shoulder then butted him with his head. He could feel himself coming loose from the tree, although the rope around his ankles held him back.

Then Michael darted his fists and seized two handfuls of the ropes that swung around Paul's chest and fell back, pulling hard. With his foot to Paul's chest, he kicked Paul backwards against the tree, aiming blows on his scar.

Winded, Paul was squeezed back against the trunk of the tree by one rope that still caught him around the stomach. He wrestled to keep fighting but Michael was out of reach now, standing just out of range and bracing himself with the ropes.

"Got you," Michael panted, crossing the two ends of the ropes, giving them a deft twist and spreading his arms to drive the knot down against Paul's chest. When he was sure that Paul was trapped again, he knotted the rope a second and third time and lunged forward with a powerful blow to strike him.

Paul tensed himself, but Michael paused, his hand hovering above Paul's vocal chords. Slowly the rage in his eyes took on a new tint, and he dropped his eyes to Rachel's body.

That was exactly what Paul had been hoping to avoid. He lunged forward at Michael again, but the blond man wasn't interested. He lowered his hands and smiled at Paul's struggles. "She did call the police after all, the little chit. But Craig is up there explaining to the officers how I drove you to a mainland bar for a friendly chat hours ago. Even if they do search my property, they won't find you here—either of you." His eyes wandered down to Rachel again.

Paul saw that the combination of the drugs and alcohol had heightened Michael's sense of power and obscured his judgment. He tried to speak, but the words came from his dry throat like puffs of wind.

Michael merely cursed at him as he leaned over the unconscious girl and lifted up a handful of her inky dark hair. There was no response from Rachel. Paul watched miserably. He had no weapons left to stop the man, and they both knew it.

"She doesn't mean that much to me," Michael mused, toying with her tresses. "But even so…" He inspected the back of Rachel's calves with a finger. "Quite a dish. Made for our pleasure, wasn't she? Tell me, did you really love her, or did you just want to—"

He paused and looked up at Paul. "You really love her, don't you?"

His eyes were cold. "Too bad for you."

Rachel woozily resurfaced into consciousness, and found her cheek pressed against the gritty stone floor of the cave. Someone was behind her, talking. His smooth, steady voice made her skin crawl. Now the distinction between nice and good was chillingly clear.

"You think she came back here for you? No, she came back here because she's hungry for what I can give her."

It was Michael's voice. She felt a sudden urge to vomit. He was wrong. She had no taste now for anything from him. But when she tried to push his hands away, she found that she couldn't move. His knee was planted on her back, pinning her down.

Michael chuckled. "You know what I'm going to do now, clown? I'm going to eat her alive in front of you. And man, you are going to watch me."

She tried to wrest herself away, but he merely laughed at her. He had a hand over her mouth, and was working a gag down her throat. Becoming aware of his other hand tracing a line from her neck slowly down her back, as though he were deciding where to start cutting her open, she tried to jerk herself away. He squeezed her neck once more, cutting off her resistance abruptly, and black bees swarmed around her head, stinging her with sharp pricks of light.

She tried to scream as he started pulling up her skirts, but all that she could manage was a strangled gasp through the gag. It was as if her throat was full of sand.

Then she became aware that Paul was crying out in a strange, gravelly voice, but she couldn't understand what he was saying. Nonsense syllables with an odd, familiar resonance. Over and over again he was crying them, struggling against his hoarseness, louder and louder.

He's saying the rosary in Japanese, she recognized.

The words had an effect on Michael. He hissed, "Shut up!" when Paul began. But when Paul defiantly cried the words again, something in Michael seemed to snap.

He got to his feet, screaming at Paul to stop. And as he did, Rachel twisted to her knees and scrambled up towards the exit of the cave. But Michael put her into a headlock. Scratching his arms and tearing through the gag, she bit his forearm, hard. He got his arm out of her mouth and started to shake her. Paul kept intoning his prayer in a high cracked voice, more and more insistently, and Rachel felt the power of words storming the heavens, and was sure, although she didn't know how, that the words would not return void—

And then suddenly a new voice broke in, a roar of battle-hardened fury.

"Let go of my daughter!" Dad bellowed, seizing Michael by the shoulders and throwing him against the wall of the cave. Rachel saw her enemy crumple to the ground, out cold for the second time that night.

Winded, she staggered towards Paul, and collapsed on the ground by his bare feet.

Then Dad was lifting up her head, saying anxiously, "Rachel? Are you all right?" The gag was pulled out of her mouth, and she breathed, relief flooding over her. She knew they were saved.

"Help Paul," she managed to say.

She became aware of Prisca, standing with her back to the entrance of the cave and hollering, "Hey! Mr. Policeman! We're over here! Yes, on the side of the cliff! There's a hidden cave over here! Wait, I'll come and show you."

☾

Paul was grateful, and happy. He sat in the police boat, clothed again, rubbing his wrists and trying, but not too hard, to stay awake. There would be police reports to make in the morning, and probably more grief to go through with the arrests of the night, but right now, he was free, having been released with some hesitation by the paramedics who had come to the island. After a long drink and a plunge into the bay, whose salt water soaked his cuts in a stinging but healing bath, Paul felt certain, and had argued with them, that most of the effects of his ordeal would be erased after sleep, but they still wanted him to come to the hospital the next day.

But right now he could simply be happy. Colonel Durham sat across from him in the boat, one arm around Rachel, and the other arm around Prisca. The moon shone above them, and her light danced on the water. Paul yawned, and grinned up at the moon.

"Thank you," he said.

"I know who you're really talking to," Rachel spoke up from beneath her dad's arm. Her sea green eyes sparkled at him.

Colonel Durham didn't ask, but he grinned at Paul. Then he reached across, and unexpectedly tousled his hair, just as if Paul were his son.

"We've got to get you cleaned up," he said. "You won't believe what's written across your forehead."

"Don't tell me," Paul said cheerfully, but he saw that Rachel's face had grown somber.

"It's not fair," she said. "That word's not true, for one thing. It wasn't right that you had to—go through this—when I'm the one at fault."

"Don't take all the credit, Rachel," Prisca put in. "All of us made mistakes."

"But Paul's the one who suffered most for it," Rachel said.

Paul flushed. "Don't worry about it," he said.

"But it's not fair," Rachel said again, looking over the bay.

"It's okay," Colonel Durham said. "He's a man. He can handle it. Every good man has to take that sort of stuff once in a while."

Paul nodded, thankful for the articulation, and felt himself losing consciousness. He yawned. "There's only one thing I ask, Rachel."

"What's that?" she said, turning to look at him once more, her lovely face still grave.

"Try to be a whole person. Not just a night person, or a day person. Be the kind of person who can live in both. Like a person is supposed to do." He yawned again. "Sorry if this is a little incoherent. But that's all I ask."

He thought he heard Rachel say, "Is that all?" but now, being fully asleep, he couldn't answer her.

Rachel observed that Paul remained essentially asleep for the rest of the night. Of course, by this time, it was early Saturday morning. Sallie and all the girls were awake when the escaped captives and their rescuers returned. Paul roused himself long enough to get out of the police boat, thank the officers, and be mobbed by a mass of crying, ecstatic girls who had been sure they would never see him alive again. Rachel had to grin as she watched him, his lids constantly edging down over his eyes, attempting to be civilized and aware and respond to the dozens of breathless questions. She half-expected him to pitch forward, snoring, at any moment.

But he was shepherded into the house by his admirers, and Sallie insisted on making up a bed for him on the couch. He thanked her, his head slumping forward, and Colonel Durham said, "Stop pestering him now, girls. He's exhausted."

Paul staggered appreciatively onto the couch, attempted to say something that sounded like good night, and plunged forward, dead to the world again.

"What did they do to him?" the girls asked Rachel anxiously after they had tiptoed out of the living room. They had, of course, noticed the obscene word which was still faintly scrawled across his forehead.

Rachel attempted to explain what she had witnessed as she wobbled over to the kitchen table, feeling more than slightly exhausted herself.

"That is so sick," Tammy said angrily. Debbie got up from the kitchen table and slipped out of the room.

"Girls," Colonel Durham said from the corner. They all looked at him, suddenly silent and guilty, remembering that until tonight, he had little knowledge of the events that had led up to this night's catastrophe. He opened the cupboard. "Does anyone want something to drink? Rachel?"

"Yes please," Rachel said, suddenly realizing how thirsty she was. She lowered herself into a chair. The others also asked for drinks, and their dad pulled out glasses and poured juice and water for everyone. Debbie came back in, took a coffee mug, and went over to the sink. Sallie, still in her bathrobe, handed around the glasses until everyone was settled.

When everyone was sitting down with their glasses, Colonel Durham pulled out a chair on one side of the table and sat down, rubbing his graying hair.

"Well," he began, looking around at them, a bit hesitant. "I'd very much like to hear the whole story, if any of you want to tell me. Your mother and I have been mostly in the dark, until you all stormed into our bedroom at two this morning."

Sallie nodded. Cheryl raised her hand. "I have one question," she said, "how much did Paul tell you?"

"Nothing," Dad said, spreading his hands. "I asked him if he could find out from you girls what was going on, and he said he would, but only if he was free to not tell me anything until you girls were ready to tell me. So I've been waiting, and praying, and I don't know very much at all."

Rachel's face reddened. "That's what Paul said the other night to me," she said. "That he wanted us to tell you ourselves."

"Well, will you?"

Rachel looked at the other girls for the final decision. Brittany was nodding her head emphatically, and Melanie, Cheryl, Lydia, Rebecca, Tammy, Taren, Linette, Miriam, and Prisca were all doing the same. She noticed again that Debbie was missing.

"All right then," she said. "Cheryl, you were there at the beginning. Why don't you tell them how it got started?"

Cheryl looked at Rachel a bit surprised. At first she looked as if she would object, but then seemed to change her mind. "Well," she said, "it all started when a few of us decided to rearrange our room one night."

Everyone in the family was listening to her intently. Rachel drained her glass, and unobtrusively rose from the table. After a few minutes, she stepped into the dining room, looking for Debbie.

Rachel found her in the living room, kneeling next to Paul's head. She had a coffee mug of warm water and a small washcloth, and was cleaning his forehead carefully. He was still blissfully asleep.

The ugly word was mostly erased. Debbie worked slowly. "I'm trying not to get soap in his eyes," she explained.

"Are you sure you're not bothering him?" Rachel asked.

"I asked him and he said to go right ahead," she said. "I don't think he even knows I'm doing it any more."

Rachel sat down in an easy chair, put her hand on her chin, and contemplated the sleeping man, grateful to see him comforted. What a remarkable person he was. Her first assessment of him, made a bare few weeks ago, had vastly missed the mark. Paul's goodness—for he was good, not just nice—was of a different quality—less easy to categorize, tame, and dismiss. He hadn't been content, either, to remain apart from them, untainted in his goodness, but had insisted on going out and getting himself mixed up with their own brand of badness. And she had seen what it had done to him.

Yet he had accepted it. She could tell he didn't resent her, despite the spasms of pain that momentarily knitted his sleeping brow.

"Sorry," Debbie whispered. "I'm almost done."

She rubbed even more slowly. "Rachel, what did that word mean?"

"You don't want to know," Rachel said wryly. "It wasn't true, anyway."

Meeting Paul had done something to her, and she wasn't entirely sure what it was. But she felt certain that she was never going to see the world in the same way again.

Now her own eyes began to grow heavy, and she put her head back against the chair. The last thing she saw before she drifted off was Debbie kissing Paul on his cleaned forehead and patting his hair.

But once she closed her eyes, the stupidity of her actions and the pain and anguish she had caused came back to her. She put her head against the cushions of the chair and wept again, her tears hot on her cheeks, this time asking for forgiveness. Somewhere in that misty land between sleeping and waking, it was granted, and she fell asleep.

With everything that had happened, Rachel should have slept in. But something woke her up before nine in the morning.

She found herself in bed, and was confused for a moment. She didn't remember coming up to bed, but after a few moments, recollected her sisters and Sallie helping her into some welcome softness at some point during the night.

Slowly, she opened her eyes. The girls' bedroom was warm and air was heavy with the sounds of gentle breathing. Carefully she moved away from Debbie, who was snoring peacefully on the other side of the bed.

Cheryl slept in the other double bed, her arms protectively around her youngest sister Linette, who still looked like a baby when she slept. Tammy and Taren were lumps of blankets crowned with strands of blond hair. Miriam, her arm thrown over her dark hair, breathed deeply in her top bunk bed, and Prisca was sleeping fitfully in the bottom bunk, half-laughing to herself in some dream. Lydia's arm hung over the side of her top bunk, and Rachel tucked it back on the bed. Becca lay on her back, the covers up to her tilted nose. Brittany slept like a guy, the blankets over her head and her bare feet thrust out of the covers.

Below her on the bottom bunk, Melanie was curled up on her pillow. Her face was perfectly content, and she smiled in her sleep. Touched, Rachel stroked her cheek with the side of her finger, and her sister sighed and turned over. Rachel couldn't help smiling at her. Melanie's heart was unburdened at last.

Rachel was still wearing her midnight butterfly dress, which, despite its trials, was in fairly decent shape. But after having slept in it, it felt to her like a tight cocoon. She wriggled out of it, relieved, and put on her denim blue dress. *Paul liked this dress on me*, she thought, and felt an unusual tremor in her stomach.

I'm never leaving you again, she had said to him fiercely, sometime last night, or this morning. And she vividly remembered her hands touching his distressed face. There was something there she didn't want to let go of.

But she was suddenly conscious that this was the daylight, not the phantasms and terror of the nighttime. Things were different here—different religions, different churches, differing paths of life. There were obstacles here, too—more prosaic and discernible, but still obstacles. But Paul had asked her to live in both the night and the day.

In the bathroom, she carefully brushed her hair, cleaned her teeth, and studied herself in the mirror. *What would Paul think of me now? After everything that's happened?* She didn't know what to expect.

At last she stole downstairs and tiptoed to the living room, to look again on the sleeping man.

But all that greeted her in the living room, bright with fresh sunshine, was a tangle of blankets, and no body.

Dumbfounded, she stood still. For an instant she almost wondered if she had been right—if Paul, as she had thought of Michael last night, wasn't really a human being, but something else, something beyond human. But that was silliness.

She hesitantly turned away and went into the kitchen. Her father was up, at a sunny spot on the kitchen table, drinking coffee and reading his Bible. He turned when she came in.

"Good morning, Rachel."

"Good morning," she came to him, put her arms shyly around him, and kissed him. "Where's Paul?"

"He's already up and gone," her dad said with a smile.

"Gone?" she repeated, dismayed.

"To church. He just left a moment ago. He said he just had time to walk to morning Mass, so he left."

"Oh."

He took her hand unexpectedly. "Rachel, I've decided to step down from leadership in our church. What do you think about that?"

She paused, holding his hand. "I think that would be wonderful, Dad."

"The more I've been thinking about it, the more right it seems to me. You girls are growing up so fast. Before you know it, you'll all be out of the house. So I want to take advantage of the time left and spend more of it with you and your sisters. I'm convinced that God wants this of me. And I'm ready."

His eyes were solemn. She bent down and kissed him, feeling a sweet happiness come over her. "Thank you, Dad. I think that's just what our family needs."

"Good!" he said, kissing her cheek and letting her go. "Would you—" He started to say something else, but she cut him off, unintentionally.

"Dad, can I ask you something?"

"Go ahead." He didn't seem to mind that she had interrupted him.

"Can I—" she looked away, towards the door, where Paul had left. "Can I go—?"

"With Paul?" he asked. "To church?"

She nodded.

He seemed to be a bit disappointed, and she realized he had probably been about to invite her to join him for morning devotions. But then he seemed to make up his mind.

He squeezed her hand again and smiled a knowing smile. "Go with that young soldier, Rachel."

Nevertheless, she didn't let go of his hand right away. "Dad, are you sure?" she asked, uncertainly.

"Go with him, daughter," he said, smiling sternly. "That's an order."

Without another word, she kissed him on the cheek, turned, and ran out of the house.

The sun was moving swiftly up into the blue sky, and the bay breeze was gusting merrily as she ran down the driveway to the gravel road. Her sandaled feet slapped against the brown pebbles, and her hair kept blowing in her face, but she didn't care. As she rounded the curve, she saw him far ahead of her, walking easily. The bend of his muscles, his brown hair fluffed by the breeze. She called his name.

I'm never leaving you again.

He turned, and she raced towards him, scattering pebbles behind her. Her breath was catching in her throat, and she laughed, almost giddy with the exertion. She had never run after anything this fast, she was sure.

And as she came closer, she saw his face, first startled, and then wondering, like a child's, and then he understood. And a grin lit up his face like she had never seen before, and he held out his hand to her.

He knows, she realized. *He knows. And I know, too. I know that I know. I know goodness. It has a name.*

☾

And so in time, to the rejoicing of all, the soldier and the oldest princess were married, and the eleven younger princesses danced at their wedding.

— Grimm

The End

ℭ 𝔄 little 𝔄bout This Book...

The great philosopher Dietrich von Hildebrand once said that if beauty and goodness are separated, then a curious disembodiment of the culture takes place. Goodness becomes abstract and merely moral, perhaps even boring; and beauty appears to be mere sensual glamour, a distraction, and perhaps even evil. For of course, said von Hildebrand, goodness and beauty are in their essences the same thing. As human beings, we need goodness to be incarnated as beauty so that we can more easily love goodness.

After I pondered these words for some time, I began to wonder: how could you possibly cure someone for whom goodness was boring? As a cradle Catholic, I had grown up knowing many jaded Christian teenagers who were sure that they knew "all about *that* stuff," Christianity, and they were sick and tired of it. To them, goodness was truly boring. What could be done for them?

To try to figure out the answer, I wrote this novel.

So right at the beginning, I have to acknowledge my debt to von Hildebrand, whose thoughts set me on this path, and also to Dr. Benjamin Wiker, who pointed out the disastrous consequences to the soul who finds goodness boring. Without the writings of these two men, this book would not exist.

I'm also very grateful, once again, to the collage of friends and family who helped me with this book, primarily my own brothers and sisters, and my friends Ben Hatke, Nicholas Marmalejo, and Andrew O'Neil. Ben helped me with the juggling parts, Nick helped me with the aikido, and they both helped Andy choreograph that marvelous fight scene at the climax of the book. I'm never going to forget watching them stage the battle in the living room of our old house: truly memorable!

Again, my friend Dr. Frank helped me with the medical facts for the book, and my chiropractor Dr. Scott Berman helped me with the "alternative medicine" parts. My brother Paul Doman (Captain, National Guard) and friend Rick Morgan (Retired Senior Master Sergeant, Air Force) assisted with the military scenes. Rick and his wonderful wife Cathy, who are parents of teenaged girls, also gave me useful and illuminating recommendations on parenting. (Cathy and her daughter Caitlin also sent over two delicious dinners during the final editing stretch, which was a wonderful blessing!) And although I had Rachel ask her father not to share his insights with his friends on p. 175, I am grateful that writer Elizabeth Foss chose to share her own epiphany on parenting teenagers with her readers., since it partially inspired that scene.

Jean Vencil, Elizabeth Hausladen, and Pastor Greg Wright all helped me enormously by reading the book and commenting on the Protestant aspects in the story. So did Ken Fast (a former Mennonite). As a Catholic, I am grateful for their perspective.

Special thanks to Caroline Miller for modeling for the cover photo. All other images were courtesy of iStock Photo, and almost all the fonts were from the great calligraphers at the Scriptorium. Two exceptions were the title font (A Yummy Apology) and the Little People dancing under the moon. The latter is a freeware font created by Emerald City Fontwerks. All fonts and images were used with permission.

Other readers who gave wonderful advice included Michaela Berquist, Anna Hatke, Alyssa Hichborn, Katie Tietjen, Mary Clare Robinson, and Nancy and Sarah Brown. And I must give a special note of thanks to screenwriter and writing instructor Janet S. Batchler who went over and over my opening scene with me until it worked. Since I tried for five years to fix it on my own, I am so very grateful.

I cannot begin to express my gratitude to my husband Andrew, who put many hours into editing and revising this book, as well as arguing to convince me to tighten rambling or unnecessary scenes. I owe him so much.

My children Caleb, Rose, Marygrace, Thomas, Joan, and Polly were also so patient with me during this whole process. Also I am sure my son Joshua was praying for me from Heaven. I'm thankful for all of them.

And most of all I'm grateful to the man Who is the only person I know who can cure us of the illusion that goodness is boring: my Savior, our Lord Jesus Christ. It was a privilege to write this book. I am glad to have been given this story to tell.

About the Author

Regina Doman lives near Front Royal, Virginia with her husband and their six children.

More information about her Fairy Tale Novel series can be found at www.fairytalenovels.com. Regina always welcomes email, feedback, and questions from readers.

www.fairytalenovels.com